"Celebrate Shelley Freydont's new mystery series in Celebration Bay, a city of festivals where the event coordinator plans everything. Except solving murders."
——Janet Bolin, author of the Threadville Mysteries

"*Foul Play at the Fair* is a fun romp of a story about Liv Montgomery, who gives up her irritating life of handling bridezillas and finds the perfect job in Celebration Bay, New York, with her Westie, Whiskey. A delicious read filled with interesting characters and good times."
——Joyce Lavene, coauthor of
the Missing Pieces Mysteries

"Event coordinator Liv Montgomery is doing her best to squash any obstacles to a successful Celebration Bay Harvest Festival, and when a body crops up, she's not going to let her plans be plowed under."
——Sheila Connolly, national bestselling author of
the Orchard Mysteries

Foul Play at the Fair

Shelley Freydont

BERKLEY PRIME CRIME, NEW YORK

THE BERKLEY PUBLISHING GROUP
Published by the Penguin Group
Penguin Group (USA) Inc.
375 Hudson Street, New York, New York 10014, USA

Penguin Group (Canada), 90 Eglinton Avenue East, Suite 700, Toronto, Ontario M4P 2Y3, Canada
(a division of Pearson Penguin Canada Inc.) • Penguin Books Ltd., 80 Strand, London WC2R 0RL,
England • Penguin Group Ireland, 25 St. Stephen's Green, Dublin 2, Ireland (a division of Penguin
Books Ltd.) • Penguin Group (Australia), 250 Camberwell Road, Camberwell, Victoria 3124, Australia
(a division of Pearson Australia Group Pty. Ltd.) • Penguin Books India Pvt. Ltd., 11 Community
Centre, Panchsheel Park, New Delhi—110 017, India • Penguin Group (NZ), 67 Apollo Drive,
Rosedale, Auckland 0632, New Zealand (a division of Pearson New Zealand Ltd.) • Penguin Books
(South Africa) (Pty.) Ltd., 24 Sturdee Avenue, Rosebank, Johannesburg 2196, South Africa

Penguin Books Ltd., Registered Offices: 80 Strand, London WC2R 0RL, England

This is a work of fiction. Names, characters, places, and incidents either are the product of the author's
imagination or are used fictitiously, and any resemblance to actual persons, living or dead, business
establishments, events, or locales is entirely coincidental. The publisher does not have any control over
and does not assume any responsibility for author or third-party websites or their content.

FOUL PLAY AT THE FAIR

A Berkley Prime Crime Book / published by arrangement with the author

PUBLISHING HISTORY
Berkley Prime Crime mass-market edition / September 2012

Copyright © 2012 by Shelley Freydont.
Cover illustration by Griesbach/Martucci.
Cover design by George Long.
Interior text design by Tiffany Estreicher.

ISBN: 978-0-425-25155-3

BERKLEY® PRIME CRIME
Berkley Prime Crime Books are published by The Berkley Publishing Group,
a division of Penguin Group (USA) Inc.,
375 Hudson Street, New York, New York 10014.
BERKLEY® PRIME CRIME and the PRIME CRIME logo are trademarks of Penguin Group
(USA) Inc.

PRINTED IN THE UNITED STATES OF AMERICA

10 9 8 7 6 5 4 3 2 1

ALWAYS LEARNING   PEARSON

For Judi McCoy, writer and friend,
who loved dogs and left us far too soon

Chapter One

....

Liv Montgomery wiggled her toes in her new Sperry Top-Siders and breathed in the fresh country air. The day was crisp, the sun was shining, and Liv felt great. It was hard to believe that only a month ago she'd been standing in the Plaza ballroom, sleep deprived and patience hanging by a thread, while the bridezilla from hell ranted at her because the oysters they were serving at the reception were Atlantic, not Pacific.

Even after Liv showed her the order sheet where she had signed off on Atlantic oysters, the woman continued to yell. Liv had gritted her teeth and wondered how soon she could get out of her four-inch heels from hell.

The bride, now the wife of some poor soul who had disappeared into the men's room right after the first dance, made one final dramatic gesture, throwing both arms wide and taking out a waiter and two thousand dollars' worth of Dom Pérignon.

And something in Liv snapped. She'd had enough. She was sick of bitchy bridezillas, desperate housewives, anything-but-sweet sixteens. She wanted a job with normal hours, where she made nice people happy, where she could get out of those damn heels.

She packed up her clothes and her dog and headed north.

Now she was the official event coordinator of Celebration Bay, New York, a town that took its name seriously, where she could wear Top-Siders and take her dog to work.

"Pretty nice place to live, huh?" she said, looking down at her Westie terrier, Whiskey.

Whiskey pulled at his leash and, after snuffling through a patch of grass, claimed the base of a nearby parking meter.

Celebration Bay was an idyllic village on a lake that, as the locals told her, wasn't big enough to be "great," but was big enough for them. It was big enough for Liv, too.

It was the last week in September, and the monthlong Harvest by the Bay Festival was culminating in a weekend fair. Up and down Main Street, gaily painted shops sold food, knitted goods, coffee, and souvenirs. The surrounding trees were turning golden and red, and the breeze off the lake carried the aroma of baking down the street.

The sound of hammering rang in the air, and Liv stopped to look across the parklike village green where the setup committee was constructing booths for the one hundred vendors and entertainers who would line the sidewalks that weekend. A bright, multicolored tent had been erected at the far end for music, skits, and magic shows.

Nearby, a children's area would feature bobbing for apples, pumpkin painting, and a go-fishing booth. There would be a farmers' market, hayrides, three-legged races, and cider pressing exhibitions. The surrounding stores and restaurants would open early and close late.

Liv let out a satisfied sigh. Her new life, her new job. It was just perfect.

As she stepped off the curb, Janine Tudor's cream-colored Cadillac sped by, barely missing Liv's new shoes. Liv jumped back to the sidewalk. *Almost perfect.*

She waited until she was sure Janine was not going to repeat the drive-by, then hurried across the street. Recognizing the bakery, Whiskey pulled her along the sidewalk past the dainty tables and chairs outside the Apple of My Eye Bakery and through the open door.

"Morning, Liv," said Dolly Hunnicutt from behind the counter. She was wearing a pink gingham dress with puff sleeves and a white ruffled apron tied around her ample waist. Her honey-colored hair was pulled back into a bun at the nape of her neck. Some of the residents took their reputation as the soon-to-be-most-popular festival destination in New York State more seriously than others.

"And don't you look festive today," Dolly added.

"Is that a good thing?" Liv asked, wondering if she'd gone overboard with her forest green corduroys and autumn plaid jacket. Whiskey had refused to participate in her new wardrobe madness, even though in an aberrant moment, she'd ordered him two scotch plaid winter sweaters from an online doggie catalogue.

"Why, of course it is. You're wearing harvest colors. Those trousers bring out the green in your eyes, and your hair shines like burnt sugar."

Liv wasn't sure what burnt sugar was, but it didn't sound too appetizing. She'd always thought her hair was dark brown.

"I have some nice lemon scones this morning. Lord knows we'll all be sick of apples before we switch over to pumpkin season after this weekend."

In the last two weeks, Liv had eaten apple pie, apple turnovers, applesauce, apple butter, and something called apple pandowdy. "Lemon scones sound delicious. I'll take two, though I can't keep this up. I've already had to increase my daily run from three miles to four."

"Pooh. The way you run around, you'll work it off in no time. But if you keep feeding Ted . . ." She clucked her tongue.

"I always treat my assistants well. The secret of my success."

"Well, bless you. Janine used to run him ragged. But don't you go overboard and spoil him."

"I won't." Liv glanced up at the pink cupcake-shaped wall clock. "Gotta run." She took the bag of scones.

Whiskey, who had been sitting patiently at her feet, his face upturned to the counter, barked.

Dolly laughed. "I would never forget such a sweetie." She handed Liv a smaller paper bag.

"Just a little D-O-G biscuit recipe I've been working on. Shaped like little bones, they're so cute. And no sugar. I'm going to talk to Sharise over at the Woofery about maybe stocking them for her clients."

"That's a great idea. You may have a whole new industry on the horizon," Liv said.

Dolly beamed, and Liv and Whiskey hurried next door to the Buttercup Coffee Exchange. The proprietor, Betty Ford, known as BeBe to distinguish her from the other Betty Ford, was waiting at the door with a large latte and a decaf tea. BeBe was a lush thirtysomething, half country girl and half urban entrepreneur. She and Liv had bonded the first day Liv had come into the store.

"Saw you coming. Knew you'd be in a hurry this morning." BeBe handed Liv the cardboard carton of drinks. "And I saw what Janine just did. Somebody oughta tell her nobody wants sour grapes at a harvest festival."

"Well, I did take her job."

"No reason to try to run over you. If she wanted to keep being the town's event coordinator, she should have done a better job. She was driving us to the poorhouse, and everybody knows it, whether they say so or not. I'll put the coffee and tea on your tab."

"Thanks, BeBe. You're a dream."

She'd made the right decision to move here, Liv thought as she hurried toward her office in town hall. Celebration

Bay was the epitome of Yankee ingenuity. It had survived several wars, the depression, a flu epidemic, and two recessions. When the cannery, the major source of employment in the county, closed, they threw a party. Fifteen years later, Celebration Bay was a thriving destination vacation spot, delivering family entertainment at affordable prices.

But the festivals had grown too big for volunteers, and when Liv saw the ad for a full-time event coordinator, she jumped at the chance to do something really worthwhile. For the most part, people were congenial, helpful, and polite. And if they liked getting their own way, well, who didn't.

Ted Driscoll was already at work in the outer office. He was a man of a certain age, tall and thin with thick white hair, mild blue eyes, and a dry sense of humor. He also had his finger on the pulse of Celebration Bay gossip. That alone made him indispensable. His computer skills and willingness to work on Saturdays made him a gem.

He stood up as Liv entered, and Liv, being a well-trained dog owner, dropped Whiskey's leash. Whiskey darted forward, and Ted leaned over and vigorously scratched behind both doggie ears. "Who's my favorite daw-aw-awg," Ted yodeled.

"Arr-roo-roo-roo."

"My favorite daw-aw-awg."

"Arr-roo—"

Liv rolled her eyes, deposited the scones and coffee on Ted's desk, and picked up a thick manila folder.

"I'll be in my office when you two goofballs are finished," Liv said. Neither goofball paid any attention to her as they yodeled through their morning ritual.

Liv's office was a big square room with two tall sash windows and a high ceiling. The walls were painted an unwholesome beige, though someone had tried to spiff things up with travel posters of Bermuda. Liv meant to do a little redecorating as soon as she got this first festival under her belt.

Ted came in with a tray, set it on her desk, and sat down across from her. Whiskey followed, his treat from Dolly held delicately between his teeth. And, finally remembering that he'd been trained at a very expensive obedience school, he headed for his pillow where he stretched out and made short work of Dolly's dog delicacy.

Liv glanced at the tea tray. In addition to the hot drinks, the scones arranged on two china saucers, the knives, forks, and paper napkins, today a folded newspaper lay on top. "We're getting way too civilized, Ted."

"Never, but the newspaper is strictly business." He handed it to Liv, who unfolded it to the front page. It was the local weekly, the *Celebration Clarion*.

" 'Fishing Suspended to Protect Spawning Salmon'?"

"Next page."

Liv opened the bifold paper. An article on tractor advancements, a report on the county fair, a Weight Watchers meeting announcement, a twofer coupon for Otis Deal's Texas Wieners. On the opposite page was an article about arrowheads found by a Boy Scout troop while hiking in the foothills. And below it was a half-page advertisement for the Harvest by the Bay Festival and a listing of the weekend festivities.

The ad was strictly clip art, designed by her predecessor, but there were no obvious mistakes; dates, times, activities were all there. She lifted her eyebrows at Ted.

"As I understand it, the ad should have been a whole page, not half."

"I don't suppose there's an invoice?"

Ted shook his head. "Janine didn't keep records."

Liv sighed. "I'll go have a talk with"—she looked at the masthead—"Mr. Bristow. I should meet him anyway if we're going to be doing business in the future." She checked her iPhone. "I have to go out to Waterbury Farms. Joss wants me to see the antique apple press exhibit that he's put together before he opens it to the public this weekend. Then

I'll stop by the Miller farm to get an ETA on the corn maze for Haunted October, but I can drop by the newspaper office this afternoon."

"Be sure to get there before three or he'll have closed up to go fishing."

Liv rolled her eyes. "So that's why festival news got bumped for salmon eggs." She entered the *Clarion*'s address into her address book.

They worked their way through the folder, dividing up jobs until there was one paper left. "Zoldosky Brothers," Liv said thoughtfully. "The jugglers?"

"Yep. I saw their Airstream drive by on my way to work. Probably going out to Andy Miller's farm. That's where most of the vendors and entertainers camp." Ted reached for the paper. "I'm glad they got here early. I'll have to get out there and remind them that they're paid a very nice fee and panhandling is strictly forbidden. I'd ask Bill Gunnison to go out but he's down with sciatica."

"A hell of a time for the sheriff's back to go out," Liv said. "Do you think he'll be okay by Saturday? I might be a bit overzealous, but Manhattan doesn't have the monopoly on perverts, pickpockets, and psychopaths."

"No," Ted agreed. "But we usually lock ours in the attic."

Liv choked on her coffee. "Don't do that," she said, blotting coffee off the manila folder.

Ted raised his eyebrows, all innocence.

"I'll talk to them. I'm going out there anyway."

Ted hesitated. "Okay, but make sure to take Andy with you. The Zoldoskys are ex-carny folk. They come every year and never cause any trouble, but they're a bit rough around the edges."

"Not to worry. You should have seen some of my clients in Manhattan. Money and an East Side address don't automatically give a person good taste or good manners."

Ted barked out a laugh. "Hon, you're a breath of fresh air. But you don't need to do everything yourself."

"I know. It's a nasty habit I intend to break . . . once the harvest festival is a resounding success. Then I'll go into strong-arming-for-help mode for Halloween."

Liv gathered up hard copies of the permit forms and added them to the manila folder, which she slid into a canvas shoulder bag.

"If I leave Whiskey here, you have to promise not to keep feeding him."

Ted widened his eyes innocently. Whiskey cocked his head—innocently.

"If you get fat, I'll have to send you to doggie boot camp."

"Maybe we can get a twofer," Ted said, patting a nonexistent stomach.

"Behave. Both of you."

Liv managed to hide her grin until she reached the hallway. She couldn't imagine any of her former Manhattan colleagues, even the dog lovers, putting up with a dog at work, much less enjoying him. She loved her new job.

She stopped in the ladies' room for a quick look in the mirror: makeup, neat, understated; slacks, loose jacket, casual but businesslike; hair . . . burnt sugar? Whatever. She twisted it onto the top of her head and fixed it there with a claw clip. Even more businesslike, in case she needed the extra clout with the Zoldosky brothers.

Her first stop was Waterbury Farms, two miles out of town on the county road. It was a working farm, but its claim to fame was the Waterbury store. The store had taken over the original cider mill when they built a larger, updated mill a mile away. There was still one huge working press housed behind a plate glass window where visitors could watch the apples being pressed into juice. The mill's fresh cider and cider doughnuts had been reviewed in magazines up and down the East Coast.

Liv pulled into a parking space at the front of the red clapboard building. Even on a midweek morning there were several cars in the lot. There was an additional parking area around back. Plenty of room for the weekend overflow. And if they had someone directing traffic, things should go smoothly.

That was the area Liv was most concerned about. Ted had told her of gnarled traffic jams and fumes smelling up the park as cars waited for parking spaces.

Not on my watch, she told herself. She didn't have much experience directing vehicular traffic, but she had a plan that she would present at the Traffic Committee meeting that night.

She slid her bag across the car seat and went inside. She was immediately surrounded by the sweet aroma of apples and frying doughnuts. Joss Waterbury, dressed in denim overalls and a red plaid shirt, was a walking advertisement for the American farmer. He was manning the doughnut maker, but he handed off the job to his teenage daughter, Roseanne, when he saw Liv.

"I got the back room all set up for the antique exhibit. I think you're really gonna like it. Educational as well as fun."

He led her down an aisle between wooden shelves that were filled with foodstuffs, books, and kitchenware, and past the electric cider press. Liv couldn't help but slow down to watch the chunks of apples rushing out of the giant delivery tube into the cloth-covered frames, the juice running out the bottom into troughs that would carry it away to be processed.

"Kinda mesmerizing, ain't it?" Joss said.

"It's fascinating," Liv agreed.

They stood watching for a few more seconds; then Joss started off again.

"You're about to step back into history," he said, gesturing to a room that until a few days ago had held quilts, T-shirts, and homespun linens, as well as a huge granite apple mill.

"I hope you're going to lead the tour yourself," Liv said. "You just sent a shiver up my spine." She stepped inside and took in the collection of old and unusual devices. Machines with slatted barrels, metal colanders, and giant hand cranks. An apple saucer, a fermentation vat, and a row of pottery cider jugs.

"This baby," Joss said, stopping by an old cast-iron and wooden press, "dates back to the late eighteen hundreds." He ran a hand lovingly over the round press wheel. "Took three of us to get it in the truck."

"Where did you find it?"

"Buddy Powers's got an 'antique' place over on Route 9. Mostly junk and such a mess that you couldn't find nothing if you tried. Except I knew he had this; he tried to sell it to me for a fortune years ago. Course, nobody ever bought it. When you got this idea for an exhibit, I remembered him. Went over there and got it for a song.

"Now, this one," he said, moving to a much larger contraption that was about five feet high and spread out over several feet, "is on loan from Fenway Farms up the road. Belonged to Fenway's grandfather. He don't want it, but his wife won't let him get rid of it. So he was happy to oblige."

Liv peered into the collection barrel, then examined the heavy iron press and the series of cogs and wheels along the side.

"How exactly does it work?" she asked.

"It works on the same principle as the big electric press, only you do it by hand." Joss flipped a heavy iron latch. "You put your apples in this funnel. Then you position the stone disc on top." He grabbed hold of a heavy-looking crank handle. "You turn the crank, which presses the stone down and crushes the apples. Takes forever. Even with the big double ones."

"They're safe, aren't they? No kid could get a mashed finger or anything?"

"No," Joss said, as he returned the latch to the iron eye. "I'll have them locked off, though I'm thinking about having hourly demonstrations on the weekends. Just a little added attraction."

A man after her own heart, Liv thought.

"I think this is going to be real interesting." He shoved his hands in his jeans pockets and looked around. "Might even build on an extra room and keep an eye out for some unusual mills to add to the collection. Found something real nice on eBay the other day. Shipping it would break the bank. But you never know."

"Well, I'm sure it's going to be a big hit," Liv said.

No one was home at the Miller farm, but Liv could see the field where a handful of trucks and trailers were already settling in for the weekend.

A battered silver Airstream trailer was parked at the farthest edge of the field near the woods and away from the other vendors. She drove across the field, following the tracks made by the trailer. She parked several yards away and read the sign painted on the side in large black letters. *Zoldosky Brothers.* And underneath, *Juggling, Tumbling, Balloon Animals.* She beeped the horn to warn them they had a visitor.

When no one appeared, she got out of the car.

The trailer had two metal steps leading to the door and two small windows on either side, covered by thick curtains. There was a pickup truck parked next to the trailer, so someone must be home.

"Hello?" she called as she approached the trailer. "Hel-lo-o."

The hair on the nape of her neck lifted; she could feel someone watching her, but when she turned around, no one was there. She suddenly felt very isolated at the edge of the woods; the few other vehicles were too far away to even hear her if she screamed.

Wuss, she thought. She turned back to the trailer; the curtain abruptly fell back across the window. So, she hadn't imagined it; someone *was* watching her.

She climbed the two metal steps to the door and knocked. "Mr. Zoldosky? Anyone home?"

Nothing. But she knew someone was in there, and now that she'd made the trip, she wasn't going away without talking to one of the brothers.

She knocked again, louder and more persistent.

This time she heard movement inside. A scrape, a crash as if something heavy had fallen over. Another crash. Maybe this wasn't a good time to be calling. Bill Gunnison would just have to hobble his way out here or wait until Saturday when the brothers would be in town.

Liv backed down the steps and turned to go.

The trailer door crashed opened. A bloodcurdling scream split the air. Liv whirled around as a body rolled down the steps and fell in a huddle at her feet.

Chapter Two

Liv held back a scream as the body uncoiled and sprang to his feet. He stepped back on one foot and made a rolling flourish with his hand as he bowed.

"Velcome."

His bow was more Uriah Heep than court jester, and his accent was as phony as the worst off-off-off Broadway play. The Zoldoskys were probably from Brooklyn. He tilted his face up and winked at her.

Tumbler, right, thought Liv, sucking in air. He was a lanky man with dark, slicked-back hair and was dressed in dirty work pants and an even dirtier T-shirt.

A second man appeared in the doorway to the trailer, and Liv automatically turned toward him. He was a smaller man with lighter hair. His face was disfigured, the nose crushed and bent to one side. His left cheek was flattened and scarred by some kind of terrible accident. Liv had to fight the instinct to look away.

"Mr. Zoldosky?"

The man disappeared inside and shut the door.

"And you are?" The tumbler slowly eyed her from head to foot and back again. His eyes stopped on hers. They were hard and dark and . . . calculating.

Liv forced a smile. "Liv Montgomery, event coordinator for Celebration Bay."

"Liv Montgomery," he said, drawing the syllables out as his eyebrows drew together.

"I came, Mr. Zoldosky, to—"

"I am Anton Zoldosky." The deep voice sounded in her ear; the breath touched her skin and sent a chill up her back. She jumped, twisted around, and came face-to-face with another dark-haired man. He was older and stockier than the other two brothers. His hair was thinning and long enough to curl behind his ears. Craggy eyebrows hid deep-set eyes. And he was incredibly light on his feet. She hadn't even noticed his approach.

Liv regrouped and looked him straight in the eye. He wasn't that much taller than her five feet six. "As I was saying, I'm Liv Montgomery." She turned slightly to include the tumbler, but he'd vanished without a sound.

Anton jutted out his chin. "I heard you," he said, in an accented voice that sounded entirely real. "But you are not the other lady."

He must be talking about Janine. "No. The trustees brought me in from New York City," Liv said, positioning herself so that her back was to the trailer. She didn't want any more Zoldoskys creeping up on her. "They realized that it was time to hire a professional."

"Ah, a professional." There was a glint in his eye that made Liv glad she was standing in a sunlit field and not some back alley at midnight in Manhattan. This was one intimidating family.

But Liv was used to intimidating bullies, though they were usually better dressed. She cleared her throat. "Yes. I came by to introduce myself and welcome you to this year's festival."

"And do you meet every one of the vendors personally?"

"As many as I can." At least, she would make it her business to vet each and every one of the participants from now on.

"And you chose to meet the Zoldosky brothers first." Another glint of his eye. There was no mistaking his meaning now; it was pure malice.

Liv gestured around the field. "You're one of the first ones here."

"Ah, zoh we are."

"I also wanted to take this time to remind you to reread your agreement with the town. The rules will be strictly enforced this year." She smiled. "Especially the ones on soliciting funds outside of the contract."

He looked momentarily disconcerted.

"No panhandling," she said. She considered taking the time to reiterate the rules one by one, but decided against it. Two men were walking out of the surrounding trees and headed toward the trailer, presumably two more brothers. As they got closer, Liv could see that one had his arm in a sling.

And suddenly Liv had seen enough of the Zoldosky family. "Enjoy your stay here. I look forward to seeing your act in town. Good-bye."

She headed toward her car, measuring her steps to let Anton Zoldosky know she was not so easily cowed. She heard the low rumble of laughter behind her and forced herself to stop at her car and wave good-bye. Then she jumped inside and locked the doors.

Anton Zoldosky stood with his feet apart, his fists planted on his hips, and his eyes on Liv. The original Zoldosky had reappeared and was juggling three brightly colored scarves, his mouth pulled up in an almost rictus-looking grin. The smaller brother hadn't reappeared, but the brother with the sling had joined them and was staring after her car. The last brother was nowhere to be seen. Liv didn't stick around to find out where he'd gone.

Five of them. And all of them unfriendly. Liv's hands were actually trembling as she bounced through the field to the road. They usually did that only when she was hanging on to the shreds of her temper. But this was different. Anton Zoldosky had definitely been trying to intimidate her. And had pretty much succeeded.

She'd let them get to her, and that was so unlike her. Though in her defense, the Zoldoskys weren't like the people she usually hired for an event—caterers, waiters, and bouncers all wanting to be actors.

And they certainly weren't like the self-centered, demanding, and richer-than-the-mint clients she'd left behind. The Zoldoskys looked like they could do bodily harm if they wanted to. Actually, she imagined that a few of her former clients were capable of doing bodily harm, or at least hiring someone to do it for them, though she was pretty sure none of them had ever taken out a contract on an event planner.

She wasn't so sure about the Zoldoskys.

The *Celebration Clarion* was housed in a little white cottage that made Liv think of John Boy and the Waltons . . . until she got closer. The green shutters were peeling, the porch sagged, and the house looked uninhabited.

She pulled out her iPhone. Checked the time. Only two eighteen. Charles Bristow should still be there. She fished the newspaper ad out of her shoulder bag and walked toward the house. The porch creaked as she stepped across it, and she had to search before she found the bell, which was a brass handle set in the center of the door. She gave it a twist and heard two loud rings, but no accompanying footsteps.

After a minute or so, she tried the knob. The door opened, and she peered into a gloomy room that seemed stuck in transition between parlor and reception area.

"Mr. Bristow?"

Hadn't she just done this a half hour ago? At least she could rest easy that Mr. Bristow wouldn't come somersaulting out of his office. The Bristows had owned the paper since 1910, and though she imagined that the original editor had long ago departed for that printing press in the sky, Charles Bristow Jr. had to be getting up there.

She listened; heard a regular, rhythmic sound echoing from the back of the house. Someone was snoring. She followed the snores through the front room and into another dim room that had probably once been a bedroom but was now crammed with computer equipment, a large printer, stacks of paper, and a long couch occupied by a recumbent man.

The folded sections of a newspaper covered his midsection. Long legs and big, beat-up work boots stuck out from the bottom edges. An open double section covered his face and ruffled with each breath.

"Mr. Bristow?" Getting no response, Liv gently poked him where his arm should be.

A grunt, a snort, and he settled back into his rhythmic breathing.

She didn't want to give the old guy a heart attack, but she had stuff to do. She grasped the toe of his boot and gave it a shake.

There was spluttering. And movement beneath the paper. A veritable boxing match with the news, and Mr. Bristow bolted upright. "What?"

"I'm sorry," Liv began.

He batted away the paper and scowled at her.

Liv forgot the rest of her apology. Charles Bristow unfolded from the couch, dropped his size-thirteen work boots to the floor, and sat up, staring at her from beneath a shock of dirty-blond hair. His blue eyes were slightly dazed but growing more focused by the second. He was closer to thirty-five than eighty-five, and he was stomach-twisting gorgeous—if you liked the scruffy type.

"Mr. Bristow?" His name came out in a squeak. Liv cleared her throat, took control of the situation. "Mr. Bristow. I'm sorry to interrupt your nap." *Not that someone this young and virile and in charge of a newspaper should be sleeping on the job.*

"Then why did you?" His voice was a baritone, gravelly from sleep. Maybe he'd been out on a story the night before.

Liv stuck out her hand.

He looked at it, then crossed his arms.

Liv dropped her hand. The man might look like the prince out of a Disney movie, but he was rude, uncouth, and, from the looks of the office, a lazy slob to boot.

"I'm Liv Montgomery."

"How nice for you." He heaved off the couch and, scratching his head, wandered over to a cluttered countertop and a coffee carafe that held two inches of something that looked like motor oil. He rummaged around until he found a paper cup and poured the sludge into it.

"Okay, Liv Montgomery. What the hell is so urgent that you had to wake me up? Town hall on fire?"

She looked around for a light source, found a lamp periscoping up from piles of loose papers, and turned it on. Charles Bristow blinked hard, then let out a long, deep yawn.

Not only was he lazy, he was ill-mannered and badly dressed. Both elbows of his plaid shirt were shredded threads; his jeans were in even worse shape.

Rein it in, Liv. Be nice.

She unfolded the newspaper to the ad. "The festival committee placed what was supposed to be a full-page ad in the *Clarion*." She handed him the paper, which he reluctantly took and even more reluctantly looked at. "As you can see, this ad is only a half page."

"So? A Boy Scout found a cache of arrowheads up by Dawely's Point. Possibly of Mesolithic origin. That would be a first around here. I co-opted a little space from the ad. Big deal. Who the hell did you say you were?" He tasted the coffee, made a face, and put it down on top of a mountain of papers.

Liv had to resist the urge to move it somewhere safe.

"My name is Liv Montgomery, as I said before. I'm the new event coordinator in Celebration Bay."

"Oh yeah, the résumé from the big city."

"Excuse me?"

"Just so you know, I voted against you."

"You? You're on the board of trustees?"

"Yep."

How could this . . . this big oaf be her boss? She'd met the other trustees, but not him.

"Boggles the mind, don't it?"

His lapse in grammar didn't fool her one bit. He was just being obnoxious.

"Mr. Bristow."

"Call me Chaz. Everyone else does."

"I just bet they do," she mumbled.

"What's that?"

"Chaz." She smiled her calm-before-the-storm smile. If he wanted to play, she'd play . . . for a minute or two. It wouldn't hurt her to keep her claws sharpened. She might need them if she had to go up against the Zoldosky brothers again.

"Now, about the ad. We depend on you to disseminate information about the festival; therefore—"

"Honey, it's a local paper. Trust me, everyone knows when the damn festival is."

"We'd also like visitors to the area to have the information available to them."

"Speak for yourself." He sat down on the couch, looking as if he had every intention of resuming his nap. "Hell, you can't take two steps without running into one of your posters. Anyone with half a brain can figure it out."

"That's not the point."

"It is to me."

"If you don't care to support our activities, you could at least fulfill your contractual obligations with the festival."

He snorted. "Did Janine tell you we had a contract?"

"Well, no, but that will be remedied immediately."

"No need."

Oh, yes, there was. She wondered how many other citizens had been stiffing the festival like Charles Bristow was doing.

He yawned. "Nice to have met you. I'm sure you can find your way out. You didn't have any trouble finding your way in." He lay down and pulled the newspaper over his head.

She yanked it off again. "When an organization pays for a service, said organization expects to receive that service."

"Oh, nag nag nag. If I wanted a wife, I would've bought one." He snatched the paper from her hands. "And FYI, you haven't paid me." He smiled up at her, clearly thinking he'd gotten in the last word.

"For how long?"

"Let's see. You still owe me from Memorial Day weekend. Oh yeah, the Strawberry Festival, Arbor Day. I think that's it. Nope, there was Midsummer Mardi Gras, too."

"That's over three months of advertising."

"Janine knows how to hold a grudge."

Liv was so tempted to ask him what he'd done to Janine, but she bet she could guess.

"If you'll send in copies of the invoices, I'll see that you are duly compensated."

"Do you always talk like a court stenographer, the party of the first part . . ."

Only when she was pissed . . . or nervous, and she was currently both.

"The party of the second part, the hambone connected to the leg bone . . . duh doo doo di doo . . ." He lay down and covered his face with the paper again.

This time Liv left him to it. She removed the precariously

balanced cup of coffee and saw herself out. She heard his, "Have a nice day," follow her as she shut the front door.

It was late afternoon by the time Liv picked up Whiskey from Ted and set off at a trot across the green toward home. She opened a can of dog food and fed Whiskey, took a carton of leftover Chinese from the fridge, and headed to her bedroom, where she quickly changed clothes and reapplied her makeup while she ate. She grabbed her keys and purse from the foyer table.

"Gotta go," she called. "Traffic Committee meeting, but as soon as this weekend is over we're getting back into a routine."

She decided to walk to the meeting. It was a lovely night, and she hadn't gone for a real run in days. She struck off toward town hall at a brisk walk.

The meeting went well, but it was still after ten when they adjourned, and even Liv's Top-Siders were beginning to pinch.

Fred Hunnicutt caught up to her as she walked out of the meeting room. "Well, that's the quickest we've gotten through that meeting ever, and we have you to thank for it."

Like his wife, Dolly, Fred always had a ready smile and a compliment. They even resembled each other, stocky and well padded, except Fred was nearly bald.

"Thanks," Liv said and waved to several committee members as they made their way to the street. "It was touch and go at first; Manhattan has nothing over Celebration Bay for bandying opinions."

"I expect we do a little better than them. We've been fighting over the same things for a couple of centuries, but you handled them like a pro. First time anybody ever did a spreadsheet and flowchart on traffic. I think everybody was so surprised they forgot to argue. Dolly won't believe her eyes when I show up before midnight. Where's your car?"

"I left it at home. It's only a few blocks and this may be one of the last mild nights we get, if Ted is to be trusted."

"We might get a few more. And where was Ted tonight?"

"I gave him the night off. Between showing me the ropes and getting his own work done, he's been working overtime. And we're just going to get busier over the weekend."

"Well, I'm going your way. I'll walk you home."

"Thanks." They cut through the park, following the path between the half-finished booths.

"I think this is going to be the best one yet," Fred said. "Kinda dark, though."

"It is tonight," Liv agreed as they stepped into the shadows between two circles of light cast by the cast-iron lampposts. "But the booths and the smaller trees will all be festooned with white and orange lights. Plus all the stores and restaurants will be lit. We'll be fine."

"You sure do think of everything."

"It's my job."

"Yeah, but you also enjoy doing it. I can tell."

"I do." It was just as many hours as she'd worked in the city. There had been snafus and frayed tempers, and she knew there would be more before the harvest festival was over and they set up for Halloween. But she *was* enjoying it. It felt right.

She had a sneaking suspicion that she'd found her home.

Liv stopped when they got to the gate of the picket fence that surrounded Fred and Dolly's cottage. Like all the houses in downtown, it was impeccably kept, freshly painted, and as charming as a postcard.

"I'll walk you on home," Fred offered.

"Thanks, but it's only another block; you go in and surprise Dolly."

Fred smiled and Liv felt a little envious, wondering how it would feel to have someone smile like that over her after twenty-five years of marriage. She couldn't even imagine someone smiling like that after a few dates.

Event planning and longevity in relationships did not mix. "Go on inside."

"If you're sure."

"I'm sure, but thanks. Tell Dolly I'll see her tomorrow."

As he opened the gate, something moved in the shadows.

"Fred," Liv whispered, grabbing his arm. "Over there, someone is in your driveway."

"Where?"

"There." Liv pointed just as the shadowy form of a man slipped into the hedge that ran along the property line.

"Probably one of the teenagers taking a shortcut."

Two houses down a pickup truck started up and sped out of sight.

Fred walked out into the street and peered after it. "It doesn't look like any truck I know of. I better go in and check on Dolly. You come, too. I don't want you alone out here until we make sure there's nothing wrong."

Liv didn't argue.

Fred opened the gate, ran ahead, and flung the front door open. "Dolly? Dolly? Where are you?" He rushed into the living room, Liv right behind him.

Dolly appeared in the doorway to the kitchen. Her hair was down; she'd changed out of her gingham and was wearing a purple velour tracksuit. Her hand was pressed to her chest.

"Thank heavens, you're here. There was a man—a Peeping Tom—at the window. Oh Fred, he didn't look human."

Chapter Three

....

"I'm calling Bill Gunnison right now." Fred gave his wife a reassuring hug and steered her toward Liv. "Do you mind staying until Bill gets here, and then I'll walk you home?"

"Of course I'll stay. Why don't we sit in the living room, Dolly? Can I make you some tea or something?"

"No, dear, I'm all right. It was just such a fright. And now to drag poor Bill out when he's down with a bad back."

Bill Gunnison showed up ten minutes later. Fred opened the door, and the police chief slowly shuffled his way into the room. Normally he was a tall man, well over six feet, with grizzled gray hair and twinkling blue eyes. Tonight he was bent over at the hips, which made him almost the same height as Fred.

"Oh, Bill," Dolly said. "You shouldn't have come out. You sit right down."

Bill crooked his head up to look at her. "Thanks, but I'm better standing." He managed a smile and fumbled inside his jacket pocket for a tape recorder. "You don't mind if I use this?"

Dolly shook her head, and Fred came to sit beside her.

Bill mumbled into the tape recorder, then lifted his head back to Dolly. "Now, tell me what happened."

"I was in the kitchen doing the dinner dishes when I heard a noise outside. It sounded like a raccoon was getting into the trash, so I went to the back window to look out, and he was there at the window staring right at me. Not the raccoon, the man."

Bill nodded and winced. "Can you describe him?

Dolly shook her head. "He didn't look human. More like a ghost—no, a skeleton. He was all white with black holes for eyes. Then his mouth opened and I think he laughed at me. It was awful."

"Sounds like he was wearing a mask, didn't want to be recognized, maybe."

"Recognized? But we don't know anyone who goes around looking in people's windows."

"Dolly, you'd be surprised at what some folks will do. Anything else?"

Dolly shook her head. "I ran out of the kitchen, and then Fred and Liv came in and we called you."

Bill twisted his head to Fred and Liv. "You two see anything?"

"Liv saw someone in the driveway, but when I looked he was gone."

"Ms. Montgomery?"

"I saw someone moving along the driveway. Then he, or she, slipped through the hedge and was gone. But a few moments later, maybe half a minute, a truck started up down the street and took off. It might have been coincidence but . . ." She shrugged.

"I didn't recognize it," Fred said. "But it was dark—gray, green, maybe blue. Not sure, just that it was dark; these days I don't see so good at night."

"Yeah," agreed Bill. "We're all getting that way."

"Middle age," Fred said. "Though Dolly here says we'd

have to live to be over a hundred if this is middle age." He smiled fondly at his wife. "And I hope we do."

"You're embarrassing Ms. Montgomery." Bill turned to Liv. "Anything else?"

"That's all. We came inside and Fred called you."

He clicked off the tape recorder and slipped it back in his pocket. "I'll talk to the neighbors tomorrow. Maybe someone saw something, or can at least tell me whose truck it was."

Fred stood up. "Thanks, Bill. Sorry to call you out when you're all banged up."

"Glad to do it. Ms. Montgomery, are you staying here tonight?"

"No, I was on my way home. And please call me Liv."

"You're welcome to stay here if you're nervous about being in that carriage house alone."

"Thanks, Fred, but I'm from the city. I can take care of myself." She could; she had the black belt to prove it, but she welcomed Bill's offer to drive her home.

He pulled all the way into the driveway of the old Victorian house and stopped in front of the carriage house Liv rented from the Zimmerman sisters, Edna and Ida, two retired schoolteachers who lived in the main house. Liv had fallen in love with the little cottage the first time she saw it. It had a cozy living room with a small fireplace, a separate bedroom, a tiny kitchen and bath, and was surrounded by trees and silence. It was close enough to the old Victorian for Liv to feel safe but not so close as to become a source of gossip. Not that she had anything to hide. Unfortunately.

Tonight she was glad of the proximity, and though she declined Bill's offer to search the premises, she let him walk her to the door.

"Are you sure you don't want me to take a look around?"

"Thanks, but I'll be fine. Plus I have Whiskey to protect me."

Bill twisted his neck to see her better. "Whiskey?"

Liv smiled. "Yes. Can't you hear him on the other side of the door?"

Liv unlocked the door and was met with a bouncing, jumping, barking, white whirlwind.

"This is Whiskey, my Westie terrier. Whiskey, meet Sheriff Gunnison."

Whiskey and Bill cocked their heads at each other. Sizing each other up as only two men could do, regardless of what species they were.

"I'll just wait here while you let him out for a minute."

Realizing he was being given a carte blanche, Whiskey scampered past them and disappeared into the shrubbery. He returned a few minutes later, looking satisfied and without any small animals to present to his mistress.

"Good night, Bill. Thanks for seeing me home."

"Go inside."

She did and locked the door. Then she scooped up Whiskey and stood at the window until Bill drove away.

"A Peeping Tom," she said.

Whiskey cocked his head and licked her face.

"I know—not something you run into on the fifteenth floor of a Manhattan high-rise." She pulled the curtain shut with one hand and carried Whiskey back to the bedroom.

He squirmed out of her arms and headed for his doggie pillow.

"Okay, but if a Peeping Tom comes to our window, I'll expect you to protect me."

Whiskey yawned and settled down to sleep.

Liv quickly brushed her teeth and hopped into bed, listening for sounds of footsteps outside her window; all she heard were the contented snores of an unworried pooch.

"I hope you're right," she murmured, and snuggling into the comforter, she fell asleep.

Saturday morning arrived, cold and crisp. Cars and trucks were juggling for space as people unloaded their wares and set up their booths and tents. Bright pennants flapped in the early-morning wind. Somewhere a flute was playing an Irish tune.

Liv and Ted stood on the town hall steps, Ted holding her clipboard while Liv cupped her latte in both hands to warm her stiff fingers.

"Don't worry. It will warm up as soon as the sun gets over the mountains, and all will be right with the world."

"At least there have been no new reports of Peeping Toms," Liv said.

"No, but there was a brawl last night at Soapy's Roadside Grill out on the county road."

"I'm not counting that as a Harvest by the Bay incident."

"I wonder who it was?"

"The fight?"

"The Peeping Tom. I don't recall ever having one of them before." He chuckled.

"There's something amusing about some pervert staring in your window?"

"No, but I was just thinking. . . ."

"About what?" Liv coaxed. Ted knew everything about everyone, but he made you work for it.

"It's kind of a strange coincidence that it was Dolly's window he chose to peep through."

"Why?"

"Back when Dolly was in high school, the boys used to sneak up to her bedroom window and watch her. And don't you dare tell her I told you."

"Dolly?"

Ted nodded. "I know it's hard to look at her and think anything but jolly grandmother, but she was a looker in her day, the first girl to have"—he made a gesture with his hands—"padding in all the right places."

Liv smiled. "Ted, I'm shocked. Were you one of those boys?"

"Heavens, no. I was too mature for that. Plus I was a few years older than that crowd. Now, Joss Waterbury. He and his younger brother, Pete, had more than one fistfight over her. They both had it bad for Dolly."

"You're kidding. I don't think I've met Joss's brother."

"He ran off right after high school. Or should I say right after Dolly disappointed everyone by marrying Fred Hunnicutt. Never came back. Good riddance to bad trash." He looked thoughtful, then smiled. "Now you know the real story of Dolores Vanderboek Hunnicutt."

"I'll never look at Dolly the same way again."

"Come on, let's go check out the fruits of our labor." They walked across the street and into the green where booths lined both sides of the walkways. They passed a trio of strolling troubadours and sampled local honey on little squares of homemade whole wheat bread.

Liv stopped to watch two ladies from A Stitch in Time Fabric and Quilting who were sewing a colorful patchwork quilt stretched taut on a large rectangular frame.

"The pattern is called Holiday Harvest," said one of the ladies.

These people sure knew how to carry out a theme, thought Liv as she admired the tiny stitches delineating leaves and acorns. "It's beautiful," she said.

They moved on to an apple-saucing demonstration, then a table set up for pumpkin painting and a bobbing-for-apples station with four huge half barrels filled with water and apples. Liv tried not to think of the sanitation rules that were being broken. It was a take-your-chances situation, and plenty of kids and some adults were having a blast leaning over the barrels, their hands behind them, chasing the floating apples around the surface.

There were homemade jams, pickled watermelon rinds, pies and cakes. A caricaturist. A man who played tunes on half-filled beer bottles. A magician and an Uncle Sam on stilts.

"Recycled from the Fourth of July," Ted told her.

Carts of cotton candy, candy apples, roasted peanuts, and funnel cakes dotted the pathways. The smoke from cooking sausages, frankfurters, hamburgers, and corn dogs thickened the air and tempted the nose.

At the fork in the sidewalk, the Zoldosky brothers had set up a colorful plywood proscenium. The brother with the disfigured face sat off to the side blowing up balloons from an air canister. Anton was tossing bowling pins to one of the other brothers. They were both dressed like Heidi's grandfather, complete with Tyrolean hats. Anton finished by throwing the pins high in the air and catching them one by one.

They bowed to the smattering of applause and the third brother, dressed in a clown's outfit, a white face, and a pointed red hat, replaced the other two and began juggling three brightly colored scarves. Though his face was painted, Liv recognized him right away. It was the same juggling Zoldosky who had somersaulted out of the trailer and scared the crap out of her. And those had to be the same scarves he'd been juggling as he watched her drive away from the Miller farm. He caught Liv's eye and winked as he snatched the pink, orange, and green scarves from the air and tossed them up again.

Liv gave him a perfunctory smile and started to move on, but Ted was staring as if it were the most entertaining thing he'd ever seen. The juggler turned his back and, still juggling, walked behind the flats while Anton once again took the stage.

"Ready to go?"

Ted shook himself. "What? Oh, yeah. I think we should

get by the farmers' market. There was a little bickering about sites this morning, though I'm sure Fred took care of it."

"Still, I should check it out. You can stay and watch the jugglers if you'd rather," she teased.

"No. I thought . . . No. I'm done."

But as they reached the street, Ted stopped. "Do you mind going by yourself? I just remembered something I should take care of."

"No problem. I'll catch you later." Liv started across the street, then realized Ted still had her clipboard.

She turned to stop him, but he was already gone. Then she caught sight of him backtracking his way across the green.

"Ted," she called, but he didn't hear her. She sprinted after him.

She was only a few yards behind him and was about to call out again, when he ducked behind the Zoldoskys' stage. Odd. She'd told him she'd taken care of the panhandling problem. But what else could have sent him back?

She was into delegating responsibility, but she needed her clipboard. She followed him behind the stage set just as Ted grabbed the arm of the tumbling Zoldosky.

The tumbler tried to knock his hand away, but instead of letting go, Ted pulled him closer, until the man was raised on his toes, and they were almost nose to nose.

Liv stared. This was her mild-mannered, gentlemanly assistant? She couldn't imagine what was going on, but she knew better than to interrupt. This was no panhandling altercation. This, whatever it was, was personal.

The balloon-making brother came around the far end of the proscenium and stopped. Ted dropped his hands, the tumbler stumbled backward, the brother ducked out of sight, and Ted strode off across the grass and was swallowed up by the crowd.

Astounded, Liv looked back at the tumbler; he was starring straight at her. Then he, too, turned and walked away.

On her way to the farmers' market, Liv tried to erase what

she'd just witnessed. At least Ted hadn't seen her. No one liked to have their less-than-stellar moments witnessed by their boss. But she couldn't help wondering what it was all about.

Later, when she saw Ted long enough to retrieve her clipboard, he didn't mention the Zoldoskys and neither did she. She didn't see him again until ten o'clock, when the last booths closed down. Most of the entertainers had long ago departed, along with most of the tourists. Only the Zoldosky brothers had remained to collect their stage and equipment when vehicles were allowed into the park for the vendors to pack up for the night. The permanent stores were dark; only the restaurants were still open, catering to the die-hards.

"Great work," Ted told her.

Liv yawned. "Sorry. You, too."

"See you bright and early. Eight o'clock?"

"Barring any disasters."

"God forbid. Good night."

"Night," Liv said and walked across the empty green toward home, wondering if she'd imagined the whole confrontation.

Whiskey was waiting for her by the door. Bits of leaves and muddy paw prints littered the foyer floor.

"I see you've been helping Miss Edna in the garden. Come on, let's get you cleaned up. The floor can wait."

Ten minutes later Whiskey was stretched on his bed gnawing on a rawhide bone. Liv turned out the light, crawled into the bed, and fell into an exhausted sleep.

It seemed like she'd hardly closed her eyes before her alarm went off. She groped for it in the dark, slapped at it, but it kept ringing. Then she realized it wasn't her alarm clock but her cell phone.

She sat up and peered at the clock. "Five o'clock? This better be important."

She turned on the lamp and pressed send. "Hello?" she croaked.

"Liv, it's Ted. We have a problem."

She was already out of bed and pulling her bureau drawer open with one hand.

"I'm at Waterbury's farm. I think you'd better get out here right away."

"I'm on it. Is everyone okay?"

"Not exactly."

"What do you mean? Joss? Amanda? One of the kids? Fire? Ted, talk to me."

"Just get over here. Drive carefully." He hung up.

Liv pushed her feet into sneakers and grabbed her new flannel jacket. Whiskey yawned, stretched, and settled back to sleep.

"You lucky dog," she whispered and tiptoed out of the room.

It was barely light outside and the grass was wet with dew. She drove as quickly as she could, the windshield wipers swiping out an arc of visibility in the condensation.

Lights were on in the farm store when Liv pulled into the parking lot. No flames, no ambulances. A burglary? She prayed she wouldn't walk in to a trashed store and broken cash register.

Ted met her at the door. "Bill is on his way," he said as he pushed her through the empty and—as far as she could tell—intact store. "At a snail's pace. I thought you should know what's happened before . . ." He trailed off as they reached the door to the antique cider press exhibit.

Joss stood with his back to them, leaning over the 1880s antique press. He turned as they entered, and Liv saw what he'd been looking at.

A man was stuffed into the barrel. His arms and legs hung over the sides and his middle was pinioned by the round cast-iron apple press. A pink scarf was tied over his eyes and a shiny red apple was stuffed into his mouth. He was still wearing his clown suit and white face makeup.

At first Liv thought it was a gruesome joke, but one look at Ted and Joss and she knew this was for real. Mr. Zoldosky had juggled his last scarf.

She heard a car door slam and hoped to heaven it was the police.

Joss lifted his head, then looked at Ted. "That's Bill."

"Most likely."

"I have to know."

"Then be quick about it."

Joss knelt down and reached toward the body.

Liv opened her mouth and tried to say, *Don't touch anything*, but nothing came out.

Joss yanked the apple out of the mouth and dropped it to the ground. The mouth gaped open, like a silent scream, and Liv's stomach turned.

Joss didn't seem to notice. He snatched the blindfold away and scrubbed it across the man's face, revealing a smear of skin and a streak of blood. A gurgling sound erupted from Joss, and he fell to his knees.

"What is it?" Liv asked just as Bill Gunnison hobbled through the door.

"Jesus H. Get away from the body. Don't you people watch television?" Clutching his back, Bill hurried closer, peered at the dead man. "Damn," he muttered under his breath. He stepped closer and bent stiffly over the body. He looked back at Joss. "Is that? It couldn't be . . ."

"Well, it is," Ted said, sounding as gruff as Liv had ever heard him.

"Damn and damnation. Still, you shouldn't have touched him."

Joss pushed himself to his feet with Ted's help. "I know, but I had to know."

"Know what?" Liv asked, exasperated, nauseated, and beginning to panic.

Joss made a strange hysterical laugh. His voice cracked, and he covered his face with his hands.

Ted squeezed his arm and came to stand by Liv.

"What's going on?"

"Remember me telling you about when Dolly was young?"

"Yes."

Ted lifted his chin toward the dead juggler. "Well. That's Joss's brother, Pete."

Liv frowned at him. "Joss's brother? I thought he was a Zoldosky brother."

Chapter Four

....

"If only he were," Ted said, shaking his head.

Liv stepped closer and peered over Bill's shoulder. There was a definite resemblance to Joss. The dead man was thinner, rougher looking; life had not been kind to him. And neither had death. Blood smeared his cheek and made a sickening contrast with the white greasepaint.

And even more sickening was the fact that was slowly seeping into Liv's brain. The man didn't hit his head and climb into the barrel for a nap. Someone had put him there, the same someone who had hit him over the head hard enough to kill him. Because, now that she had forced herself to look closer, she could see the bloodied, matted hair above his right ear.

Her stomach roiled, and she swayed on her feet. Joss's brother had been murdered.

Bill straightened and shuffled to face them. Perspiration had broken out on his forehead. "Joss, when do the rest of your people come on shift?"

"What?" Joss blinked hard several times. "Most of the

guys are over at the new mill already. The first shift starts at five. Donnie and I set up everything here; then Ronnie and Earl Weaver come in around eight thirty to run the electric mill for the tourists."

He ran a big hand over his face, leaving a streak of white paint and blood across his cheek. "Fiona Higgins keeps the register, and I hire a couple of teenagers to help out on the weekends. They come in at nine."

Bill looked around the room. "I'm sorry, Joss. But you better call them all and tell them not to come in today."

"I . . . Of course."

"Ted, you and Ms. Montgomery take Joss back to the house and wait for me."

"I'll make the calls," Ted said and took Joss's elbow.

Joss pushed him away. "I'm not leaving. That's my brother. Good God, that's my brother," he repeated as if it had just sunk in. "What the hell is he doing back here and dressed like a goddamned clown?"

Liv realized that he'd been working at the store all day yesterday and hadn't been in town to know about the jugglers.

She doubted if anybody would have recognized him after thirty years. It wasn't until Joss had removed the whiteface that he recognized him. And though Liv could see the resemblance between the two brothers now, she would never have guessed it without seeing them together.

She glanced at Ted and remembered his reaction to the jugglers the day before. She'd called his name twice to get his attention; then he'd gone back to confront the juggler. For what reason?

Joss was shocked, but Ted didn't even seem slightly surprised. Was that because he'd recognized Pete the day before?

Ted caught her eye, looked away. "Come on, Joss. Let Bill do his job."

"I don't understand," Joss said, holding his ground.

Neither did Liv. What was Pete doing in Joss's store? He

must have come straight from the festival since he was still wearing his costume and makeup. The store would have been closed by then. If he wanted to see his brother, why didn't he go to the house?

And that is for the police to figure out, she reminded herself. Solving a murder didn't come with her job description. Though she'd have to do something about stopping it from becoming public knowledge. If it got out that there was a murderer loose, it could kill the weekend. It could kill the town's reputation and their main source of income as surely as someone had killed Pete Waterbury.

There was a commotion outside, the sound of footsteps, and three faces appeared in the doorway.

Bill Gunnison groaned. "Folks, could you all move back? This, I'm sorry to say, is a crime scene."

"A crime scene?" Amanda Waterbury, still dressed in a robe and curlers, pushed her way past her son and daughter, who'd stopped in the doorway and were staring in open-mouthed horror. "I can't have a crime scene here. You'll have the inspectors closing us down." She stopped abruptly, obviously seeing the body for the first time.

Her hand went to her mouth.

"Don't be sick," Bill barked.

She shook her head, her eyes bulging above her fingers.

Donnie Waterbury moved his mother aside and stepped into the room. "Dad, what's going on? What happened? Who is that?"

Bill forced himself to stand a little straighter. The man needed backup—literally. "If you'll all just go into the other room."

"Who is it, Mom?" Roseanne Waterbury's cinnamon-red curls bobbed as she tried to see around her brother, Donnie. She saw the body, screamed, and began to cry.

Bill grunted in exasperation, or pain, or both. "Amanda, please take Roseanne and Donnie back to the house. This is no place for them or you."

"But what happened? Who is it? What's he doing in the apple press?"

Liv felt a hysterical giggle rise to the surface. She pushed it back down. A man was dead. Joss had lost a brother, and Liv had to do something before it cast a pall over the festival. And she didn't have a clue where to start.

"Oh my God," Bill groaned. "What are *you* doing here?"

They all turned as Andy Miller rushed into the room. He was dressed for the fields but he stuttered to a stop when he saw the body, and his face turned whiter than the victim's makeup.

He shook his head as if waking from a bad dream. "I heard it on my police scanner. I thought if there was trouble, I could help. I never thought. Oh my God." He dragged his John Deere cap off his head, revealing thinning corn-silk hair. "Oh my God. What on earth happened?"

"That's what I'm trying to ascertain," Bill said, holding on to his patience. "So, if you really want to help, you can take all these folks up to the house. Maybe make some coffee."

"But—"

"Now."

The sound of another arriving vehicle pulled Bill's concentration.

Bill's eyes rolled to the back of his head. "And if that's the crime scene van, tell 'em to park around back."

"Sure thing, Bill. Anything I can do." Andy herded everyone toward the door, but Liv hung back, absently staring at the body while her mind reeled off the implications of the crime as she made contingency plans for directing tourists away from the farm store.

"Ms. Montgomery? Liv?"

"What?"

"You really need to leave, too."

"Oh, of course, but . . . Bill, at the risk of sounding callous, I need to do something about this."

"You? Oh, you mean about the festival. Well, we can't let people in here today. They'll have to close."

"I realize that, but I don't want to have people panicking when they learn that a murder has been committed."

Bill winced, but Liv wasn't sure whether it was from pain or the idea of murder in his town. But she noticed he didn't contradict her. Pete Waterbury had definitely been murdered.

"It could have disastrous results for the festival and everyone who depends on it for their livelihood." The rumor that a murder had been committed on the premises might cause a full-blown panic, keeping visitors away in droves. Not to mention what it would do to Waterbury Farms's reputation. But if a murderer was still running loose, it could have tragic results.

"I'll have someone put up the chain across the entrance. There's a Closed sign attached to the chain."

Liv had noticed the two short posts on either side of the entrance. The chain and sign would be good enough to keep out cars, but what the hell was she going to do to stop the speculation?

She looked back at the body, trying to feel sad that a life had been lost, but mainly feeling angry that the Zoldoskys had brought this on the town.

"Bill—"

Several crime scene detectives came in. The head man gave Liv a look before turning to Bill. "Were you first on scene?"

Bill cleared his throat. "So to speak."

"Body been moved?"

Bill glanced at Liv. "Yes. In an effort to ascertain if the victim was alive."

The man turned to Liv. "Did you find the deceased?"

Liv shook her head. "No. I was just leaving." She scurried out of the room.

She had to force herself not to skulk behind the open door and listen to what the detectives said. It wasn't morbid fascination. She needed to get reassurance from the police that the murderer wouldn't strike again.

As if anybody could predict that.

She walked up to the house, looking around her for God knew what. The murderer hiding behind the hay bales? A murder weapon? A note saying, This is the only person I'll kill so don't worry.

Stop it; you're acting stupid. You need all your wits today. Just because this is your first murder doesn't mean you can lose it. You have a responsibility. Liv let herself in the open back door and stepped into what she imagined was a typical farm kitchen, with colorful curtains and lots of counter space for making family meals. Only today there was no bustling activity, no cozy warmth. Everyone was sitting around the long farmhouse table silently watching Joss stalk up and down the room like a cornered moose.

Ted poured her a cup of coffee and motioned her to a chair.

Liv didn't much feel like sitting down. She'd rather join Joss in his pacing. She knew she should say something, but after Joss's reaction to his brother's body, she was afraid that condolences would be out of line.

Amanda Waterbury watched her husband, her frown growing more intense as the minutes went by. Finally she broke her silence. "For heaven's sake, Joss. Talk to me. Did you know Pete was here?"

Joss shook his head.

"I just don't understand," she persisted. "Why now? Are you sure it was him?"

Ted came to stand by her chair. He patted her shoulder. "It was Pete. No doubt about it. You and Joss need some family time, time to talk to the kids and help them through this. As much as I hate having to bring this up, we need to decide what to do about the store."

"That's what I came for," Andy said. There was a shredded napkin on the table in front of him. "I wasn't just being ghoulish. I didn't even know. . . ."

"Of course not," Amanda assured him.

"When I heard the police call, I was afraid Joss had

gotten hurt or somebody was sick. I thought I could help out. I know how much we all depend on this weekend, and I figured if for some reason you couldn't open the store today, I'd come over to offer you space in my stand at the farmers' market. I had no idea that it would be . . . this."

He swallowed hard. "And that still goes. I'll be glad to take cider and doughnuts and any goods you want, put 'em in my stand. It won't be as good as having the store open, but you won't lose out on everything."

"That's so thoughtful of you, Andy," Amanda said.

Andy looked down at the table, his face working. "Hell, you'd do the same for me. Have done. That's what neighbors—friends—are for. Being there for each other when the going gets rough."

Joss finally stopped pacing and turned to the others.

Liv's breath caught at how much Pete Waterbury resembled his brother, even in death.

"I appreciate it, Andy, but I doubt if they'll even let us back into the store, much less load anything out." He heaved a sigh. "I thank you just the same." He stared past them, a man utterly deflated; then he banged both fists on the table.

Everyone jumped; silverware and china rattled.

"Thirty years. Thirty years he's never showed his face here, and when he finally comes back, he brings trouble with him."

Roseanne burst into tears. Donnie bit his lip, looking as if he might explode. And looking very much like his father.

"We'll get through this," Andy said.

Liv looked at Ted. He nodded toward the door. She stood up.

She stopped by Amanda's chair. "Bill is putting up the chain and the Closed sign. Would you like me to add something? Due to bereavement?"

"That's a joke," said Joss and leaned heavily on the table, his head drooping. "Damn him. Damn him to hell."

Chapter Five

....

"Whew," Liv said when she and Ted were outside.

Ted didn't comment, just looked toward the farm shop where the police photographer had arrived to take pictures.

"I guess he didn't get the message to park around back," Liv said.

"You're not going to keep this from spreading."

"Well, I can try." Liv took out her cell phone. "Who is the least gossipy person we can rely on to put a strike-through on the posters?"

Ted frowned. "Besides you, me, and Joss, I guess that would have to be Fred Hunnicutt."

Liv pressed a few keys and Fred's number came up. It took a while for him to answer.

"Is there a problem?" he asked in a sleep-groggy voice.

Liv realized it was only six o'clock. "You might say so. I can't explain now but the Waterbury store has to close for the day. I need you to get someone to strike out the venue on the posters. Just say, 'Closed for family reasons.'"

"What's wrong? I can't remember a time when Joss closed the store. Even when he and Amanda went on their second honeymoon to Niagara Falls a few years back. Something happen to the store? Not a fire?"

"No, no. Nothing's wrong with the store. It's just a family issue. I'll explain when I get to town, but can you just get this started for me?"

"Sure. I'll round up a couple of teenagers to help."

"Thanks. I really appreciate it."

"Is everything all right? Where are you?"

"I'm on my way." She hung up before he could ask any more questions. She turned to Ted.

"You'd better get back." He nudged her toward her car. "Things will spread like wildfire. Andy isn't the only person with a police scanner. I'd say every other house has one, and if they're still listening, which I'm sure they are, they'll know more about what's happening than we do."

Liv pressed her fingers to her forehead.

"Liv, if you can manage without me, I'll stay here for a while. I imagine Bill will want to talk to me. Then I'll help Andy load up his truck if Bill will release any of the goods. Otherwise, Joss will lose a bundle of money this weekend."

"Sure. Take whatever time you need." Liv hesitated.

Ted frowned at her. "What? If you need me in town, just say so."

"You're indispensable, but stay here and do what you can. I'll manage."

She had a sudden déjà vu. Ted telling her to go ahead without him and returning to the park to confront Pete Waterbury. Was he doing the same thing today? Getting rid of her because he had something specific to do that he didn't want her to know about?

She gave herself a mental shake. Of course not; he just wanted to be there for his friends. This was what violence did. Made you doubt everyone, even your closest friends.

"Joss doesn't seem to like his brother much. I get that, but why is he still so angry? The fight over Dolly was decades ago and Joss seems happily married; he has a great family."

"People around here have long memories."

That was something she didn't want to contemplate. She'd been in Celebration Bay for only a few weeks, and already she was getting to know the people, considered some of them friends, and didn't want any of them to turn out to be murderers.

And most of all, she didn't want to have to admit that there was a serpent in her newly found Eden.

"I'll see you in town."

Ted started. "What? Oh, yes, I'll try to move things along here and . . . Later." He turned and strode back to the house.

Liv waited until he was inside. The door closed and Liv was stabbed by the knowledge that she was an outsider. Of course the others had known one another for years, and she had no desire to be catapulted into their private lives. Besides, they were depending on her to keep this under wraps and make the weekend a success. And the first thing she needed to do to make that happen was talk to Bill. She headed toward the parking lot.

Bill Gunnison was coming out of the farm store with another man. He was not in uniform, but considering he was wearing dark trousers and a sports shirt, Liv surmised he was a detective, not a neighboring farmer. The two men stood talking for a minute, then shook hands, and the detective walked around to the back of the building.

"Bill?"

Bill looked up with a frown. "Bad business, this," he said.

"It is," Liv agreed. "I know you must be busy, but I need to ask you some questions."

"Liv, you know I can't discuss—"

Liv held up her hand, stopping him. "I don't want details, but I do need to know if you think it's safe for people to be in Celebration Bay today."

"Not much way of keeping them out. At least not without ruining a lot of folks' weekends, not to mention the financial loss to the town."

"And the town's reputation," Liv added. "But if there's a murderer loose . . ."

Bill sighed heavily. Gritted his teeth. "Well, between you and me, it looks like a crime of passion, though I'd be beholden if you don't pass that around."

"It did seem rather symbolic, didn't it? The scarf over the eyes, the apple in the mouth, like the monkeys."

"Monkeys?"

"You know—see no evil; speak no evil."

"Hmm." He frowned at her. "Funny you picking up on that."

She shrugged. "Attention to detail. It's an event planner's bête noire."

"Come again?"

"It's a pain in the butt, but I can't help it. It comes with the territory."

Bill nodded. "Well, if you notice anything else, please bring it to me before you say anything to anybody else."

"Of course. But do you think people will be safe? Do you have enough staff to investigate the"—she swallowed—"murder and provide security for the festival? Should I ask the traffic volunteers to be extra vigilant?"

"Good God, no." He glanced at his watch. "I'll handle it, but you'd best be getting into town. Things are bound to get out even if everyone's sworn to secrecy. I'd appreciate it if you'd do what you can to keep it under wraps until tomorrow."

Tomorrow, when most of the tourists would be gone. "Absolutely. I—"

He opened the car door for her. "And even then, no details. Mum's the word. If we want to catch the killer."

"Of course." She suddenly had a hundred questions, but she could tell Bill was anxious for her to leave. Reluctantly she climbed into the car. He shut her door and strode over to where a chain rested on the ground.

She would do what she could to staunch the gossip. It would be a disaster if Celebration Bay got the reputation of being a dangerous town.

Bill gave her a two-finger salute as she turned onto the road, then pulled the chain across the entrance behind her. As she drove away, she saw him heading for the house.

While Liv showered, her mind chewed at the events of the morning; the phone call, the shock of seeing Pete Waterbury pinned by the apple press. Joss's reaction.

The man disappeared for thirty years and came back now? Of all days, of all weekends? Liv had a hard time not taking his reappearance personally, which she knew was ridiculous. There were people in town who might have real reasons to be upset by his return. She just hoped—hell, she prayed—that none of them had murdered the man.

To her mind, the most likely suspects were the Zoldosky brothers. All four of them looked perfectly capable of committing murder. But she'd watched enough *CSI* and *Criminal Minds* to know that killers had a way of camouflaging themselves. Sometimes hiding away and sometimes hiding in full view until the geniuses of television prime time caught them.

As much as she liked Bill Gunnison, even without his sciatica, he just didn't seem like the high-tech, high-IQ, sophisticated profiler that always caught those malefactors. And Bill and a few deputies and officers had to patrol the whole county and the festival as well as investigate. She'd have to look into hiring special security for future events.

Especially in light of what had happened.

She dried her hair while she tried to organize the coming day, but she just kept coming back to the murder. She couldn't wrap her mind around it. Why? Why now? It just kept nagging at her. It was the strength as well as the bane of event planners, the attention to detail, predicting problems and solving them before they arose, being able to antici- pate complications and prepare for the road ahead. And in the worst case, dealing with problems beyond her control before the ramifications became too monumental to fix.

But Liv was at a total loss to understand or fix the events of this morning. She'd just have to wing it, because nothing, not even murder, was going to mess with her town, her fes- tival, her new life.

She grabbed a granola bar and opened the door to the garden. "Whiskey, I gotta go. Come here, buddy. Come on." Whiskey bounded out of a rhododendron bush and shot past her into the kitchen. She put her recharged batteries in her walkie-talkie and grabbed her canvas bag. When she got to the door, Whiskey was already there.

"Sorry, baby, but you have to stay home again. We've got trouble in Celebration Bay. I'll ask Miss Edna to take you for a walk later."

She squeezed out the door and locked it, and when she turned around she saw a little terrier face pressed to the living room window, looking pitiful. "Sorry," she said again. Even though he got more attention and exercise here than he ever did in Manhattan, he could still make her feel guilty.

Before she reached the end of the driveway, she heard her name being called. Miss Ida was standing on the front porch of the main house, her arms crossed over a light green twinset.

"Morning, Liv. We heard you go out early this morn- ing and—"

Miss Edna opened the front door and stepped onto the porch. "Sister, Liv is busy. Get to the point."

Miss Ida pursed her lips. Liv knew what was coming.

"We were listening to our police scanner this morning," she said. "And heard there was a commotion out at the Waterbury farm. They sent the sheriff out."

"That was just after you left," added Miss Edna, looking formidable in a tweed jacket and blue jeans. "But twenty minutes later they called for the CSI unit. What happened? And don't tell us you weren't out there. Where else would you have gone at that hour?"

"Now, Sister. It might not be any of our business. We just want to be sure no one was hurt. And if we should call Amanda to see if she needs help."

"None of the Waterburys were hurt," Liv said. "I can't say more. I have to get back to town."

"A robbery?" asked Miss Ida.

"I don't think so. We'll have to wait to hear from Bill Gunnison."

"I suppose so," Miss Ida said.

"Now I really have to run." Liv waved. "Can you let Whiskey out for a bit? I may be gone late."

"Don't worry about a thing. We'll take good care of him."

"Thanks," she said, heading for the street.

Miss Ida waved and smiled, but Miss Edna scowled after her. Ida might be satisfied with Liv's prevarication, but it was obvious that Miss Edna wasn't so easily fooled.

As Liv walked to downtown, she noticed that the posters had already been altered to reflect the closing of the Waterbury farm store, the name crossed out in thick black marker and replaced with: Closed Today, Family Emergency.

Fred had given just enough information to quell the complainers without raising suspicion or alarm.

A handful of vendors were setting up, getting an early start before their cars and trucks were banned from the area. None of the stores were open, though she could smell something delicious wafting from the direction of the bakery.

She glanced at her watch. Nearly seven. Two hours had passed since Ted's phone call. Such a short time in which so much had changed.

She shuddered and crossed the street. Dolly's wasn't open yet, but the lights were on at the Buttercup.

"It'll be another second," BeBe said. "I just turned on the steamer a few minutes ago. Didn't get to talk to you yesterday, but Ted said that you're the one that spotted Dolly's Peeping Tom."

"I just saw him running across the lawn."

"Probably one of those kids from the hills. They're always coming down into town to do their mischief." She opened a spigot and the steam screamed.

Liv jumped.

BeBe shot her a look as she placed the milk carafe under the spigot and the milk bubbled to the edges. "I don't want to shoot myself in the foot, but are you sure you need the caffeine this morning?"

"Positive," Liv said over the steamer. "I'm just feeling the stress. Caffeine helps stress."

"If you say so." When the milk was foamy, BeBe reached for a medium-size paper cup, pressed a double shot of espresso into it. "Do you know what is going on out at Joss and Amanda Waterbury's?"

"Some family emergency," Liv temporized.

"Someone sick? Not Amanda, I hope. She had really bad pneumonia last winter."

"No, Amanda's fine. I don't know the details. Just that they had to close today."

Her new job, her new home, and already she was having to lie. Liv's stomach turned sour. Even though she had done her share of hedging the truth in her old situation, she'd really hoped to avoid it here. Of course, she hadn't had to deal with murder back in Manhattan.

Sometimes life was just weird.

"Well, let me know if you hear anything." BeBe waved her out just as Fred Hunnicutt, wearing the orange vest of the traffic patrol, came in the door.

"Morning, Liv. What's going on up at Joss and Amanda's? I tried calling but no one answered. Nothing too terrible, I hope."

Depends on how you felt about Pete Waterbury, Liv thought.

"Joss ain't sick, is he? I saw him last night, and he just didn't look like himself."

Liv's attention perked up. She knew she shouldn't ask. Too much curiosity could set off a flood of speculation, but she couldn't miss this opportunity.

"How did he look? The flu, maybe?"

"No, I don't know. Just not like himself." He stopped to give his order. "Two medium house blends with milk, one black with two Sweet'N Lows."

BeBe nodded and began to pour coffee, but she stayed close enough to overhear anything they said.

"Kind of distracted, like maybe he was worried about something. It could be the flu, but the flu wouldn't close him down."

"When was this?" asked Liv.

"Well, let's see. It was toward the end of the evening. He came to pick up Donnie and Roseanne. They were supposed to meet him by the Methodist church. Joss was standing out front, but the kids were late. Roseanne came up while we were talking, but she hadn't seen Donnie. They took off across the park looking for him. I had to get on over to the bakery to pick up Dolly. Didn't want her going home alone."

So Joss was looking odd; maybe he was worried about his son or maybe he'd seen and recognized his brother.

"Hope it wasn't nothing with Donnie."

"Oh, no." Liv caught herself. "I'm sure someone would have heard if Donnie was hurt or something."

"More than likely." Fred reached in his pocket for money. "Hard to keep secrets in Celebration Bay."

They parted at the sidewalk. Liv dissected their conversation as she walked to her office. A strange choice of words. "Keep a secret," as if Donnie might be doing something he shouldn't. And maybe he was, but at that point, at least it hadn't been murder.

Which made her think of Ted saying that Pete Waterbury had left right after high school, that he and Joss had fought over Dolly. How would Dolly feel if she knew he was back and that he'd been murdered here?

She came to an abrupt stop, and coffee spurted through the container opening. What if the Peeping Tom had been Pete Waterbury? She thought back to that night, and Dolly saying that he didn't look human. Black holes for eyes and mouth.

Not a teenager up to mischief, but Pete Waterbury in whiteface. Up to his old pranks? Surely Dolly hadn't recognized him. Or had she? And told Fred, who told Joss when they were standing in front of the church waiting for Roseanne and Donnie.

Ridiculous. Her mind was running away with too little information and too much imagination. She had a festival to run and visitors to keep safe from a possible psychopath.

Everything looked as bucolic and festive as it had the day before. Of course, it was still early. Hopefully everyone was too busy getting ready this morning to have time to listen to their police scanners. And what was it with that? Liv sometimes listened to music on the radio in the mornings, but she didn't really get the appeal of starting your day with the snap, crackle, and pop of police communications.

She studied the park where the vendors were unpacking their wares. She wondered if the Zoldosky brothers had been told yet. And what was their story? Why was Pete Waterbury impersonating a Zoldosky and why were the real Zoldoskys letting him use their name?

Too many loose ends. Liv hated loose ends. They could sabotage a party or event with the snap of your fingers. Some things were out of her hands, but she could make sure everything else was secure.

Usually Ted opened the office, but today Liv walked into a dark, chilly room. She kept her jacket on while she drank her latte and organized her paperwork. She wondered when

Ted would be showing up and caught herself listening for the sound of footsteps in the outer office, but no one came.

She reviewed the contracts and invoices for the weekend, made sure all accounts were paid to date and no vendors were in arrears. She got out the checkbook to write the final checks to the entertainers, who were paid half on arrival and the second half at the end of the weekend.

She opened the checkbook to the last page of stubs. The bottom check was gone but nothing was written on the stub—no payee name, no date. Liv thought back. The last check she remembered writing was the one above the missing check, for additional garbage pickup. She checked the next page. All three checks were there with Ted's signature.

Maybe Ted had taken one for emergencies, but since both of them had to sign for it to be negotiable, that seemed unlikely. She'd have to ask him when he came back from the farm.

She was just finishing up when church bells began ringing, calling worshippers to nine o'clock services. She went to the window and looked out. A steady stream of people was entering the two churches on the square.

The people in Celebration took their celebrations, their families, their friends, and their religion seriously. Liv knew she would have to make an appearance in one of the churches soon if she were ever to be really accepted.

She had never been a consistent churchgoer. She never seemed to have the time, except, she realized now, in her busiest party seasons. Thanksgiving, Christmas, Easter, when she really didn't have time to go but couldn't resist the music and the message those holidays brought. Maybe there was a nascent churchgoer hidden inside her.

But for now, she had a festival to run. She put her cell phone and wallet in one pocket of her jacket and her walkie-talkie in the other. She shoved a stack of survey sheets into her canvas bag. She'd hand them out to the vendors later this morning and pick them up at the end of the day. The

questions were posed to give the committees a better idea
of the efficiency and convenience of the facilities. There was
a Web page where the surveys could be filled out online, but
at Ted's suggestion she'd decided to supplement that process
by one she could collect at the end of the day. Strangely
enough, not everyone was willing to go online to answer.

She left the office and cut through the alley between
Bay-Berry Candles and the Bookworm, the new and used
bookstore, to the municipal parking lot where the farmers'
market was already doing a healthy business.

The sun was just breaking and clear skies had been promised by the weather bureau. Rows of tables, tents, trucks
with their tailgates down, and cars with their trunks open
displayed produce. Some sellers had elaborate custom-
painted signs and special display boxes constructed to show
off their wares. Others had simple folding tables loaded with
local produce: apples in more varieties than Liv had ever
seen, pumpkins of all sizes, squash, funny-shaped gourds,
crisp broccoli, frilly kale, cabbage, cauliflower, shiny purple
eggplants, fresh and dried herbs, jars and jars of honey and
homemade preserves.

Liv found Andy Miller's stand strategically placed at the
end of the second aisle, near the street and the sidewalk that
people used to return to their parked cars or wait for the shuttle
that would carry them to lots farther from town. A basket of
corn, homegrown onions with the soil still clinging to them,
gourds, and the last crop of green beans sat at one end.

The other half of the table held a pyramid of Waterbury
cider bottles and jars of apple butter and grape jellies that
Amanda had made. There were no doughnuts, and Liv
knew everyone would be disappointed, but at least the day
wouldn't be a total loss.

Andy handed a paper bag to a woman with a double
stroller, and the woman rolled babies and produce away,
revealing Roseanne Waterbury standing behind the table
next to him.

Her rusty curls had been subdued into a long braid behind her back. She was wearing tight, low-slung jeans and a tight ribbed tank top with the obligatory flannel shirt tied around her neck.

Even with the sun up, the day was still chilly. The girl must be freezing for fashion. It made Liv feel a little better to see that she wasn't at home traumatized by the death of an uncle she'd never seen.

Roseanne smiled shyly as Liv walked up but evidently thought Liv would want an explanation. "Mom and Dad made me and Donnie come. I don't think they wanted us around with the police there." She slapped her hand over her mouth and looked quickly around.

"What police?" Janine Tudor, self-appointed society matron of Celebration Bay and former event coordinator, walked up to the stand and glowered at the little group clustered around the produce.

Of course Janine, of all people, would be in hearing distance. Liv plastered on a smile and turned around.

Janine was a tall, thin woman—Liv had never seen her eat anything but lettuce and rice cakes—with a frosted face-framing haircut that was always impeccably styled. (It was public knowledge that she went to a hairdresser in Albany every six weeks, no one in the county being expert enough for Janine's tastes.)

Today she was wearing a rust-colored pencil skirt and a goldenrod jacket. Both were obviously well made, but they reminded Liv of a seventies kitchen. Janine carried a brown leather handbag that matched her three-inch heels.

"What's happened now?" she asked accusingly, directing the question at Liv.

"Sorry," Roseanne said to Liv, making it worse.

"What police?" Janine repeated. "At your house, Rose? Was there a robbery?" She looked from one person to the next, her eyes stopping and staying on Liv.

Fred shrugged. "I'm kind of curious myself."

Andy suddenly became very busy rearranging the cauliflower display.

"No robbery," Liv said. "Just a little emergency; everything should be back to normal soon."

"So why were the police there? Is that where Bill Gunnison is? Just what is going on here? And who is protecting the town?" Janine's strident voice had attracted the attention of the people at the next stand, which was just what she intended. She'd been determined to make Liv look bad from the day she had arrived.

One of them came over. "What's all this talk about the police?"

"It's nothing," Liv told him. "But if you all keep saying 'police' at the top of your lungs, we won't have a visitor left in town."

"Oh," said the newcomer, whom Liv finally placed as Dexter Kent, owner of the garden center out on Lakeside Road. He leaned in closer and everyone followed suit.

Liv suddenly felt claustrophobic. "Look," she said, casting a quick glance at Andy and Rose, warning them to back her up. "It will all be cleared up, but it's best if we leave it until tomorrow and concentrate on selling today."

"Yeah," Andy said, picking up his cue. "No big deal. Let's sell some produce."

Liv smiled and said good-bye, but when she was several vendors away she turned back to the group. Their heads were together, customers ignored. She had no doubt that they were pumping Andy for the details.

Their choice; their loss if people started bailing on the afternoon. Hopefully, they were savvy enough to keep it among townspeople and not let it drift to the tourists' ears. Though she didn't have such hope for Janine's good sense.

She was sure to use the murder to make Liv look bad. Liv for the most part had been able to ignore Janine. In the scheme of things, she didn't hold a candle to some of the witches Liv had dealt with in the city. But if Janine started hurting the town, Liv would show her just what an ex-Manhattan event planner was made of.

Liv walked back to the park where everything seemed perfectly normal. So far, so good. With any luck they'd get through today without the news leaking out.

She was surprised to see the Zoldosky stage set up and Anton and one of the brothers practicing their act as if nothing were wrong, only today instead of bowling pins they were juggling odd objects: an ax, one bowling pin, and a plate. The disfigured brother was sitting in his normal place, twisting a yellow balloon into an elaborate form.

Their presence seemed a little coldhearted in light of Pete's demise. Of course, Pete wasn't really a brother, and Liv guessed whatever his relationship to them was, they weren't mourning him.

As she watched, another figure sauntered toward them and alarm bells clanged in her head. Of all the people she didn't expect to see at the festival, didn't want to see, the laziest newspaper editor in New York State, today of all days, had decided to do his job.

And Liv had to stop him.

Chapter Six

....

"Mr. Bristow!" Liv hurried to head him off.

He looked up and a wary expression invaded his face. His hair was sticking up and he hadn't shaved. He looked like he hadn't slept the night before; his face was drawn and his eyes were puffy. His jeans were baggy and his multi-pocketed khaki coat looked as if it had been smeared with—blood?

Liv's step stuttered. No. Not possible. Was it? Her hand automatically went to her walkie-talkie.

Right, Liv. What are you going to do? Bash him over the head with it? He surely didn't have a motive for murder. The man couldn't have been more than five years old when Pete Waterbury left town.

People around here have long memories, Ted had said. But not that long.

"Mr. Bristow," she said, coming to a stop in front of him. She was vaguely aware of Anton Zoldosky looking up from where he'd just taken a bow. The balloon brother had stopped twisting his animal shape and stared. And the other brother came to stand by his side.

"Ms. Montgomery," Chaz drawled.

On closer inspection, she saw that the stains were indeed a combination of mud and blood. There was a dirty handkerchief tied around two of his fingers.

Now that she had his attention, she wasn't sure what to do with him. She had to draw him away from the Zoldosky brothers on the outside chance that he wanted to ask them questions about the dead man. But she didn't want to draw him too far from the crowd in case he'd actually murdered Pete Waterbury.

She was saved by the cavalry, in the person of her assistant, Ted. She breathed out a sigh of relief.

Chaz Bristow raised one eyebrow at her.

"Morning, Chaz," Ted said just as easily as if he hadn't seen a murdered man in situ just a few hours before. "Any luck?"

What? Ted was in league with Chaz Bristow? Hell, even a lazy editor would take this info and run. It would be all over the front page tomorrow. Liv gave Ted a stern look, which made him frown.

"Sorry, I didn't mean to interrupt," Ted said.

"You're not interrupting," Chaz said. "At least, I don't think you are. Did you want something, Ms. Montgomery?"

"Oh, I was just saying hello . . . and . . . wondering if you'd like me to answer any questions about the festival. You *will* be doing an article on it for the *Clarion*, won't you?"

"Yes, Ms. Montgomery. But I don't think I have any questions for you at this time. Actually, I was on my way to talk to the Zoldoskys."

"No!" Liv blurted. "I mean, wouldn't you like to do a piece on the farmers' market? I could take you over." It was the first thing to come to her head. And the farthest venue from the jugglers.

"There's a farmers' market just about every weekend from May to October. I think maybe it would make boring reading."

Unlike the fishing reports, Liv thought grumpily.

Ted was grinning.

"I'll just come back later," Chaz said and started to ease away.

"What happened to your hand?" Ted asked, indicating the bandaged fingers.

Chaz shook his head. "Stupid. Sliced them during a hell of a fight last night."

Liv started. Pete Waterbury had been hit on the head. Not knifed. She'd seen the matted hair and the smear of blood left by the handkerchief. Bristow must have been in a bar brawl or something equally distasteful.

"Big one?"

"About eleven pounds."

Eleven pounds? What?

"But he fought like a tiger, tangled himself up in the rushes so bad I had to cut the line and a couple of fingers." He held up the bandaged hand.

"Better get them cleaned up."

"I will. I was on my way home, just stopped to tell Junior to come by and get his half of the catch." He turned to Liv. "Not only is he a whiz at balloon animals, he knows where to find the best night crawlers."

Liv shivered. "Night crawlers?" They sounded hideous.

"Don't tell me they don't have night crawlers in Manhattan." Chaz exchanged a grin with Ted.

"Sure we do," Liv said. "And other low-life types. But I try not to frequent those kind of places."

Chaz barked out a laugh. "I don't know what the board of trustees was thinking." He shook his head. "Boggles the mind."

"He's just goofing on you, Liv," Ted told her. "Night

crawlers are earthworms; they come out at night, and they're the perfect bait for catfish."

"Catfish?"

"Yeah. Where did you think I was? Trawling the local bars?"

"Of course not." Not exactly. Though she had to admit trawling bars was better than committing murder. He'd been out fishing. Of course. Where was her mind? "I thought fishing was canceled because of spawning salmon."

"Not night trawling," Chaz said, looking at her speculatively. "Though it's nice to know you read my humble rag."

Liv ground her teeth into a smile. "Well, I won't keep you. Are you coming, Ted?"

"I'm all yours. Better go look after that hand, Chaz." Ted joined her and they started across the lawn toward town hall. Liz forced herself not to look back to see where Chaz Bristow had gone.

"What was all that about?" Ted asked.

"What?"

"The run-in with Chaz? You really don't like him, do you?"

"Oh, he's all right, I guess. He's just so blasé about everything, for which I suppose I should be thankful. When I saw him going toward the Zoldoskys, I was afraid he'd learned what happened and was going to interview them."

"Oh, so you've heard about him."

"Who?"

"Chaz."

"Just what you told me. I figured the rest out all by myself. No great stretch."

"Really," said Ted. "Just what did you figure out?"

"Besides the fact that he's a slob, lazy, and goes fishing at night? Are there more fascinating details I should know about?"

"Nope," Ted said. "None at all."

"How are the Waterburys holding up?" Liv asked.

Ted opened the town hall door for her. "I suppose the answer would be, as well as can be expected. Though no one ever expected this." He turned on the lights to the office and they went in. "Joss hasn't heard from his brother in over thirty years. Not a postcard or a phone call, according to him. Then suddenly to show up dead in his apple press . . . It doesn't make any sense." He looked around the office. "We forgot to pick up breakfast."

"Rats," Liv said. "Dolly hadn't opened when I passed by earlier, and I was on my way there when I ran into Chaz."

Ted looked up, eyes twinkling, "And everything else flew right out of your head?"

Liv gave him a sour look. "Yes, but not in the way you're thinking. I was trying to avert disaster. I mean, we don't need murder spread all over the front page."

"Won't be able to stop people from talking, Liv. This is Celebration Bay. Gossip is our meat and potatoes."

Liv dropped into her desk chair. "How could this happen? I'm sorry for Joss's loss, of course, not that he or the Zoldoskys seems to be mourning Pete's demise. But think of the ramifications for the town. And—not to sound selfish but—for me."

"You?"

"My first event here and there's a murder. Everyone might think it's my fault." She sighed. "See, I told you: selfish."

"Never, but if it's any consolation, Pete Waterbury is no great loss. He was a bully and a conniver when he was a kid. I don't think he'd changed at all."

"I just wish he'd gotten killed in some other town."

"I do, too. There's bound to be trouble ahead."

Liv looked up. "You mean somebody who lives in Celebration Bay may have killed him?"

Ted smiled ruefully. "Never slow on the uptake, are you?"

"No," said Liv. "It's a necessary skill for survival in a territorial, competitive business. But in this case, I think ignorance would be bliss." She sat up straighter. "They usually suspect the spouse or, in this case, the brother? Lord, you don't think Bill will arrest Joss?"

"Not unless he has just cause."

Liv eyed him speculatively. "You think he might have just cause?"

"Joss might have a motive for killing him. Like a lot of people in this town. Including me." Ted's mouth twitched. "I'll go get breakfast."

"Ted. Come back here." It was too late; after dropping that bomb, Ted slipped out the door and was off to the bakery.

"Arghh," Liv growled at the closed door. "I hate it when he does that."

"Just how many people in Celebration Bay had a motive to kill Pete Waterbury?"

Liv and Ted were sitting at her desk, Liv's second latte of the day before her and two sour cream crumb cake squares placed on the china plates.

Instead of answering, Ted took a bite of his crumb cake. Liv wasn't even surprised. She just waited patiently until he finished chewing, then gave him an aggrieved smile.

"What was that?"

"I said, how many people here wanted Pete dead?"

Ted blinked. "Well, that's putting it a bit harsh."

"Just tell me." She held up her hand. "I know you won't divulge any of your own intimate details, but spill on the rest of the folks, okay? I've got a town's reputation at stake here."

Ted washed his cake down with a sip of tea. "Well, let's put it this way. Nobody liked him."

"And?"

"Well, he stalked Dolly until her father threatened to go after him with a shotgun. She was only fifteen at the time. But don't get excited. Mr. Vanderboek died about four years ago. And besides, that's all hearsay, because I was away at school at the time."

"Boarding school?"

"College."

"Oh. Who else?"

"He used to pick on the smaller kids. Andy Miller took a few good beatings from him."

"Andy? I'd hardly call him little. Wiry, maybe."

"I guess I mean younger, smaller." Ted shook his head; his eyes took on an unreadable look. Was he thinking the same thing she was—that Andy had showed up just after the body was discovered? But she just couldn't see Andy committing murder.

"What about Bill?"

"We all got bussed to the same high school, but Bill lived down the road at Hadley's Crossing; he didn't hang out with any of us much. Surely you don't think Bill killed him."

"More like he wouldn't want to arrest any of his friends."

"He'll do what he has to do, whether he likes it or not."

"What about Fred?"

Ted brushed crumbs off his fingers and thought. "He was a year or two ahead of Dolly. So he must've been twenty when Pete disappeared for good."

"He'd disappeared before that?"

"A few times. Like I said, he was just no good. And from such a decent family, too. Just goes to show you." He shook his head. "All I know is that after that last time, he never came back. It was a bad business."

"What? Was there something about the last time that was different?"

"Liv, it was a long time ago and best not thought about. He was just bad. Nobody liked him, but they'll all show up for the funeral because Joss is well respected and the Waterbury family has been here for generations." He stood up. "Now, I have work to do. I have this slave-driving boss. . . ."

He gathered up the dishes and cups and headed for the outer office.

"Ted?"

He paused and turned around in the doorway.

"Who do you think did it?"

Ted shuddered dramatically. "All I can say for sure is it wasn't me."

And Liv had to be content with that.

She spent the next few hours collating stats that had already been collected, reading the comments left on the Celebration Bay website, and organizing her report for the wrap-up meeting Monday evening. She made several forays outside to check on the climate, both weather-wise and gossip-wise. The weather was cooperating, and after a few admonishments to stop speculating in public and to think of the money they'd lose if they became the pariah of event towns, the gossip climate also calmed down.

At three o'clock, Liv left to collect the surveys and make the final payments. She stopped by Ted's desk on her way out.

"Did you take a blank check?" she asked.

"No. Is one missing?"

"I think so. There's no documentation, and I can't remember anything after the Dumpster check. Though I didn't go back to see if we skipped something."

"Not to worry. I'll take a look and check the numbers against the bank statements."

Liv waited until the Zoldoskys took a break before she handed over their payment to Anton. He took it without a word, looked at it, folded it over, and stuck it in the pocket of his vest.

"I'm sorry for your loss," she said, not being able to think of any other way to say it but feeling she should.

"No loss."

"I . . . If you don't mind me asking . . . We know who the deceased is. Why did you let him pose as your brother?"

"He is not my brother."

"Yes, I know, but everyone thought he was."

He puffed out air and shrugged. "I cannot help what everyone thinks. I never said he was my brother. No one asked me. I hired him when Serge broke his arm. I told this to your sheriff and now I tell it to you."

He turned his back on her.

Liv left, not feeling the need to say good-bye and hoping they wouldn't be back the following year.

By six o'clock trucks and vans were pretty much packed up. Tourists had moved to the permanent stores and restaurants as they prolonged what was left of the weekend. Most of the surveys had been returned, and from what Liv could tell from a quick skim, most vendors had been satisfied with the facilities and the traffic.

Ted joined her as she watched the Zoldoskys fold up their proscenium and tie it to the trailer roof. The equipment trunks and air tank for the balloons were placed inside. The balloon maker climbed in back with one brother, and Anton and Serge climbed into the front seat.

Liv breathed a sigh of relief when the trailer pulled away from the curb.

"I'm not sad to be seeing the back of them," she said.

"Don't start celebrating yet," said Ted. "Bill told them not to leave town."

Chapter Seven

....

Dolly was strangely reticent when Liv and Whiskey stopped by the bakery the next morning. She hardly looked at Liv as she sliced off two large pieces of blueberry coffee cake, then reached down to absently pat Whiskey on the head. He nudged her hand and she shook herself. "Oh dear. What was I thinking? I almost forgot your treat." She rummaged below the counter and came out with one of her special dog biscuits. Whiskey licked her hand before taking it.

Liv had been worried about gossip, but this silence was worse. Whiskey sensed it, too.

"Dolly, is something wrong?"

Dolly's eyes flitted around the empty bakery; then she leaned over the counter toward Liv. "Is it true? Did they find Pete Waterbury's body in Joss's store?"

Liv sighed. The word was out, and there was no use in denying it. "Yes. It's true."

Dolly shook her head slowly. "It's bad news. Bad. Why did he have to come back here?"

"I wish he hadn't," Liv said.

"Don't you go feeling sorry for him. He was as rotten as they come. Poor Joss. He was like a father to Pete. When old man Waterbury died—dropped dead of a heart attack, fell right off the tractor—Joss took over running the farm and being head of the family. But he couldn't do nothing with Pete. He was just bad. And now he comes back after all these years and makes trouble for Joss again."

"Again?" Liv asked. "Did he make trouble for Joss before?"

"Oh, time and again, but the last was the worst."

Liv leaned closer. The bell tinkled and the front door opened. Dolly jumped as if she'd seen the ghost of Pete Waterbury walk through the front door, but it was Fred.

"Came by to see how you were doing," Fred said to Dolly, but not before Liv caught him giving his wife a stern look. Fred didn't want Dolly talking to Liv. Or maybe he just didn't want her talking to anybody.

Liv put on a smile she didn't feel. "I'm glad to see you this morning, Fred. I didn't get a chance to thank you last night for all your help and going beyond the call of duty."

Fred jerked his chin in acknowledgment, almost as if the reaction was out of his control.

There was an awkward silence, and Liv didn't feel like she could push them to talk without jeopardizing their new friendship.

She took her bakery bag from the counter. "Thanks, Dolly. See you tonight, Fred, at the wrap-up meeting?"

"Sure thing," he said.

As soon as Liv was outside, she turned to peer through the window. Fred was speaking intently to Dolly, and Dolly looked like she might cry. He wrapped her into a hug and Liv turned away. Was Dolly distraught over Pete's death? Couldn't be. Was she afraid?

Liv ducked into the Buttercup, wondering what reaction she'd get from BeBe.

"Don't know the man, but I didn't move here until 'ninety-eight," BeBe said, reaching for a paper cup. "Everybody says he was no good, so I guess I'll take their word for it. But, Liv, do they know who did it?"

"Not that I know of," said Liv.

BeBe shuddered. "Kinda makes you want to keep looking over your shoulder, doesn't it?"

She pushed the cardboard box with Liv's regular order across the counter.

"BeBe, has Dolly ever mentioned anything about Pete Waterbury?"

"Dolly?" BeBe pulled a face while she thought. "No, not that I remember. Why?"

"Nothing. She just seemed upset this morning."

"I think we're all pretty upset."

"True," Liv said. And Liv had an awful suspicion that it was going to get much worse before it got better.

Ted was waiting for her at the office door. He and Whiskey went through their yodeling routine; then he looked at Liv. "Mayor Worley's called a trustees meeting this morning at ten. You and I are invited."

Liv closed her eyes as acid filled her stomach. "Any particular reason?"

Ted took the cups and pastry from her. "He's in a panic. Afraid he won't be reelected if he gets the reputation of being soft on crime."

"It just happened two nights ago."

"I know, and I don't know why he's worried. He's been the only candidate for the last twelve years. It's not like anybody else is dying for the job."

"Does Bill have any leads yet?"

"I wouldn't know."

They sat down at the desk. Ted turned the coffee cake over and wrinkled his nose. "Dolly seems off her game this morning." He held up the burned bottom.

"She was definitely upset. She asked me if it were true. I told her yes. Then Fred came in while I was there and she got more upset."

"Hmm." Ted bit into his coffee cake and chewed slowly.

Liv waited for him to swallow. "Would you like to elaborate?"

"Actually, no, I wouldn't. I think it will be better if we all sit back and let Bill do his job."

"Is there any other alternative?"

"Liv, hon, you're in upstate New York. There are lots of alternatives and none of them good."

"You mean vigilante stuff?"

Ted shrugged, sipped his tea.

Liv waited; she was learning to be patient and let Ted take his time.

"In this case, I don't think anybody cares if the murderer is found. Nobody who knew Pete will mourn him, and those who don't will follow everyone else's lead."

"Are you're saying they might obstruct justice?"

"Possibly. More likely, they might decide to nudge justice in a beneficial direction."

"And that would be . . .?"

"Let's just say that if I were one of the Zoldosky brothers, I'd be watching my back."

Liv was still thinking about Ted's statement when they walked across the hall to the meeting room. He stopped her outside the door.

"You look worried. Surely a big-city girl like you can handle a little trustees meeting."

"Of course. It's just I like it here and I don't want anything more going wrong."

"Just be yourself."

Liv had to smile. "I always am."

"That's my girl." He opened the door and they went inside.

Three of the trustees were seated in a semicircle around a raised dais, all older men whom Liv had met when she'd interviewed for the job. The fourth trustee was again absent; Chaz Bristow had probably gone fishing.

She and Ted took their places alongside the other three.

"Very nice weekend," said Roscoe Jackson, a diminutive gentleman with a comb-over and a three-piece suit.

Liv smiled. "It was, wasn't it?"

"Too bad it had to get spoiled." Rufus Cobb scowled and chewed on his mustache. "We just hope you're not gonna have second thoughts about your job here."

"Not at all," Liv assured him. "It's unfortunate but something that none of us could have predicted or prevented."

Jeremiah Atkins, the third trustee and president of First Celebration Bank, shifted in his seat to look at Liv. "Unfortunately, that seems to be the case."

Liv was taken aback. Surely he didn't expect her to predict murder? She was an event coordinator, not a psychic.

The door opened and Mayor Gilbert Worley came in. Gilbert was short, fat, and friendly. He had graying, brilliantined hair and a gold tooth that glinted when he smiled. Today he was frowning.

Janine Tudor followed him in and took a place on the dais next to him.

"What's she doing here?" Liv whispered to Ted. "She isn't a trustee."

"Oh, I'm sure she's here to cause trouble. Don't let her rattle you."

Liv dipped her chin and gave him a look. "Not a chance."
Ted grinned.

The mayor took his seat and looked over the room. "I see that most of us are here and—"

"Where is Charles Bristow?" Janine shot an accusatory look around the room, as if she thought they might be hiding the newspaper editor. "Really, if he isn't going to take this job seriously, he should resign."

Ted lowered his head and whispered, "And she'd be glad to take over for him. If she starts talking about civic duty, we'll be here all morning."

"He might not be back yet," Roscoe said. "I know he was taking a hire out night fishing."

"Fishing," Janine said contemptuously.

Liv heard the mayor sigh. He was probably envying Charles Bristow at the moment. Much more of Janine's caustic behavior and Liv might consider throwing a pole or a rod or whatever in the water, herself.

"Perhaps someone should call him and remind him of his responsibilities."

The door opened and all faces turned toward it. Charles Bristow wandered in right on cue.

"Good, Chaz, you made it," the mayor said.

"Mr. Mayor," he said, managing to ignore Janine completely. He nodded to the others, covered a yawn with a less-than-clean hand, sprawled onto the nearest chair—which happened to be the one next to Liv—and winked at her.

Damn, she bet he'd been standing outside the door waiting for his entrance. She couldn't help but admire his cheek.

"There are two items I want to discuss today," the mayor continued. "I'm sure by now you've all heard the news of Pete Waterbury's death."

Everyone nodded solemnly except Chaz, who said, "Who is Pete Waterbury? Any kin to Joss?"

"His brother."

When Chaz looked blank, the mayor said, "He left town years ago. But he was murdered night before last, here in Celebration Bay."

Roscoe nodded. "They found him in Joss's store."

"I heard he'd been stuffed into the apple press," Rufus added. "Whoever heard of such a thing."

Chaz glanced over to Liv, who looked at her hands. She wasn't about to volunteer any spurious details. She'd find herself quoted in the next edition of the *Clarion*.

"Huh," said Chaz, who laced his fingers over his abdomen and settled down into the padded chair.

The mayor cleared his throat to get everyone's attention. "First let me say that other than that particular item, the harvest festival was a resounding success. And we have Liv Montgomery to thank for making things run so smoothly."

Janine looked like she had just swallowed a bug.

"Thank you," Liv said. "I couldn't have done it without Ted and all those who participated. Everyone was extremely cooperative and enthusiastic, and I think we can look forward to many more successful events." Liv mentally crossed her fingers, just in case this was going to turn into a Lynch Liv mob.

"We've already begun to implement improvements that will allow us to expand coming events to include more venues and accommodate more visitors."

"Good news in this economy," the mayor agreed.

"I think we all know what a good job Ms. Montgomery has been doing," Jeremiah said. "But I think we need to discuss how this incident might affect our future. The festivals have boosted our economy, given the town a real revitalization, but maybe they're growing too big."

"I hadn't thought about it like that," Roscoe said.

"No way," Rufus said. "It's just a coincidence. Coulda happened anywhere."

Liv frowned.

The mayor looked thoughtful.

"Well, I must say," Janine said. The room seemed to shrink. "We never had a murder when I was running the events."

So that was why she was here. She wanted her old job back. Liv had seen it coming, but she wasn't really worried. Janine couldn't have pulled this weekend off with all the help in the world, and Liv thought most of the trustees knew it.

"Now, Janine," the mayor began.

Janine threw up her hands and turned on him. "This is just what I warned you would happen. How can you expect some city girl to come in and understand the nuances of— of—small-town life?" She jabbed a maroon-painted fingernail at Liv. "And she brought the dangers of the city with her."

Ted snorted.

Janine glared at him.

Next to Liv, Chaz Bristow seemed to have fallen asleep.

"I just hope she hasn't caused irrevocable harm. How do we even know she'll stick it out—providing we allow her to stay on."

They all looked toward Liv.

"Signed a contract," Chaz said without opening his eyes.

"Oh, for heaven's sake," Janine said. "Anyone can break a contract. She's created a mess and she'll leave us high and dry. You mark my words. She won't last until Christmas. Then where will we be?"

Chaz sat up. "I for one will be glad for the peace and quiet. Are we going to vote on something? Because if we're here just to listen to Janine rant, I've got a paper to put out."

"Actually, there is another reason I asked you all here," the mayor said.

"Bet he didn't invite Janine," Chaz said under his breath.

Liv glanced at him, but his eyes were closed.

"I know he didn't," Ted answered on her other side.

Liv twisted her head toward Ted, but he was looking straight ahead, the picture of the attentive assistant.

Great, thought Liv. She was getting a play-by-play commentary in stereo.

The mayor cleared his throat. "Bill Gunnison has asked to speak at the committee meeting this evening." His Adam's apple jumped as he swallowed. "He's going to ask that anyone with information about the, uh, incident come forward."

"Meaning he don't have a clue." Roscoe nodded wisely.

"It was probably one of the itinerants," Rufus added. "Don't see how we can stop things like that from happening."

"If I may," said Liv at her most formal.

Beside her, Chaz mumbled something about hambones.

She ignored him. "I will be adjusting the current contracts to include a section for background. We will vet everyone who signs a contract with the town."

"And just how do you propose to do that?" Janine shot her a don't-get-comfy-in-your-desk-chair look.

"Can you do that?" asked the mayor.

"We don't have the means to do a thorough background check on everyone," Liv began

"I didn't think so." Janine sat back, satisfied.

"But I have access to search engines that can red-flag anyone who might have a questionable past, or if any of their statements that don't ring true. An arrest record, financial difficulties, incorrect address. For example, we might have had warning that something was amiss when the Zoldosky brothers showed up with five brothers instead of four."

"Isn't it illegal for a regular person to do that?" Roscoe asked.

"Not for what we'd be looking for," Liv said. "It's all public information."

"That's just spooky," said Rufus. "You can really look all that stuff up?"

"Yes, and I'm surprised that you haven't instituted this before." *Take that, Janine.* "I can find out when you were born, where you live, when you bought your house, if you own one, how much your taxes are, your phone number. I can even see what's growing in your backyard. It's all public record if you know how to look."

"That just ain't right," Rufus said.

"We, of course, would not abuse the ability, but only use it to insure that we won't be harboring any felons or other"—she paused to glance at Chaz—"lowlifes in our midst. It isn't fail-safe but it will help."

"That sounds like an excellent idea," the mayor said, looking a lot happier.

"At least now you'll know how many Zoldosky brothers there are," Chaz mumbled.

"I'm going to sic Janine on you," Liv whispered back. She just caught the hint of his smile in her peripheral vision.

"It does sound good," Jeremiah said. "I think Liv should start now and see what she can find out about Anton Zoldosky and his brothers. It seems mighty suspicious, them allowing Pete Waterbury to pose as one of them in order to sneak back into town to do God knows what."

Holy moly. Were they going to ask her to "nudge" justice toward the Zoldoskys to prevent anyone in town from being charged with murder?

She took a breath. "I'm sure the police are already running background checks on all the Zoldoskys, and they have much more sophisticated means to do it."

"Don't mean they're gonna look."

"Of course they will," Ted said. "Bill Gunnison wants to catch the murderer as much as anyone."

"Just so he catches the right one," Roscoe said.

"Oh, he will," Jeremiah said.

Liv wondered whether he was right. Bill Gunnison didn't want it to be a local person any more than the rest of them. But would he go so far as to try to railroad the Zoldoskys?

"What do you think Pete was up to?" Rufus asked, pulling on his mustache.

"Up to no good," Roscoe said. "Caught him more times than I can count helping himself to whatever he wanted in my store. I was just starting out and couldn't afford to lose that much to theft. Fortunately Joss Senior was willing to pay for it. Kept Pete from getting arrested as a juvenile. Now I think maybe we shoulda just let him take his punishment. Maybe he would've turned over a new leaf and not be lying dead today."

Jeremiah shook his head. "Not your fault or Joss Senior's. The boy was just bad. It sometimes happens, even in families like the Waterburys. I'm just glad Joss Senior didn't live to see what finally happened, but it's a sorry shame that Joss had to deal with it on his own. Just a sad business all around."

"Well, I say Bill Gunnison oughta take a good look at the Zoldoskys. They were probably in on it together," Roscoe said.

"On what?" Ted asked.

"On whatever it was they were planning."

Chaz rose to his feet. "Well, if that's settled, I have things to do." Without waiting for an answer, he headed for the door.

"Well," Janine said as soon as the door closed behind him. "I don't think we should hold another festival until Liv can assure us that she can create a safe environment for tourists. All we need is to get a reputation for being a town where people get murdered."

Liv was stunned, and it took her a second to respond. When she did, she had to raise her voice to be heard over the others' reactions.

"This town depends on the income from the festivals. And Halloween is a big moneymaker. Christmas and ski season are even bigger. It would be disastrous for our local economy, not to mention morale, if we have to cancel."

"That's right," said Rufus. "We can't just stop. People are expecting us to put on a good event. They've made plans. Corrine Anderson says the inn is booked solid for every weekend through February. And my B and B is filled up, too."

"Well, it won't be if one of your guests is murdered in their bed," Janine said.

Liv stood up. "Janine, you're not helping with this hysterical attitude. I may be a city girl in your mind, I may be young, but I was an established and respected professional in Manhattan. I'm now committed to my life in Celebration Bay. And I resent your casting aspersions on my intentions, my honesty, or my fortitude."

"Well, really—"

"Unfortunate events happen everywhere. Hopefully, the Zoldoskys brought this trouble with them. But either way

I'm here to stay and I'm sure the county police and Bill
Gunnison have every intention of keeping us all safe."

"Brava," Ted said under his breath.

"Yeah," said Rufus.

"Bill has the entire county to patrol," Jeremiah pointed
out.

"I realize that and I've already begun putting a proposal
together to hire an outside security firm for the larger weekends that would coordinate with the county police."

Ted raised his eyebrows at her.

Well, she would start on it tonight.

"How soon can you do this?" the mayor asked.

"I'll crunch some numbers, consult with the sheriff, and
get back to you with some figures. In the meantime—"

"In the meantime," Janine snapped, "I move to cancel
all further activity."

Ted cleared his throat and the others turned to look at
him. "Janine, dear. You're not a trustee. And only a trustee
can make motions."

Roscoe and Rufus nodded.

Janine shot him a look that could cool the Javits Center.
She turned the glacier on the mayor.

"Well, perhaps Janine has the right idea," Mayor Worley
said. "There's two weeks before the big Halloween weekend.
If the murderer is caught by then, we'll hold the events. If
not . . ." He shrugged and looked apologetically at Liv.
"We'll have to rethink our position."

Janine didn't look totally satisfied. The mayor had left Liv
wiggle room, but she had no doubt that Janine would do what
she could to sour the rest of the inhabitants about Liv's plans
for the future. Liv just had to make sure they found the killer
first.

Chapter Eight

....

"I can't believe what just happened," Liv said as she paced the small area in her office. "They hired me to grow the festivals, not cut back on them."

"Not to worry," Ted said.

"Don't worry? You heard the mayor. He wants to cancel Halloween. You don't do that and recover easily. And we have great momentum right now."

"He doesn't want to cancel Halloween or any other festival."

"Then why—"

"He wanted Janine off his back. If he were serious, he would have called for a vote."

"Are you sure?"

"I'm sure. Being soft on crime might not keep him from being reelected, but undermining the town's major source of income will. And he knows it."

"What is Janine's problem? Is it just me she hates?"

"Mainly she feels humiliated."

"She was a volunteer. You needed a professional. You advertised. There's nothing to be humiliated about."

"I know that, you know that, but Janine is a horse of another color."

"A horse isn't the animal I was thinking about to describe her."

"She's that, too."

"Is there something I should know about her and Mayor Worley?"

"Nothing interesting. She's best friends with his daughter, Caroline. And Caroline, at thirty-something, is still daddy's little girl."

"Does she live here? I don't think I've met her."

"In Albany. She visits occasionally for the Junior League and the Garden Club, but doesn't generally mingle with the rest of us mere mortals—including her father."

"Poor Gilbert." Liv plopped down in her office chair. "So what do you suggest we do?"

"Carry on as usual."

"In that case, since I can't close out on the harvest festival until after tonight's meeting, can you bring me the files on the Halloween vendors? I'll start vetting them right away."

"They're already on your desk. And while you're doing that, I'll go get us lunch."

At the word "lunch," Whiskey appeared from under the desk and raced around the room.

"Pastrami?" Ted said in a singsong.

"Arr-roo-roo," Whiskey answered.

"You ate already," Liv said. "Pastrami's fine."

"I'll take Whiskey with me," Ted said.

Liv raised an eyebrow. "Do not feed him," she said, and not expecting to be heeded in the least, she went back to the records.

Fortunately there were only ten outside vendors for Haunted October. And most of them were deliveries. The weekend food and drinks tents were manned by volunteers from Celebration Bay.

When all ten checked out, Liv clicked out of the search program, cleared the history, and hid the program. No way was she going to have people hacking into her research or using her computer to do background checks on their neighbors.

"No one comes up as an ax murderer," Liv said when Ted returned with two giant Reuben sandwiches from Buddy's Place, the diner on First Street.

"Good. Feel better?"

"Marginally, but this is as far as I go. So don't worry; I won't be looking you up." She smiled slyly. "Though it is an intriguing idea."

"Don't expect I'm in there," Ted said.

"Everybody is in here. I just wish I had thought to check out the Zoldoskys. God knows I ran background checks on everyone I employed in the city."

"Well, don't beat yourself up over this. No one has ever vetted the vendors before."

"We will from here on out. Though you might say the horse is already out of the barn."

Ted looked amused. "You're beginning to sound like a real country girl."

"And I'd like to stay one."

"I wouldn't worry. My guess is we made more on this harvest festival than we ever have. That alone should insure you a place in history."

"Thanks, but I just want to make sure I don't become history."

"Eat your sandwich."

"So what do you think?" Liv asked after swallowing a bite of the best Reuben she'd eaten north of Katz's Delicatessen.

"About?"

"About the Zoldoskys as most favored felons."

"Definitely a possibility. Not necessarily the way it actually happened."

"Do you think it will get picked up on the wire?"

"A measly, small-town murder? I doubt it."

"I suppose we should be thankful. What about the *Clarion*? Reporting it might give its sales a boost. I'd hoped to speak with Mr. Bristow after the meeting adjourned but no such luck. Though I guess it's a good thing he left before the mayor made his threat to cancel the next event. From my brief contact with the less-than-energetic editor, he'd probably be happy to see it end."

"Hmm," Ted said, ruminating over a bite of his sandwich.

"How worrisome could he be? Surely he won't report that two of the trustees practically asked me to find evidence that would point to one of the Zoldoskys as a murderer. Hopefully he won't rouse himself to do any interviews about the murder."

"I wouldn't worry about Chaz."

She didn't want to worry about Chaz Bristow; she didn't even want to think about him. She just wanted this murder to be solved quietly and quickly with the least amount of fanfare. But could she trust Chaz Bristow to sleep through the investigation?

"Hon, you'll give yourself wrinkles if you keep scowling like that."

"Should I salt the hills with some more arrowheads?"

"What on earth?"

"To distract the editor of the *Clarion* from too much speculation about who murdered Pete Waterbury?"

"Trust me. He'll just bury it in the police blotter that takes up a corner of the third page on each fourth week of the month. In case you haven't noticed, he takes life on his own terms."

"I noticed, and I suppose I should be happy that he's so

lackadaisical. But I was hoping to get a little more enthusiasm from him on reporting the town's events."

"You write the copy and he'll probably run it."

"Why on earth did he ever agree to run the newspaper?"

"He was the last Bristow, so he inherited the paper and the job of editor."

"Which reminds me," Liv said. "Between the Peeping Tom and the murder, I forgot that we seem to owe Chaz Bristow for ads dating back to the spring. Is there any way we can check to see what we have paid him?"

"You can ask Janine."

"Oh, thanks. You want to ask her?"

"Not me. That's definitely one for the boss."

"I assume he would have been paid out of the festival account? We should be able to go back and find the checks for what he was paid for. And we can look for that missing check while we're at it."

"I'll get the checkbook." He returned a minute later with a blue canvas checkbook and handed it to Liv.

"This could take all afternoon." Liv turned to the first page and looked at the first three check stubs. "Do we always advertise in the *Clarion*?"

"It depends on the date and if Janine was on her high horse or not. It might be easier to look at back issues to see where the ads occurred. Or just take Chaz's word for it."

"I don't think so."

"He's honest. And he's got a mind like a steel trap."

"A fish trap, maybe."

Ted chuckled. "Well, regardless, he won't mind waiting for a few days."

"Unlike the Zoldosky brothers. I assume they're still here."

"Oh yeah, and not happy about it."

"Do you know if Bill found out anything besides the fact they never told anyone that Pete was a Zoldosky?"

"You mean if they were in on it with him, whatever it was, like Roscoe suggested?" Ted said in a deadpan.

Liv cringed. "Well, not exactly, but it does seem odd that he had just signed on with them when they were on their way to Celebration Bay. Maybe using them as a cover? To do what?"

"I'm sure Bill will get to the bottom of it."

"Aren't you the least bit curious? Or do you have insider information that you're not allowed to share?"

"Neither. Shall we move on to the preparations for Haunted October?"

"If there is a Haunted October." Liv wrapped up the remaining half of her sandwich and pushed it aside. She picked up a stack of invoices and glanced at the first one. "Okay. The tents are rented and guaranteed for weekend after next."

"Andy said he'd have the corn maze open to the public by this Thursday and will have the Maze of Madness ready to go for the next three weekends."

"I'm not sure how that works," Liv said. "You walk through with a flashlight and things jump out at you?"

"Pretty much. The maze is not for the faint of heart. It only operates late at night and you have to be over twelve to go inside. We get a lot of college kids from the area. During the day you just get cornstalks and decorations, G-rated.

"The Fenways have already volunteered to do the hayrides this year if Joss decides it would be too much for him and Donnie and Roseanne. I thought I'd give them a few days to assimilate all this and get the funeral arranged before they have to decide."

"They're going to have a funeral?"

"They'll have to. Pete was family. And family gets a funeral. I imagine it will be small, without the wake. But I doubt they'll be able to stop folks from bringing food and visiting."

"I don't guess you've talked to Bill since yesterday morning?"

"Nope. I don't envy him. Don't envy him at all."

"You think he'll railroad the Zoldoskys?"

"One of them may be guilty."

And even if they weren't, it was beginning to look like the Zoldoskys were headed for a rough time. Liv had to admit she was a little spooked to see how quickly the town had closed ranks against outsiders. After all, she was an outsider herself.

The Harvest by the Bay Wrap-Up Committee meeting was packed and noisy. Normally, at least for the four meetings Liv had attended, they set up tables in the empty room and discussed things in a round-robin fashion. Tonight the tables had been pushed aside and chairs were set up haphazardly in rows, but no one was sitting down.

"Where did all these people come from?" Liv asked Ted as they entered the assembly room at town hall. "We never had this many people in the other meetings. Is this normal?"

"Well, we generally have the subcommittee heads attend, but my guess is you've got a town meeting on your hands."

"Town meeting. On *my* hands? What town meeting?"

"Liv, is it true they want to close down the festivals?" Dexter Kent's voice cut through the din.

All faces turned toward Liv.

"Is it?"

"They can't do that."

"Our livelihoods depend on it."

Liv held up both hands. "Everyone sit down and I'll tell you what I know." She could brain Janine Tudor for causing this trouble.

"*This* town meeting," Ted said as he guided her toward the raised platform at the front of the room.

For a split second she longed for one nasty bridezilla instead of what looked like nearly a hundred desperate townspeople. But only for a second. As she looked around at the familiar faces, and the not-so-familiar faces, she knew she was looking at her new life, her new friends. And they were looking to her to save their bacon.

"Please sit down," Liv repeated as she reached the center of the platform. Ted had pulled a chair to the side of the stage and sat down. He was placing it in her hands. Not a cop-out, but a show of faith.

"Evidently you've heard about some of the suggestions that were brought forward at the trustees meeting this morning."

"Is Gilbert Worley out of his mind?"

This question was followed by loud support.

"If you'll all keep calm, I'll tell you exactly what was discussed." She hoped she wasn't breaking some trustee rule. But this had become bigger than four men and a mayor. All of whom were merely human and hopefully wanted the best for their town.

"It isn't fair," cried a solitary voice.

"What's going to happen to all us farmers who depend on the market to sell our produce?"

Liv took a breath. "I'll answer all of your questions as well as I can, but since we all have one major concern, let me address it to everyone."

"Everybody sit down." Fred Hunnicutt, bless his heart, was the voice of reason. Everyone sat down amid a shuffle and scraping of folding chairs.

"Let me just say, first off, that you all did an incredible job this past month and especially this past weekend."

"For all the good it did."

Someone rapidly hushed the speaker.

"I want you to know that I left a good job in the city because I saw the possibilities in Celebration Bay, the room for growth and for success. And I intend to see that we do grow and we are successful."

"Yeah," someone shouted.

A smattering of applause.

"The trustees are concerned for everyone's safety, and this is why the suggestion was made of postponing, not ending, the events until the police investigation is wrapped up." She was choosing her words carefully, but a little voice in her head was chiding her for her cold, legalese-like speech.

"Why don't they just arrest one of the Zoldoskys—"

"Or all of them."

"Because," Liv said before things got out of hand and the committee meeting turned into a free-for-all, "the law's responsibility is to protect as well as to arrest. Or none of us would be safe. We must be patient."

"While we go broke."

"I said patient, while we continue to set up for October."

"So they're not gonna close us down?"

Liv jumped off the fence. "Not if I have any say in it. But to insure we can continue, we have to be proactive."

"You mean like bringing in the Zoldoskys ourselves."

"No!" Liv yelled, appalled. "First of all, no one is taking the law into their own hands. That would be death to any hope of continuing the festivals." She couldn't believe she had to say something like that; she felt like she was living in the Wild West. "But the festivals have grown so large and so frequent that we really need to pay attention to security."

"That's what Bill Gunnison is supposed to do."

"Yes, and he does. But he's one man with a small force who is responsible for the entire county. We can help them by setting up so that there are fewer situations where accidents or violence can occur."

"Like Joss's apple press?"

"I was thinking more along the lines of store owners making sure alleys are well lit. That everyone should have a buddy when closing late. Be friendly but not careless when meeting new people. Report any suspicious activities or behaviors immediately to the police." Should she mention that she wanted to hire a separate security force? Better to draw up a spec sheet and run it by the trustees first.

"It's a question of being intelligent." She saw Bill Gunnison enter through the back door. "Now, Sheriff Gunnison would like to address a few words to the group."

Bill walked down the crooked, makeshift aisle. His sciatica seemed to be better, since he was almost standing upright. He stepped onto the platform, and Liv moved aside to give him the floor.

"Thank you, Liv. I couldn't have said those things better myself. Vigilance is the key to safety."

"Didn't help Pete Waterbury."

"No, but Pete's death was an unusual situation," Bill said. "I guess it's no secret that the man was murdered by an unknown assailant. I'm asking anyone with any information, who thinks they might have seen something, to please come forward."

There was a rustling of chairs.

"Not now," Bill amended hastily. "I know Liv here needs to wind up the reports from September so she can get started on October. I'll be here for a while after the meeting, or if anyone prefers anonymity, they can call the tip hotline."

He nodded to Liv and stepped down.

"Okay," said Liv, moving back to the center of the platform. "If I could have the committee chairs and their subchairs and assistants down front, we'll move through this as quickly and efficiently as possible. The rest of you, thank you for coming. There's a suggestion box in the lobby for ideas on improving the event, and I'm sure Sheriff Gunnison will welcome any information you might be able to give."

There was a mass exodus to the back door. She hoped Bill didn't get bombarded with useless speculation.

The rest of the meeting proceeded without too much argument. Ted collected reports and monies, and he and Fred Hunnicutt took them to the office safe until they could be checked against receipts and taken to the bank the next morning.

When the last committee member had gone home, Liv

returned to the office to find Ted, Fred, and Bill deep in conversation. They fell silent as she entered.

"Gentlemen?" she asked, inviting information.

"Well, I'd better be going," Fred said. "You need an escort, Liv?"

"No, thanks. I need to talk to Bill for a minute."

Ted lifted his jacket off the coatrack, "Then I'll take off, too. See her home, Bill?"

"Sure."

"Well, I don't think I've ever seen those two move so fast," Liv said as soon as the door closed behind Ted and Fred. "Sort of like rats on a sinking ship."

Bill's brow furrowed.

"They were so eager to leave, I wonder if they were avoiding talking to me?"

"Nah," Bill said. "We were just talking about the funeral. Wednesday at the Presbyterian church. Joss asked us to be pallbearers."

Interesting, thought Liv. "You don't sound too happy about it."

Bill shrugged. He looked years older than he had a few days before. "Put me in a bit of an awkward position. I had to turn him down. My good friend, and I couldn't be a pallbearer for his brother."

"Because you're investigating the murder?"

"Something like. Investigations take you to places you don't necessarily want to go."

"Like?"

"Aw, hell, Liv. I can't discuss the case."

"I realize that, Bill. And trust me, I don't want any gory details. But I do need some information. The trustees are threatening to close down the upcoming events until this murder is solved. Which means it needs to be solved yesterday."

"Damn. It ain't gonna happen that easy. I've done about all I can do while I'm waiting for the damn forensic reports to come back. Murder in a small town isn't exactly a high priority."

"If we lose Halloween, Thanksgiving, and Christmas, not to mention the whole ski season, I don't know how long it will take to recover. Or if the town will be able to recover. We can't afford to take that chance, Bill."

"We're in a mess, Liv, no doubt about it." He slumped down on the edge of Ted's desk and frowned at the floor.

Liv took that as an invitation. She sat down in the armchair facing him.

"Do you have any leads? I won't gossip. I've survived the society pages of New York City. I know how to keep my mouth shut and my eyes open."

Bill's own eyes lit up. "Did you see anything?"

"No, but I talked to Anton when I took them their check Sunday. He said they'd never told anyone Pete was a Zoldosky. That was just an assumption we made."

"That's what he told me."

Liv thought back to her visit to the field, the commotion in the trailer before Pete somersaulted out. "But Pete did."

"How so?"

"Well, he didn't actually say he was a Zoldosky, but last Friday, I went out to remind them panhandling wasn't allowed. I knocked on the trailer door. No one answered, but someone was watching me from the window. Then there was a lot of crashing and banging inside; then Pete somersaulted out the door and landed at my feet. He wasn't wearing greasepaint, wasn't disguising himself in any way. Because he'd checked me out from the window and knew I wasn't someone from his past. Maybe he was even testing his disguise out on me. Because he bowed and welcomed me, I assumed he was a Zoldosky.

"Then Anton came and introduced himself and Pete disappeared. Pete never said he was a brother, but he certainly wanted me to think he was."

"Hmm," Bill said rubbing his back. "Anything else?"

Liv shook her head. "Another two brothers showed up and I got the hell out. But I stopped to look back. Pete was juggling those scarves and grinning like he'd just heard a good joke." She sat back. "I guess that doesn't really help. Just kind of substantiates Anton's statement."

"Of course, he could have lied to both of us."

"To protect himself?" Liv asked.

Bill shrugged. "Maybe, but I couldn't get anything else out of him. And I'm not gonna let them leave until I do. You didn't happen to see when they left the green Saturday night?"

Liv thought back. "They were still there at ten. They couldn't pack out their gear until after closing when the traffic crew let vehicles back in. But I didn't notice if Pete was there or not. Sorry."

"Doesn't really matter. He wasn't killed till after midnight at least."

"I did think that maybe Dolly's Peeping Tom might have been Pete made up in his white greasepaint."

Bill jumped to his feet, wincing.

"That was probably one of the hill kids; they all get rambunctious this time of year. Come on, I'll drive you home."

Surprised, Liv stood up. The mention of Dolly had galvanized him into trying to get rid of her. Which meant she wouldn't tell him about Ted's confrontation with Pete, or about Fred saying that Joss was looking weird the night of Pete's murder.

It was all just speculation, and it was obvious from Bill's reaction that he didn't want to hear anything that would point to one of his friends.

He drove her home, but they didn't discuss the murder or much of anything. But before she got out of the car, she said, "Bill I know this is awful, but you have to help me. The town is depending on it."

"I know. But I'm damned if I do and I'm damned if I don't."

"Why?"

"The state is already threatening to send in investigators."

"That would be good, wouldn't it? I mean, they have access to better equipment and faster results."

"They don't know the area or the people. They'll come in stirring up all sorts of nonsense, rub people the wrong way, accuse people who might have a motive but have never broken the law in their lives, sow distrust and suspicion, because they'll be working with a clean slate. They have no vested interest in us, just in upholding the law.

"I've seen it happen before, Liv. They might apprehend the killer, but they'll destroy this town in the process."

Chapter Nine

....

Peter Jacobsen Waterbury's funeral was held on Wednesday morning at the First Presbyterian Church. The place was packed, as Ted had predicted. Most of the worshippers came to pay their respects to the Waterbury family. At least a few came out of pure curiosity.

A simple casket was placed at the front of the church with a profusion of wreaths and flower arrangements surrounding it. The mood was solemn and silent, which was unusual for the local inhabitants. Dolly and Fred were sitting near the front, their heads bowed. Andy Miller sat with Ted, though they seemed unaware of each other.

Bill Gunnison, dressed in a dark suit, stood at the back of the church, hands clasped behind his back, either acting as a greeter or looking for a killer; it was hard to tell. His expression was somber, almost angry. No one spoke to him as they passed.

Ida Zimmerman sat on the aisle next to her sister, Edna. She nodded to Liv and indicated an empty spot between

them and BeBe Ford. Liv smiled and sidestepped her way
to the empty place.

"Nice turnout," BeBe said, moving her folded coat to her
other side. She was dressed in a muted gray dress.

Liv was glad she hadn't worn black. She wasn't sure
about local funeral fashion and had opted for a brown wool
skirt and tailored tweed jacket, one of her moving-to-the-
country purchases, and it was subdued enough not to stand
out at the funeral.

The back doors opened and Joss Waterbury guided his
wife, Amanda, down the aisle to the front pew. Donnie and
Roseanne followed, their eyes cast down at the floor. Roseanne wore a black skirt and sweater and looked very young
compared to the hip seventeen-year-old of a few days ago.
Donnie wore a black suit like his father. Dressed alike they
bore a striking resemblance to each other . . . and to Pete
Waterbury.

When they were seated, the Reverend Phillip Schorr
climbed to the pulpit. The pastor was a young man who had
moved to town a few years before. Liv wondered what he
would find to say about the man no one liked.

Not much, as it turned out. After the usual introduction
and a hymn, he read a few Bible verses and turned the floor
over to Joss Waterbury.

Joss rose ponderously to his feet, as if his dark suit were
made of lead. He seemed out of place without his overalls
and flannel shirt. Older, tired, and ill at ease.

He climbed the two steps to the chancel and stood at the
head of the coffin.

He cleared his throat. "My brother, Pete, was an unfortunate man. He just didn't fit in and he didn't care. But he
was my brother and I hope he's goin' to a place that welcomes him at last." He rested his hand gently on the coffin
and shook his head.

The organ started up. Five other men rose from their seats

and joined him, and Liv realized they were pallbearers. Andy, Fred, Ted, Dexter Kent, and Rufus Cobb.

At least Pete was going out in style.

Amanda, Roseanne, and Donnie followed behind. When they were gone, the mourners rose. Quiet talk broke out among them.

BeBe reached for her coat. "There's going to be a graveside service just for the immediate family; then everyone will meet at the Waterbury farm for lunch. I know they'd want you to be there."

"I don't know," Liv said. "It's a pretty solemn occasion among people who've known each other for a long time, and besides, I didn't make anything."

"That's okay," Miss Ida said. "Edna and I made extra."

"Besides," BeBe added. "There will be so much food nobody will notice. I'm driving Miss Edna and Miss Ida out. Why don't you come with us? Save us taking both cars."

"Thanks," Liv said. "I'd like that."

They all climbed into BeBe's Subaru, Ida up front with BeBe and Liv and Edna in back.

"Well," Edna said as BeBe pulled out of the parking lot. "I hope for Joss's sake the place Pete's going welcomes him with harp music, but for my money, I think he'll go straight the other way." She nodded her head portentously.

"Now, Edna, I had him in fourth grade," Miss Ida said from the front seat. "He was a rambunctious child, but not any worse than most of the farm boys. They were used to doing chores and playing out of doors. A lot of them found it hard to sit still for lessons."

"Pooh," said her sister. "There's rambunctious and there's plain old troublemaking. And that fits Pete Waterbury to a *T*."

"Maybe he had that attention deficit disorder, though we didn't know about such things in those days."

"Pooh. You've always made excuses for the misfits. Pete

Waterbury didn't have anything that couldn't have been cured by a few whacks on his bottom. But that Dr. Spock came along telling everybody not to spank their children, and look where it got us."

"Sister, you never spanked a child in your life."

"Well, I didn't have any, did I?" said Edna.

"No, you didn't, but not because Albert Johannsen didn't try."

"Pooh. Albert Johannsen didn't have two pennies to rub together."

BeBe glanced at Liv through the rearview mirror, her eyes twinkling. This was obviously a running theme between the sisters.

Liv pulled them back on track. "What about Joss? Was he . . . rambunctious?"

"Lord, no," Miss Ida said. "Joss was in my class four years before Pete. And those two boys were like night and day. Even though they both took after their father in looks, Joss was the stable one. He was quiet and attentive. Maybe he somehow knew he'd be having to take over the farm early on."

"Seems like," said Edna. "He won a town scholarship to go over to the aggie school at Cobleskill, but he had to come home after two years when Joss Senior starting failing. A darn shame, too. Joss Senior died two years later and Joss took over the running of the farm."

Miss Ida clucked her tongue. "Poor boy. But he's done a fine job with it. And he married Amanda Pitts from over in Elizabethville. Such a nice girl."

"By then Pete was really acting out," Miss Edna said. "A big bully. Stealing and fighting. Then what he did to that unfortunate—"

"Here we are," Miss Ida said as BeBe turned into the drive in front of the Waterbury store. Already it was filled with cars. BeBe offered to drive the sisters up to the house and then find a place to park.

"Good heavens, no," said Miss Ida. "The exercise will do us good."

But a young Latino man was standing in the yard and motioned them ahead. BeBe stopped by him and unrolled her window.

"Hi, Marco," BeBe said. "Sad occasion."

"Yes, miss. Mr. Joss, he saved you a place for your car by the house. I'll show you." He took off toward the private driveway.

"That Joss. So considerate, even in bereavement." Miss Ida sighed.

Her sister gave her a look but refrained from comment, and they went inside with Liv wondering what Pete had done to that "unfortunate" somebody Miss Edna had been about to tell them about.

The living room was packed with people. Liv followed BeBe and the sisters to deposit their food offerings among the already heavily laden dining table. Then they wove through the crowd to where Amanda and Joss stood.

Joss stood like a sentinel, but Amanda smiled warmly and took each sister's hand. "Thank you so much for coming. Joss?"

"What?"

"The Zimmerman sisters and BeBe and Liv are here."

He looked at them as if he'd never seen them before but thanked them for coming. They all murmured something and moved on.

Ted stood across the room, talking with a man whose back was turned. He saw Liv and motioned her over. "I wondered if you'd come. I meant to call you."

"BeBe said I would be remiss not to, but I feel a little out of place."

The other man turned, and Liv did a double take worthy of a Saturday morning cartoon. Chaz Bristow, hair neatly combed, fingernails clean, wearing a dark gray, impeccably tailored suit, grinned down at her.

"Go on. Say it. I clean up real nice."

Liv couldn't keep from returning that megawatt grin in spite of the solemn occasion. "I'm just surprised—"

"That I bestirred myself to make an appearance." His eyes flashed and for a second she thought she saw something that wasn't boredom. "Joss is a good man and he doesn't deserve this—" He caught himself but they both knew what he'd been about to say. "Unfortunate situation," he finished.

"No. It's really awful."

"Oh hell, here comes Janine. Is no place sacred? See you later." He disappeared into the crowd like vapor, not an easy feat for someone over six feet tall.

Janine didn't slow down as she passed Liv and Ted.

"The woman is an indefatigable hunter, but it's really a bit gauche at a funeral," Ted said under his breath.

"What does she want with him? When I went to the *Clarion* office, he said Janine knew how to hold a grudge. Is there something between them? I mean, will whatever happened in the past affect how we do business with the *Clarion* now?"

"It shouldn't." He looked over the crowd.

"You know, that's so annoying."

"What?"

"How you make me wheedle every detail out of you."

He smiled. "Just my innate dramatic sense. Can't help myself."

"Were you an actor?"

"Me? Lord, no. But I come from a long line of storytellers."

Liv frowned at him. "Is that a euphemism for liars?"

"Nope. It's the honest-to-God truth. But I thought you wanted to know about Chaz."

"Only because it's good to know your colleagues. The feud?" she prodded.

"Oh, that. Not anything interesting. Janine's been divorced for quite a few years now. When Chaz came back she showed some interest in him. He didn't reciprocate. You've probably figured out by now, Janine likes to get her way. And she's tenacious. Excuse me; I think Chaz needs help."

Left alone, Liv took the opportunity to look around the room. It was a comfortable space with cushioned chairs and a plump couch. Extra chairs had been brought in but hardly anyone was sitting down. Most stood talking in small groups, holding plates of funeral foods, eating and chatting quietly, though as Liv looked around the room she saw that people were beginning to be a little more vocal and enjoying themselves more. Respectful, but not mournful. Pete Waterbury had had his fifteen minutes of fame.

Bill Gunnison stood on the far side of the room, looking uncomfortable and ignored by all. Feeling a little out of place herself, Liv turned to study the family pictures lined up across the shelf of a dark wood bookcase. A group shot of Joss and Amanda and all five children. Hank, the oldest, ran the cider mill, Ely had a farm in Vermont, and Elisabeth lived in Plattsburgh where she taught school.

Next to that was a picture of Roseanne and Donnie as young children standing in front of a huge white pine Christmas tree. One of Donnie in his football uniform. Roseanne, standing next to her father, smiling broadly and holding a soccer trophy. It had been taken several years ago. Roseanne's red hair was held back in a ponytail and the smile showed a row of braces.

But it was the image of Joss that caught Liv's attention. He looked just like his brother had looked only a few days before. It was so obvious that Liv knew anyone who had known Joss then must have recognized Pete. Now she was sure Ted had recognized him and had confronted him. And what about Dolly? Had she known who her Peeping Tom really was? A shiver rippled through her.

"That was eighth grade. We were the Essex Junior Champions." Roseanne reached past Liv and picked up the photo.

"I never got to play soccer," Liv said. "Did your dad come to all your games?"

"My dad?" Roseanne clutched the photo frame so tightly that her knuckles turned white. "Yeah, almost always, except if he got hung up at the mill. But most of them." She placed the frame back on the shelf facing away from Liv.

Liv peered at Roseanne's profile, trying to read her emotions.

She turned back to Liv so fast that Liv stepped back.

"Mom sent me over to tell you to get some food." Roseanne rolled her eyes. "She's always trying to get people to eat. Like that's gonna solve anything."

"Does something need solving?" ventured Liv.

Roseanne gave her a look that only a teenager could manage, halfway between *Are you blind, deaf, and dumb?* and *You know exactly what I'm talking about but are treating me like a child.*

And she would be right. That was exactly what Liv was doing. And she imagined everyone else was, too. It was human nature to want to protect a child from all the ugliness in the world. But this child was no dummy. She hadn't taken the photo in order to give Liv a better look; she'd carefully removed the picture from Liv's view. On purpose, because she didn't want Liv studying the photo. Because she, too, had seen the resemblance?

Except that Pete had always appeared in public in his clown white. And now it was painfully obvious why. When could Roseanne have seen Pete without his makeup? The night she and Joss had gone into the park looking for Donnie, Pete would have still been in costume. After he was dead? As far as Liv knew, there had been no viewing. And the casket had been closed for the funeral.

"Come on," Roseanne said. "I'll take you to get a plate." She moved closer. "Take some of everything even if you don't like it. It'll hurt their feelings if you don't eat."

"Thanks for the tip," said Liv, walking with her to the dining room.

Roseanne hovered over her while she dabbed food onto

her plate. It was an amazing array of choices. Jell-O salad, brisket, chicken, meatballs, ham, vegetable casseroles, fruit salad, pickles and relishes, rolls and biscuits. When Liv was finished, her plate was filled to the edges.

"You want something to drink?" Roseanne pointed over to the sideboard where a variety of liquids was displayed, as well as another table of desserts. Liv liked to eat, but she didn't think she could do justice to all of this.

"Thanks, but I don't think I can juggle the plate and a glass. I'm more comfortable with a glass and food that comes on a toothpick."

"Is that how they eat in New York?"

"That's how we generally eat standing up in a crowd."

"Smart."

"Have you ever been to New York?"

Roseanne shook her head. "But I want to go. We were supposed to go see the Rockettes last year, but Mom got really sick with pneumonia and we had to cancel. But I want to go someday. Is it safe?"

An odd question from a girl whose uncle was just murdered in her father's store. "As safe as most places. You just have to have street smarts; don't go anywhere that doesn't look safe and don't act like a tourist."

"Do you know any Goths?"

"Um, I'm acquainted with a few."

"Have you ever been to a mosh pit?"

"Once. Mainly I just worked."

"But you met all kinds of fabulous people, right?"

"Right. Fabulous. And also a few not so fabulous."

"Like the Real Housewives?"

"Oh yeah. A lot of those."

"Did you ever see a murder?"

Liv nearly dropped her fork.

"I mean being from the big city and all. It probably happens all the time."

"Not all the time." Where was this going? Was the girl

afraid that it would happen again? "And it usually happens over drug deals gone bad, or in a domestic dispute that got out of hand."

"But it could be random, right?"

"Yes," Liv said slowly. "But, Roseanne, it's unlikely to happen here again."

"I know. Bill will arrest the Zoldoskys and it'll be over."

"Most likely. Don't worry."

"I'm not worried. I'm just . . . curious. We'd better get back." Without waiting for Liv, she took off toward the archway. By the time Liv reached the living room, Roseanne was gone.

Liv joined Dolly and Fred, who were standing with the mayor. Gilbert Worley was one of the last people she wanted to see, but at least she knew the man and wouldn't have to meet and greet people she didn't know while plowing through her plate of food.

"You'll be popular with all the ladies," Mayor Worley said, indicating her full plate.

"Roseanne showed me the ropes."

"Such a sweet girl," Dolly said.

"Terrible business," the mayor said. "Amanda says Rosie was all cut up about Pete's death."

"Even though she's seventeen, she's still just a child," Dolly said. "And to see something like that, her uncle all trussed up in the cider mill. No wonder she's upset; they shouldn't have let her inside."

So the details were out, not that Liv thought they could keep it quiet.

"I just don't know why they had to dump the body on Joss."

"And who would *they* be?" asked Bill Gunnison, coming up behind Dolly.

Dolly let out a squeak. "Oh, Bill, the way you creep up on a person."

Liv thought he'd approached more like a lame bear, but whatever.

"She's talking about those Zoldoskys, of course." Mayor Worley patted Dolly's shoulder. "Everybody'll feel a lot better once you've arrested them or sent them on their way."

"I'm working on it," Bill said. "But I don't want people deciding it's the Zoldoskys, until we have proof. I won't have people getting all riled up and taking things into their own hands."

"Bill Gunnison. We're civilized, God-fearing Christians."

"I'm sure you are, Dolly, but I wouldn't attest to a lot of folks in this town."

"How's the investigation coming?" Fred asked. "If you're at liberty to say?"

"It's in progress."

Jeremiah Atkins stepped up to the group. "Which means nothing much is happening."

"Jeremiah, you know that's the way the law works," Bill said. "And let's remember why we're here." He glanced over to Joss and Amanda, who were standing by the door and seeing a group out.

"You're absolutely right," Fred said. "It's about time we were going, Dolly. I'll get your coat." Fred went off down the hall. Dolly said good-bye to Liv and she and Gilbert went to take leave of Amanda and Joss.

"I guess I'll get going, too." Jeremiah wandered off after Fred.

Which left Liv alone with Bill. A faint, dull red slashed his cheekbones. He was caught right in the middle and she didn't envy him, and she couldn't think of a thing to say. Fortunately BeBe, Ida, and Edna were ready to go.

As Liv stood behind Andy Miller waiting her turn to say good-bye to Amanda and Joss, she looked around for Donnie and Roseanne, but they were no longer there. She caught Bill's eye for a split second before he turned and left the room. A few minutes later they were climbing back into BeBe's Subaru.

"Well, that was a nice reception, wasn't it," Ida said as they followed Andy's truck out of the Waterburys' drive.

"More than Pete Waterbury deserved, and that's a fact," added her sister.

"I'm just glad it's over," BeBe said. She honked as Andy Miller turned into the lane to his farm. Liv couldn't keep from looking into the field where the vendors had camped. In the distance, she could see the Zoldosky trailer and the gray truck parked next to it. It looked sad and lonely, and Liv felt a stab of empathy for the men who might or might not have killed Pete Waterbury.

BeBe slowed down and swung wide to avoid a man walking down the road. As they passed he looked toward them, then quickly looked away, hiding his battered face. It was the one they called Junior, the balloon maker.

"Poor boy," said Ida. "What will he do if they send the older brother to jail? I'm sure he protects him from the cruelty of the world. And I'm not so sure the other brothers will take care of him."

"Oh, Sister, you are a pushover for every stray dog, feral cat, and misfit in the world. They'll do just fine with one less brother. And the farther away from here, the better."

"Well, I'm not sure that one of them was the killer at all."

"You think it was one of us?" Edna scoffed.

"Not us, but somebody just passing through, and Pete was in the wrong place at the wrong time. Maybe he got into trouble out there at that Soapy's place."

"Wearing a clown outfit?"

Liv jerked. How did Edna know about the clown outfit? Surely Bill hadn't released that detail. Who was she kidding? The whole town probably knew all the details.

"Clown outfit?" asked BeBe, horrified. "You mean he was still dressed in his costume?"

"Where did you hear this?" Liv asked.

Ida blushed and tried to look innocent.

"We're not at liberty to say," Edna said primly.

There it was again. They were shutting Liv out because she wasn't one of them.

"You know, ladies, I'm here for good. This is my home now and I'm responsible for the success of the festivals that keep everyone employed. I wish you would trust me."

BeBe glanced over her shoulder. "You should trust her."

Edna sighed. "It was Susie Andrews over at the Bayview Diner out on Lakeside Road. She overheard two of the county cops talking about it at breakfast. Everybody knows."

Ted was right about the Celebration Bay gossip. The whole town must know what was going on.

"So has everyone agreed that one of the Zoldoskys killed him?" Liv asked.

"Let's just say everyone hopes it is," Edna said. "Though it is possible that there is someone who recognized Pete and decided to put an end to his shenanigans."

"Hush," Ida said. "No one in Celebration Bay would commit murder."

Liv studied the two sisters, wondering how two women who looked so alike, who had lived together forever, could be so different. Like Pollyanna and Eeyore.

She wanted to side with Miss Ida's compassion toward the Zoldoskys, but she was afraid that Miss Edna was right.

"Well, I say good riddance to bad rubbish. He got what he deserved. An eye for an eye. Not that it will bring back poor Eleanor Gibson's son, rest her soul."

"Eleanor Gibson?" Liv asked. It was the first time she had ever heard the name.

"She was Ted Driscoll's sister," said Miss Ida. "Her boy, Victor, went out fishing one night and never came home."

"Hmmph," Edna said. "He never came home because Pete Waterbury murdered him, and that's a fact."

Chapter Ten

....

Murder. The word bounced around in Liv's mind and finally settled on her tongue. "He murdered someone?"

"It was never proven," said Ida with little conviction. "No body and no witnesses," she added almost apologetically.

"No arrests?" asked Liv. This information cast a whole new light on Pete Waterbury's murder and the reason everyone had wanted to keep Liv out of the loop. They did know something she didn't, not that her finding out could sway things in any way.

And strangely enough, her first thought was not of the victim, or the details of what happened, or how it would play out now, but that Ted hadn't confided in her.

"Well, the boy was never seen again after that night," Edna said.

"Never?" asked BeBe. "How horrible for that poor mother."

Liv dragged herself back to the conversation. "Why do you think Pete Waterbury killed him?"

"Because of what happened before," Edna said.

"What did happen before?"

"It was a long time ago," said Ida. "Maybe we shouldn't stir it all up again."

"I don't think anyone will be able to stop it, Sister. Bill is bound to take a look at the people involved then. History repeating itself. Uh-huh."

"What happened?" Liv prodded.

BeBe pulled into the Zimmerman driveway, turned off the engine, and turned around. "I want to know, too."

The two sisters exchanged looks; then Edna said, "It seems that Victor and Andy were out looking for night crawlers when Pete and some of his bully friends accosted them."

"Andy Miller?" asked Liv.

Edna nodded. "Andy Miller."

"Beat them," Ida said barely above a whisper. "Terrible, just terrible. I remember. Andy didn't come to school for a week afterward, and even when he did, his face was all bruised and he had stitches in his forehead and his cheek. He walked like an old man. And him just a boy."

"Victor never came home at all," added Edna.

"Didn't Andy know what happened to him?" Liv asked.

"As I remember it," Edna said, "Andy told Victor to run and tried to hold them off. They found a missing rowboat down at the south end of the lake, but they never found Victor." She shook her head, remembering.

Ida sniffed. "Victor was a shy little thing, a couple of years younger than Andy. He was always getting picked on. Andy, such a sweet boy, stuck up for him, would let him tag along when he did things.

"Andy was an ideal student, always so polite. Never married, though. I think what happened just took the heart out of him."

Liv's mind was whirling. Andy beaten by Joss's brother, his friend missing, presumed killed by Pete. Andy showing up right after they discovered Pete's body. Ted and Joss standing over the body of the man who could have destroyed Joss's standing in the community, who had allegedly murdered Ted's nephew. Talk about your six degrees of separation. "They never brought charges against Pete or the other boys?"

"They couldn't," Edna said. "It was Andy's word against Pete's. And they never found the body. A few weeks later, Joss sent Pete away."

"And he's never come back until this week."

"That's just awful," BeBe said.

"And now it's all going to be dredged up again," Ida said, and opened the car door. "Well, thank you for the ride, dear."

"Dead and still causing trouble," said Edna in ominous tones. "Thank you, BeBe."

"Yeah, thanks," Liv said, getting out the other side. "I really appreciate you givng me a ride and including me."

"Don't be silly. You're one of us now. See you tomorrow." BeBe backed out of the drive.

"Would you like to come in for a cup of tea? It's been a very exhausting day."

"Thank you, Miss Ida. I would." Liv could use a cup of tea, and she needed a lot more information if she was going to navigate the town through this maze of secrets and intrigue.

She followed the two sisters up the steps of the porch and waited while Edna unlocked the leaded glass door. They settled Liv into one of the padded horsehair chairs in the parlor, and Ida disappeared into the kitchen to start the tea while Edna excused herself to get something she thought Liv might be interested in.

Liv sat in the scratchy chair looking around the old-fashioned room. She'd been in the old Victorian several times for tea, and it always was like stepping into the past. Sunlight filtered in through the side windows and several lamps cast a yellow light over the dark mahogany furniture. The head and arms of each velvet piece were covered with crocheted doilies. Ornate wooden tables filled the parlor and their surfaces held photographs and figurines and other knickknacks that made Liv's head swim when she thought about how long it must take to dust them all.

The sisters had grown up in this house and had never moved away except to go to the teachers college in Plattsburgh. According to Ted, both had been engaged to men who were killed in the war. Neither ever married and both still wore their engagement rings on chains around their necks.

When Liv had first learned this, she'd thought of it as creepy. But once she got to know the sisters, she came to think of it as not just old-fashioned, but unswervingly loyal and steadfast. Traits she realized that were all too lacking in the world she'd grown up in. Getting to know the Zimmerman sisters had given her a new perspective and appreciation of what those qualities really meant.

Edna returned, carrying two large, dark green books that Liv immediately recognized as school yearbooks. Edna placed them on the coffee table and motioned Liv to join her on the couch.

"I thought you might be interested in seeing the boys. These were taken the year before, but it was only early autumn when the tragedy occurred. They hadn't changed much."

She opened the top book and riffled through the pages. "In those days we only had two county schools, K through eight and the high school. All the children were bussed to school."

Liv had been stuck behind several school buses since she'd arrived in Celebration Bay. They stopped at every farmhouse and crossroad, and could make a trip seem interminable and probably extended the days of the kids at the end of the line by an hour or two each day.

Edna stopped at a page and smoothed the paper with her hand, almost like a caress. "This was Nita Smith's sixth-grade class." She pointed to a black-and-white group shot of children standing on tiers next to a young woman with light-colored hair. "And this is Victor Gibson." Her finger stopped on the first row, the fourth boy in. He was small for his age, with shaggy hair and soft features.

"There's his school picture." She moved her finger to the next page of four rows of rectangular photos. He wasn't smiling but stared at the camera beneath half-closed lids. Caught forever in this shy, self-effacing pose.

Ida returned at that moment carrying a tray with a plate of cookies and a teapot and cups decorated with bunches of pink roses.

Edna closed the yearbook and placed it on the side table. While Ida poured the tea, she opened the second book and placed it in Liv's lap. Liv recognized Edna immediately. The tall, spare figure, her hair in the same severe short hairstyle she wore today. She must have been in her late forties. Liv wondered if she had already accepted her future, living with her sister, growing old together in the house they'd grown up in.

"That's Andy."

Even in black and white, Liv could have picked out Andy's towhead from the rest. He, unlike Victor, was smiling, happy, carefree, and slightly mischievous.

"It was the only year I taught ninth grade." Miss Edna's voice sounded far away, as if she was remembering the woman she'd been then. Or maybe it was with pity for what had happened to those two young men.

"Andy was never quite the same after that."

"Edna, hand Liv a cup of tea." Ida's voice broke sharply into the quiet. She lifted the book from Liv's lap and closed it, then took both books to the far side of the room and placed them on a writing desk.

"No use in dwelling on the past," she said briskly. "Have a cookie, Liv."

Liv had to shake off the somber mood that had fallen

over the room. It was almost as if the sisters had exchanged roles. Miss Edna was usually the brusque, matter-of-fact, slightly pessimistic one next to Miss Ida's sentimental softness. But Ida had certainly risen to the occasion.

Edna visibly pulled her thoughts from the past. She handed Liv one of the delicate cups. "Sugar, milk?"

"No, thank you; this is fine." Liv placed the cup and saucer on the table and chose a cookie from the plate Ida held out to her.

"Say what you will," Edna said, returned to her normal brusque self. "Pete Waterbury got his just desserts." She took a cookie and bit into it.

"Perhaps," said her sister. "Only he's not the only one to suffer. This will open all those old feelings. The pain and the guilt. Joss and Andy and everyone else involved don't deserve to have to go through all that again."

"Do you think it will?" asked Liv.

"Well, it was a long time ago," said Ida. "Of course, all of them, including Bill Gunnison, were mere children then. Mrs. Gibson's been dead these twelve years and more. I doubt if anybody much remembers about it."

"Somebody did," said Miss Edna.

Liv's cup rattled against the saucer.

Ida sighed. "I don't know why on earth he had to come back here."

Edna stopped with her cup poised in the air. "Why, that's obvious. He came to cause trouble."

"Well, he's certainly done that. Will you have another cookie, Liv?"

It was too late to go back to work when Liv finally left the Zimmerman sisters. And she had too many things batting around in her head to be able to sit still. That was normal. The next few days after any big event always left her at loose ends, slightly restless after running on adrenaline for days, sometimes weeks. But today there was another element caroming around her brain. The question of who killed Pete Waterbury and how it would affect the town's future and hers.

She did the only thing that was sure to clear her mind. She changed into running gear and dropped Whiskey off to visit with Edna and Ida. The sisters enjoyed his antics and had been dog sitting just about every day since Liv had moved in. She was glad he didn't have to be shut up all day like he had in Manhattan.

"Take your time, dear," Miss Ida said as Whiskey bolted past her into the house.

Liv hurried through a few stretches and hit the streets. She took off in the opposite direction from town. She wasn't exactly sure what the etiquette of small-town funerals was. BeBe had gone back to work, but Liv thought they might look askance at Lycra running pants and a ponytail.

She chose a route that she had never run before, one that skirted the north part of town but curved back to the lake. It had less-traveled roads and was nowhere near the Waterbury farm. The sun was already on its way to the horizon and the air was chilled. She zipped up her hoodie and picked up the pace.

She ran through several blocks of residential streets. At first the homes were well kept with tended gardens, but as she got farther away from the center of town, they became more run-down with peeling paint and unkempt yards. The pavement began to have cracks and fissures until she turned into a street where there were no houses and there had been no attempt to keep the pavement traversable. Potholes cratered the two lanes, and Liv had to watch the ground in order not to twist an ankle or worse.

It was a deserted area that she recognized from her first tour of town. The old cannery, whose closing had put the town's future as a destination spot in motion, tottered on the landscape, big, empty, and forlorn. The windows were broken out and the walls were spray-painted with graffiti. Liv pulled up and ran in place while she considered the building, and a new idea took seed in her mind.

The Cannery. Shops. Fine dining. Indoor activities for winter. Skating rink? Or some other venue. It was worth putting on a back burner. The town stayed open year-round and did fairly well from the overflow ski traffic. But they could do much better without going the theme park route that some towns had taken. Using the cannery as an additional venue was definitely worth consideration.

She started out again in the direction of the lake. She could make the loop back through town and be home before dark if she kept up her pace. She cut through a vacant lot to connect with the path that ran alongside the lake to the Lakeside Inn.

This side of the lake was shadowed by the trees that lined its bank, but across the way the surface glittered with light from the setting sun. Ahead of her the shrubbery around the inn twinkled with little white lights.

Liv slowed as she reached the parking lot where the wooden boat-rental dock jutted out into the lake like something out of a Norman Rockwell painting. Most of the boats had been put in storage. *Dry dock*, she amended. You stored winter coats; you dry-docked boats.

There was a lone rowboat moored at the end of the dock, and Liv was hit with an image so strong that she actually stopped jogging. A frightened boy, Ted's nephew, Andy's friend, running from a gang of bullies led by Joss's brother. Jumping into the boat and rowing desperately to the middle of the lake in hopes of getting away. What had happened? Had the boat overturned? Did he fall into the water? Was his body still lying at the bottom of the lake?

After thirty years, she guessed there would be nothing left. Nothing but resentment.

Liv shivered, decided etiquette be damned, and cut through the inn's parking lot and back to town.

She ran past the darkened Presbyterian church, but the stone rectory was lit up and she could see the silhouette of Reverend Schorr at the kitchen window. She ran past the cemetery and crossed the street kitty-corner to jog past the block of stores just off the village green. Made a mental note to make an appointment when she passed Woofery Dog Grooming. Whiskey was thriving on country living, and a lot of country was thriving in Whiskey's fur.

A block later she reached the village green. The town was pretty quiet. Just about everyone had gone to the funeral, and she imagined that some of the closer friends were still out at the Waterbury farm.

Lights were on in the Buttercup. She didn't need coffee, but she suddenly felt like company. She decided to see if BeBe was free for dinner.

"I'd love to go eat. Not that I need to eat. But I was just going to close up, and I want to hear everything. I knew they'd ask you for tea—didn't they? I was dying to stay but I couldn't leave the store for that long."

"We should probably go to the inn," Liv said. "They looked like they could use the support. But I'm not dressed and I don't feel like changing."

"I'd rather go to Imogene's anyway. It's meat loaf tonight. And I have to confess, I'm a sucker for anything with hamburger and tomato sauce."

While BeBe closed up, Liv stretched in the warmth of the coffee bar, and within twenty minutes they were walking down First Street toward Buddy's Place.

Buddy's was a combination luncheonette and diner. It had been around in pretty much the same form since the late 1950s. The neon sign said Buddy's Place, but only tourists called it by its full name. Locally it was known as Buddy's or the Place or just Imogene's.

Imogene "Genny" Parsons, the proprietor-manager-hostess and sometimes waitress of the Place, slid off the counter stool and reached for two menus as soon as Liv and BeBe walked in.

"Well, you two seem to be about the only ones who didn't eat themselves silly at the funeral repast today. Take your pick."

A row of red vinyl booths sat empty along the windows. They chose the farthest from the door, ordered two meat loaf specials and glasses of the house pinot grigio, and returned the unopened menus to Genny.

Over meat loaf, Liv filled BeBe in on what the sisters had told her about Victor Gibson.

"I remember Eleanor Gibson," BeBe said. "I knew her son had died but no one told me he was murdered." She took a sip of wine. "Probably because I've only lived here for fifteen years."

"Off topic, but why did you move here?"

"Followed a boy."

"No kidding. Anybody we know?"

"No. He was a biker; his family lived out in the sticks near here. He took off again and I settled down."

"Amazing."

"I'd call it typical of young, stupid girls. But I recovered faster than I should have. Took out a bank loan a few years ago and opened up the Buttercup. Should make me one of the people, but not quite."

"Yeah," Liv agreed. "I've only been here a few weeks, and I don't really notice being an outsider until something like this happens. Then it seems like they all band together and close the doors."

"Just human nature, I guess. But everybody likes you, so you shouldn't feel bad."

"I don't," Liv said. "It's just I don't like surprises. And I don't want to fail this town because I lack information."

"How could *you* fail the town, just because someone who everyone hated was killed?"

"The trustees are already talking about closing down the festivals until the murderer is caught."

BeBe stopped with a fork of mashed potatoes inches from her mouth. "They wouldn't."

"I hope not, but the mayor is nervous, and things aren't really moving on the case."

"Yeah, I know. It's that forty-eight-hour thing. But is it true you have to catch the killer by then or the trail goes cold?"

"I sure as heck hope not."

BeBe reached for another roll and pulled it apart. Then she looked at Liv. "You know, we have the means in town to help Bill move things along."

"Don't look at me. Roseanne Waterbury already asked me if I knew all about murder because I'm from the city."

"No offense, but I was thinking of Chaz Bristow."

"Chaz Bri—I'm not even sure he could stay awake during an investigation; he slept through the trustees meeting."

"That's because he likes yanking everybody's chain."

"Why does he bother? It seems like he only lives to fish."

"Yeah, it does seem that way, but before he came back to run his family's paper, he was an investigative reporter."

"Where did you hear that?"

"I didn't hear it. I Googled him when he first moved back."

Liv laughed. "You didn't."

"Well, most of the men around here, the ones that still have their teeth anyway, only care about beer and darts. Chaz was good-looking and . . . I asked him out."

"I take it, it didn't work out?"

"No. He was nice enough. But way too weird for me. I never knew whether he was making a joke or being a jerk. We never . . . you know . . . if you're wondering."

"I wasn't wondering. And I admire your good taste in not pursuing him."

"Better taste than Janine, at least. Did you see the way she was chasing after him at the wake? Of all times."

"Hmm," said Liv, drawing her fork across the top of her mashed potatoes. "An investigative reporter, huh. I wonder if he was any good."

"I don't know, but he was with the *Times*."

"The *Fishing Times*?"

"The *Los Angeles Times*."

After dinner, BeBe insisted on driving Liv home. "With Peeping Toms and murderers running loose, we girls can't be too careful. Actually, no one can be too careful. I mean, right there in the store. How did Pete Waterbury get in? Did he have a key left over from thirty years ago?"

Liv frowned. "Good question. Was there even a store thirty years ago?"

BeBe glanced over at Liv. "I don't know. Does it matter?"

"I don't know." Liv was still pondering the question when they came to a stop in front of the Zimmerman house.

"I'll wait until you get in, give me a sign. Flick the porch lights."

"Thanks, but you go ahead. I have to pick up Whiskey from Miss Edna and Miss Ida."

BeBe laughed. "You know, someone might get the wrong idea if they heard you say that."

"Yeah, I should have named him Snowball or something."

"That wouldn't work. He's definitely more of a Whiskey than a Snowball."

"Well, thanks for coming to the diner with me. I'll see you tomorrow. Night."

Liv climbed the steps to the Zimmermans' porch and rang the bell. Slow footsteps and quick clicks of doggie feet, and the front door opened.

Liv squatted down. "Hi, baby. Were you a good boy?"

Whiskey planted his paws on her knees and licked her face.

"He's just a sweetheart. He helped Edna dig up the onions this afternoon. Didn't you, you rascal?" Ida beamed down at an unrepentant pooch.

"Oh dear," said Liv, and stood up. "Did he do too much damage?"

"Not at all," came echoing from inside the house. Edna appeared at the door, a book in her hand and her reading glasses hanging from a chain around her neck.

Whiskey ran back through the door and ran several circles around Miss Edna's feet. "A flirt, this one," she said and leaned over to ruffle his fur.

"Well, thanks for keeping him. If he gets to be too much, just stick him in the carriage house. He has more toys than I have room for. I kind of spoil him."

She walked down the driveway to her rental, Whiskey bounding ahead, darting in and out of the bushes and finally flashing past her as she opened the door. She poured fresh water for him, treated herself to another glass of pinot grigio, and went into the living room to open her laptop and do something she'd been itching to do since her dinner with BeBe.

She sat down and Googled Chaz Bristow.

For the next two hours she sipped wine and followed links while Whiskey lay sleeping on her feet. Neither Charles nor Chaz had a website; he wasn't on Facebook or Twitter. There were a couple of mentions in relation to the *Celebration Clarion*. Several links to sports fishing articles he'd written. And finally a mention of a Charles Bristow, investigative reporter for the *Los Angeles Times*. Which didn't mean it was the Chaz Bristow she was researching.

She pulled up Google Images. Searched through the Charles Bristows until she found an old, grainy black-and-white. She clicked on it. A newspaper clipping with a byline and a picture. Chaz Bristow had definitely been a reporter for the *Times*.

She clicked back to her search. Not only a reporter, but a very prolific one. She scrolled through the links searching for the first mention of his writing, fighting the urge to speed ahead to the recent past, hoping to get a sense of the history that had made him give it all up. His first byline was ten years before, a report of a warehouse fire in Compton, then several follow-up articles that led to a conviction of arson.

Chaz had risen steadily in the pecking order if Liv could rely on the number of times his name appeared on the byline of articles. The topics he covered and investigated grew in importance. Drug busts in south LA. Prizefight fixing. A study of Watts, forty years after the riots, the broken demographics, the anger, the gangs. It was impressive writing. Crisp, clear reporting that had to have put him in harm's way more than once. Was that why he gave it up for fishing reports in upstate New York?

Had he burned out, got fired, lost his nerve?

She was bleary eyed and yawning before she came to the last two years of his work with the *Times*. It was after midnight, the print wavered before her eyes, and she had to reread most of what she read. Pete Waterbury's funeral, the letdown of a job well-done, and knowing that she had to start on the next one in less than eight hours—not to mention knowing a murderer was still at large—had taken its toll. Her eyes shut and she gave in to her exhaustion.

She was vaguely aware of Whiskey pushing off her feet. He barked once and ran to the front window.

Liv pulled herself from a fog, vaguely thinking of Chaz Bristow. She lifted her head from the keyboard and realized she'd fallen asleep.

Whiskey barked again and tried to jump onto the chair that sat beneath the window. Liv came wide-awake. She hadn't closed the blinds when she'd gotten home that night. She shot out of the chair and, calling to Whiskey in an urgent whisper, threw herself against the wall between the window and the front door. Heart pounding, she cautiously peered around the side. She nearly jumped out of her skin at the knock behind her.

Whiskey bolted to the door and barked again. It was the middle of the night. One of the sisters? An emergency? They would have called. But a Peeping Tom or a murderer wouldn't knock. Of course, a murderer might, but . . .

Another knock, quiet, secretive.

Liv swallowed. "Who's there?"

A mumbled reply.

"Who?"

A little louder.

"Oh my God." Liv unlocked the door and peered out. Opened it wider.

Pale faced, eyes round and dark—not the Peeping Tom. Roseanne Waterbury stood in the downcast porch light, her face contorted. A shudder, a ragged sob, and she fell through the door into Liv's arms.

Chapter Eleven

....

Liv stood rooted to the floor while Roseanne clung to her, sobbing uncontrollably, and Whiskey jumped at their knees. As soon as her head cleared, Liv inched over to the window and extricated one arm long enough to pull the shades. She didn't know what this was about, or why Roseanne had come to her in the middle of the night, but she certainly didn't want anyone seeing and speculating.

"What's wrong, Roseanne? Are you hurt? Did someone frighten you?"

The girl shook her head, burying it farther into Liv's shoulder. Liv eased her away so that she could see the tear-streaked face.

"What is it?" she asked.

"D-Daddy. They arrested him. For murder."

Liv was too stunned to speak. Joss Waterbury, a murderer? Of his own brother? She had trouble believing it. But if Bill had arrested him . . . Liv gently steered Roseanne toward the couch and lowered her to the cushions.

Whiskey put both paws on the seat cushion, whining until

Liv gave him a boost up. He settled himself between the two of them, his muzzle on Roseanne's thigh.

"Rose, you need to calm down and tell me what happened."

Roseanne took a shuddering breath and the words tumbled out. "It was this afternoon after everyone went home. Almost everyone. Ted was still there . . . and Bill Gunnison." She sucked in air, hiccupped, absently stroked Whiskey's back. Whiskey snuggled closer to Roseanne, sensitive as always to someone in distress.

"Bill waited until everyone had left before he arrested your father?" At least he hadn't hauled him off in the middle of the funeral.

Roseanne shook her head, pulled Whiskey closer to her. "Not Bill," she wailed, and broke into a fresh round of tears.

This was getting them nowhere. "Roseanne, in order for me to help you, you'll have to pull yourself together."

"Then you *will* help me?"

"Uh, of course, I'll do what I can," Liv said hesitantly. How on earth could she help? Then she remembered her conversation with Roseanne that afternoon. *You must know all about murder.* Liv mentally crossed her fingers. *Please don't let Roseanne expect me to find an alternative suspect to her father.*

Well, this was a predicament. At least she could hear the girl out before she had to let her down. It would probably do her some good to talk it out, and any knowledge that Liv gained would help her strategize in the days to come.

If she were really callous—which she wasn't—she would be glad they had made an arrest. It would take the heat off her and her scheduled festivals. But not Joss Waterbury, not if it meant closing down a slew of festivals.

"Okay. Let's start at the top. Bill and Ted were still there and . . ."

"These men came to the door. They were all in suits, so I thought they'd come to pay their respects. I let them in. Me. It's my fault."

"Absolutely not," Liv said. "If they planned to make an arrest, not opening the door wouldn't have stopped them." Liv pushed a handful of red curls away from Roseanne's face and stuck them behind her ear.

"Now, tell me what you remember. They came in and what happened?"

Roseanne sniffed. Tugged at Whiskey's ear. "They stopped just inside the door and looked around the room. That's when I knew something awful was going to happen, but it was too late."

"Rosie, don't fall apart." Liv spoke more sharply than she intended, but really, this could take all night, and Roseanne's family must be worried about her. Though since it was after two o'clock, they probably didn't even know she was gone.

"Then they said, 'Which one of you is Joss Waterbury?' Daddy and Mr. Gunnison both moved toward them, and then the first guy said . . . He said, 'This is out of your hands, Gunnison.' And he sounded really gruff, a real as—jerk. Mr. Gunnison just glared at him, then looked back at Dad."

Roseanne wiped the back of her hand across her nose. Liv jumped up long enough to grab a pack of tissues from her desk. She ran a fingernail along the perforation and pulled a tissue partially out before handing the pack to Roseanne.

"Then what happened?"

Roseanne blew her nose. "Dad said he was Joss Waterbury and the guy said they wanted to ask him some questions at the police station. I'd never seen them before. Maybe they were the FBI or something like that."

"Whoa," Liv said. "Did they read him his rights?"

"You mean, like, 'You have the right to remain silent'?"

"Yes."

"No, I don't think so. No. They said they wanted to question him. He was a person of interest or something like that. But he didn't come back. He's in jail and it's all my fault."

"Stop it. It's not your fault. And he might not be in jail. He might be home right now wondering where you are."

Whiskey shimmied his front half onto Roseanne's lap and shot Liv a disapproving look. Roseanne shook her head slowly. "I stayed up after everyone went to bed. Uncle Ted had to give Momma a pill, she was such a mess. It was awful. She never loses it, ever."

"Does anyone know where you are?"

"Donnie. He said you couldn't do anything, so I told him to stay home in case Momma woke up."

"You drove?"

"I brought the truck. I have my learner's permit."

Oh great. Knowing this, Liv couldn't let her drive home by herself again, which meant Liv would have to take her or she'd have to stay overnight.

"And Donnie said he'd call my cell if Daddy got home."

Liv blew out a long breath. "You know, I think we need some hot chocolate and a snack while we think of what to do."

Roseanne's face brightened and Liv knew in that instant she had said the wrong thing. She'd meant to comfort, but Roseanne heard, *I'll help you prove your father's innocence.* And well, hell, she kind of heard that herself. She'd have to backpedal at least a little bit. "You know, I bet Bill Gunnison is down there with them and helping get your father back home again."

"I don't think so. He tried to go with them. And the guy—he must be the boss or something—said thanks but his presence wouldn't be needed. It pissed Mr. Gunnison off, I could tell, 'cause his face got all tight and he kinda lunged at the man. Uncle Ted had to grab hold of him. And that other guy just kinda smirked just like those smug outsiders on TV."

"Right," Liv said, grasping at straws. "And what always happens in those shows?"

Roseanne shrugged. "The local guy beats them out."

"Right. So let's put our trust in the sheriff—what do you say?"

Roseanne's cell phone trilled and they both jumped. "It's

Donnie," Roseanne said excitedly, and flipped open her phone.

It wasn't good news. Donnie's voice carried right through the phone. Ted had called to make sure they were all right. He had seen the truck go by and wondered what was going on. "He's on his way to pick you up. And, Sis. He's pretty pissed."

Roseanne snapped the phone shut. "I don't care what he says. You have to help me clear Daddy. They all treat me like a kid, but I can help you. I know things."

Liv had been about to stand up to go to the kitchen, but she stopped. "What kind of things?"

"I'll tell you if you promise to help me."

"Roseanne, I—"

"And you have to promise not to tell anybody, not even Uncle Ted."

Liv couldn't promise something like that. Especially if Roseanne really did know something that would help the investigation. But if she did know something, why hadn't she told the police? *Because, dummy, it might implicate her father. God, what a mess.*

"Off topic for a sec. I didn't know Ted was your uncle."

"Oh, he's not my real uncle. I wish he was instead of . . . He's really my godfather, but I call him 'uncle' 'cause he's so much like a part of the family."

"Ah," Liv said. "Why don't we go into the kitchen and put on some water for Ted's tea?"

"He'll be here any minute and—" Roseanne's mouth twisted. "It's all my fault."

The girl's distress trumped Liv's better judgment. She sat down on the edge of the coffee table facing Roseanne. "That's the second time you've said that. Why don't you start at the beginning?"

Roseanne made use of another tissue. "Donnie and I were going into town, and we stopped at Gonzo's for gas. It's out of our way, right off the highway, but it has a really good snack bar, so . . ." She recollected herself. "I went inside while

Donnie filled up, and while we were there this big silver trailer pulled up to the pump. You know, those old-fashioned kinds."

Liv nodded, encouraging her to get on with the story.

"So I'm curious 'cause it has a tumbling sign on the side, and I figure maybe they're coming to the fair. Then this guy gets out and starts walking toward the snack shop, and I do a double take. I really did. 'Cause he looks just like Daddy in that soccer picture you were looking at."

She shrugged. "That's why I took it away from you. I didn't want you to see how much they looked alike. I mean, I could tell because it's my favorite picture and I've looked at it, like, a thousand times, and it was so weird. I mean, it was like looking at my dad five years ago.

"I was standing next to the magazine rack, so I grab a copy and pretend like I'm reading it, but I'm really staring at him. He looked at me and I knew it was Uncle Pete. I knew it.

"I couldn't think what to do. I wanted to tell him who I was, but everybody in my family hates him. They don't say why, just that he's a big disappointment. But it had to be more than that, right? I mean, like, every family has somebody that's kind of sketchy, but they don't pretend like he doesn't exist.

"Then Donnie comes in and I drag him down the aisle and tell him to look. He does and gets really weird. Says that he doesn't look anything like Daddy or Uncle Pete." She made a face. "Like he's ever seen him."

"So did you introduce yourself?"

Roseanne shook her head. "Donnie said we should stay out of it. That it probably wasn't him, but if it was, he'd better watch his back, because plenty of people in town hated his guts. And he was asking for it coming back to Celebration Bay.

"I tried to reason with him, but he can be a real butthead sometimes. He got all mad and pulled that 'I'm older than you and you'll do what I tell you' crap. And he said to forget it, because I didn't know what I was talking about.

"But I did, and I knew he did, too."

She straightened her shoulders and stuck out her chin as if she expected Liv to scold her. When Liv didn't react, she went on. "The more I thought about it, the more I was positive it was Uncle Pete, so I decided to make sure."

"Please tell me you didn't confront him."

Roseanne grimaced and played with Whiskey's fur. "Well, I did. Sort of. I mean, it wasn't supposed to be a confrontation. I was just going to get a better look. I knew they'd be staying at Andy Miller's pasture, so I rode my bike over there."

Liv lifted her hand. "May I please just interrupt here to say never, ever do anything like that again. Deal?"

"Deal."

"So what happened?"

"That old truck was there, so I knew they were home. So I hid my bike in the bushes by the stream and crept closer to get a better look. I saw him coming up the path from the lake with a bucket of water. I followed alongside of him trying to see better. I thought the bushes would hide me. I was real quiet." She frowned and said in a smaller voice, "I must have made a noise, and he turned around and looked right at me.

"At first he was really mad. He dragged me out of the bushes and I was kinda scared. But he was my uncle, black sheep or not, whatever that means. So I told him who I was. Then he was much nicer."

Liv just bet he was. She imagined him playing on the girl's trust to get what he wanted, which, according to everyone in town, was to cause trouble. This was not looking good.

Roseanne paused. Liv waited, not sure she should be listening. Surely Roseanne should be telling this to Bill. But Roseanne wasn't ready to put her trust in either Bill or Ted. For some reason she'd come to Liv.

Liv smiled encouragingly, though encouraged was the last thing she felt. This story was leading right to more trouble. But somebody needed to hear it, and unfortunately that somebody seemed to be her.

Roseanne looked up, her eyes round and frightened and guilty.

Liv jumped in with both feet. "Go on."

"He was real nice after that. Offered me a soda and stuff. But I felt a little creeped out. I mean, he was my uncle, but he was also a stranger and . . . Well, I just didn't feel all that okay with it. But we walked and he started asking me questions, and I was sure not to tell him too much, 'cause suddenly I began to feel like I shouldn't be there."

She sniffed. "But he seemed nice. And he even said he'd been pretty wild when he was a kid, and he didn't blame Dad for kicking him out. That he deserved it. So I asked him why he didn't come back to make up with Dad. He said he'd thought about it a hundred times, but he was"—her voice cracked—"too afraid. And now he's dead."

Liv's conscience got the better of her. "Maybe you should tell the rest to Bill."

"No way. He's an old stick-in-the-mud. He'll just tell me to mind my own business. And I haven't even gotten to the worst part."

Oh holy moly, thought Liv.

"It's really bad."

Liv shifted to sit beside her. Whiskey sighed contentedly. Liv felt slightly nauseous. She pushed the same strand of hair back behind Roseanne's ear. "Go on."

"He said if I thought he should try to make it up with Dad, he would."

A tear seeped out of her eye and rolled down her cheek. She dashed it away with the back of her hand. "And I told him I thought he should. I mean, hell, it had been thirty years . . . and families should be together." She snatched at the package of tissues and buried her face in a handful of fluff. Her shoulders shuddered as she cried, and Liv automatically pulled her close, stroked her back.

What the hell could she say? Roseanne was no dummy.

She knew that she might have been the catalyst that would eventually send her father to jail.

"It's all right. I'm sure your dad would never hurt his brother even if he was mad at him."

"But he said Dad would never let him in the house. He'd have to surprise him and make him listen to his apology. Dad can be pretty hard-nosed. He's fair, but he's tough. You know?"

"Then Uncle Pete said I should unlock the door to the store and get Daddy to go down there where they could talk it over. And nobody would bother them. Part of me thought it was a good idea and part of me said no way. But I had told him how I wanted to go to New York but Momma got sick. And he said when we were one big happy family again, we'd all go to New York. He'd been lots of times, and it was fabulous and he knew all the best places to see. And he'd take me to the Hard Rock Café, and I—I said okay."

Liv didn't try to stop her. She'd let the girl start down this road, and there would be no stopping it until she got to the end. And Liv dreaded where and to whom that road would lead.

"So I did, but then I got nervous and told Donnie. He got pissed and told me I was an idiot. He said he'd go lock the store because Pete was up to no good. But I guess he didn't get a chance before . . ." She trailed off. "Dad was in the house asleep all night."

Dad might have been, thought Liv, but Donnie had gone to the store, and if Pete was already inside . . . Thankfully, Roseanne seemed oblivious to the fact that she may have cleared her father but had implicated her brother in the murder of Pete Waterbury.

"Promise you won't tell."

"Roseanne, you need to—"

"Promise."

Liv took a breath. "Okay, I promise, but you have to

promise me that you'll think about all this and tell Bill. It's important that they know all the facts."

"Not if it means . . . He didn't do it."

"Then the facts will help them find out who did."

Liv held and rocked Roseanne until her breathing steadied and they heard a car in the driveway. Roseanne sat up and wiped her eyes. Liv went to get the door.

"Of all the lamebrained things," Ted said as he strode across the living room and peered at Roseanne down the length of his patrician nose. "What do you think you were doing, coming here in the middle of the night?"

"Liv is going to help me find out who really killed Uncle Pete."

"What?" Liv exclaimed at the same time Ted barked, "The hell she will."

Roseanne's mouth drooped. Whiskey climbed onto Roseanne's lap. Liv stared. This fiery temper was something she hadn't seen in Ted until this awful murder.

"She promised." Roseanne hugged Whiskey to her chest. "Didn't you?"

"I—" Liv began.

"Will stay out of this," Ted finished, his expression set, his normally mild blue eyes cold as a frozen lake.

"Now, just a minute."

"Come on, I'm taking you home."

"No."

"Roseanne Elaine Waterbury. Now."

Whiskey sat up and barked. He obviously didn't like Ted's tone of voice, either. Roseanne pulled him close and shook her head, but her lip trembled.

The kettle whistled, and they all jumped.

"How about we all have a nice cup of tea," Liv said, feeling like a cross between a Stepford wife and Miss Marple. "I'll just get the tea things."

"I'll help," Roseanne said and slipped past Ted to the kitchen before he could stop her. Whiskey jumped off the couch and, after giving Ted his most disapproving look, padded after her.

Liv and Ted were left looking at each other. Liv deliberated for two seconds on whether to explain things or to avoid his questioning eyes.

"Don't upset her any more than she already is," she whispered as she and Ted followed Roseanne and Whiskey into the kitchen.

But as soon as they reached the kitchen, Ted said, "I think it's time that you explain yourself . . . and yourself," he added, turning to Liv.

Liv poured hot water into three cups, two with hot chocolate mix and one with a tea bag for Ted. "Roseanne needed to talk to someone."

"Try again. She has a whole town to talk to."

Liv hesitated, took a deep breath. "You know how people talk to bartenders? Sometimes it's easier to say things to people you don't know very well, because they have no preconceptions."

"About what?"

"Oh, Ted," Liv said, exasperation getting the better of her. "I love you dearly, but playing dense is not one of your better qualities."

Ted opened his mouth.

"Don't be angry with her, Uncle Ted. It's not Liv's fault."

Ted raised a sardonic eyebrow.

"Roseanne seems to think that, being from Manhattan, I'm an expert in murder."

"Ridiculous. What would an event planner know about murder?"

Roseanne shrugged. "I don't know, but somebody has to do something. And you and Sheriff Gunnison are just standing around with your—"

"Roseanne," Ted warned.

Roseanne huffed out a long, disgusted sigh. "Are doing nothing about getting Dad out of jail. At least Liv listens to me."

That was a stretch. A couple of sentences about funeral food this afternoon. And a garbled explanation about her father's arrest. Or non-arrest, as the case might be. But Liv wasn't about to risk losing the girl's trust.

"Let's just all sit down and discuss this rationally," said Liv, placing mugs on the table and reaching into the cabinet for something to accompany them. The only thing she found was a box of animal crackers, left over from her going-away bash the night before she left Manhattan. She poured them into a bowl and put them in the center of the table. Rosanne automatically reached for one. But Ted wrinkled his nose.

"Best I could do," Liv said. "I don't bake." *Or cook, or do any other domestic duty if I can get away with it.*

She sat down, took an animal cracker, and bit at the edge. She had some serious decisions to make, and she needed to make them soon. She couldn't tell Ted or Bill what Roseanne had told her. She just couldn't break the girl's confidence that way. She'd have to help Roseanne tell them herself. It wouldn't be easy. Roseanne refused to look at Ted, and she'd already told Liv exactly what she thought of the sheriff.

They drank their tea and hot chocolate in silence; then Ted told Roseanne he was driving her home. "No arguments. Get whatever you brought and let's go. Donnie can pick up the truck tomorrow."

Roseanne shot Liv a desperate look, then slid out of her chair. As soon as she was out of earshot, Ted said, "What was this all about?"

"Ted." She couldn't tell him; she'd promised. "I couldn't begin to say."

She saw them to the door and locked it behind them. Whiskey laid a paw on her foot.

"Yeah, I know, baby. There's more trouble ahead."

Chapter Twelve

....

Liv didn't even attempt to make it to work on time the next morning. She hoped Ted had decided to make it a late day, too.

She let Whiskey out, dressed, then went into the living room to pack up her computer. Her laptop was open. She tapped a key and the screen lit up with an article about Chaz Bristow. She'd forgotten all about her Google search once Roseanne had showed up at the door.

She sat down and scrolled through the article. Bristow was thorough. He'd ratted out one meth lab, followed the trail to a ring of labs, and was taking notes as the cops took a high-profile drug lord off to jail.

She clicked back to Google and brought up the most recent articles, written five years before, about the kidnapping of the wife of one of LA's most prominent bankers.

The banker paid several ransom demands, but his wife wasn't returned. There was speculation that she was dead. Speculation that the husband had been in on it. Speculation that it was revenge for an illicit scheme gone wrong. The husband stopped paying. Chaz's articles stopped.

Maybe that was the end of it. The cops would keep looking for a while; then it would be declared a cold case. Chaz would have been put on another story. And in the meantime the editor of the *Clarion* died and left it to Chaz.

Liv leaned back in her chair, stared at the screen until her screen saver appeared. Would Chaz be interested in pursuing the murder of Pete Waterbury? Was he already doing research? She could imagine him in his office, head bent over old newspapers, following the lead . . . right to the couch where he'd lie down and dream of catfish.

Liv huffed out a breath. There would be no help from that direction. And she should be getting to work instead of thinking about the murder.

It was so frustrating. The worst thing she usually had to deal with was the weather, an overbooked venue, or an off-season flower order that froze in an airline cargo hold. Those were the problems she knew how to deal with. She had protocol in place.

She'd once had to postpone a retirement banquet because the retiring CEO dropped dead of a heart attack before he could be feted. A week later in a new venue, she took charge of the memorial service. But she never in her wildest dreams thought she'd be broadsided by murder.

And she didn't like it one bit. And the sad truth of it was that no one had even liked the victim. He wasn't part of their community, and no one mourned him. But they were afraid of it happening again.

"Grrrr."

Whiskey barked once from the doorway.

"It's all right, baby. Just me." She got up and went to get her coat and keys, while Whiskey gamboled around her feet. "Sorry, fella. You have to stay home until I get this mess sorted out. Maybe Miss Edna will let you help her in the garden again. But. Do. Not. Dig. Up. Her. Carrots. Capisce?"

"Arf."

"And we'll go on a long walk tonight when I get home."

Whiskey cocked his head and took off for the bedroom.
If she followed him, she'd find him hiding under the bed.
To Whiskey, an evening in front of the television trumped
exercise any day.

"See ya," she called and headed to town hall.

The temperature had dropped overnight and she walked
briskly to get her blood pumping. She could have gone back
to get her winter coat, but she refused to be the first person
to give in to the cold. Liv Montgomery could take it with
the best of Celebration Bay's old-timers.

There seemed to be plenty of them on the street this
morning. It was a Thursday; there were no special activities
outside of the usual October fare, but nearly every parking
space was filled.

She passed three men confabbing on the street corner.

"Morning, Liv." Otis Deal touched his fingers to the bill
of his John Deere cap. "Heard any more about what's happening with Joss?"

Liv shook her head automatically. Why did he think she
would know anything?

"Well, it's that damn fool Bill Gunnison, letting the damn
state people come in and push their weight around," said his
shorter companion.

"I don't think he had a say in it," said the third man. "He
must be pretty darn frustrated."

"Then he should have hurried up and arrested one of the
Zoldoskys instead of going to funerals and hobbling around
like an old man."

The door to the bakery opened and Edna and Ida Zimmerman came out carrying a large bag.

"Well, good morning, Liv," Ida said. She was dressed in
a tweed skirt and sensible shoes with an old green car coat
buttoned up to her neck. "Now, you boys run along and stop
gossiping like a bunch of old women."

"Yes, Miss Ida." The three middle-aged men hightailed it across the street.

She turned to Liv. "We saw Joss's truck parked on the street last night and Ted's car at your place in the middle of the night. Did they let Joss out of jail? Did he ask you to help him?"

Of course they would know everything that went on, especially in their own backyard.

Before Liv could think of an answer, Edna took her sister's elbow and practically dragged her to the curb. "Well, I for one am not going to stand here and gossip all morning." She turned to Liv, frowned, then cut her eyes back toward the bakery, the meaning clear. Something's up. "Come along, Sister; we'd better get home before these buns get cold."

Liv smiled good-bye and stepped inside the bakery.

Dolly was bent over what appeared to be a tray of sticky buns. She was dressed in civilian clothes: khaki slacks and a pink sweatshirt. It was the first time Liv had seen her on-site not wearing one of her gingham dresses. Only the ties of the white apron gave a nod to baking.

"Good morning, Dolly."

Dolly squeaked and whirled around. Her face was chalky. She wore no lipstick and no smile of welcome.

"Sorry. I didn't mean to startle you." Which was odd in itself, considering the Zimmerman sisters had just left and customers came in all day long. Edna had sensed something was wrong, and she'd given Liv a heads-up. But what was she supposed to do?

Dolly put her hand on her chest. "I was just off in a blue study. Didn't even hear you come in." She smiled; it was forced. Liv had been around people who smiled like that for far too long. That was why she'd moved to Celebration Bay. She wanted to take Dolly by the shoulders and shake her. *Don't do this to me. I'm not the enemy.*

Or was she? Was Janine already spreading her venom?

We never had a murder before she came. She brought the evils from the city with her.

"What can I get for you?"

Some truth, some honesty, and two of those sticky buns.

"Just got these sticky buns out of the oven," Dolly said too brightly. "Ted loves them."

"Fine. I'll take two."

Dolly turned away and lifted two buns into a white bakery box. She set the box on the counter. "That'll be three twenty-five."

At least Liv was still getting the local rate. A tourist would pay that much for each bun. She counted out the change and handed it to Dolly. Dolly took it with trembling fingers.

Liv looked over her shoulder to make sure no one was coming inside. "Dolly. Is something wrong? You seem a little uneasy."

Dolly shook her head. "No, no. It's just . . . Well, this awful thing about Pete, and Joss being arrested."

"I heard he had just been taken in for questioning. That's understandable. He was a family member." Liv tried to sound reassuring but didn't really succeed.

"That's not what Harry Ellis over at the pub said. The local cops go there after their shifts. They said state detectives brought him in and are keeping him. They won't even let Bill talk to him."

Liv frowned. State detectives? Still, wouldn't it be a common courtesy to let the local sheriff in on the investigation? "What does Bill say?"

Dolly threw up her hands. "I have no idea. No one's seen him. I swear if that man—if he—oh—" She clapped a hand over her mouth.

"Dolly, what's the matter?"

"Nothing, nothing at all. I just don't know whether I'm coming or going this morning. This whole thing has just got me discombobulated."

It looked like more than discombobulation to Liv, but she couldn't force Dolly's confidence. She wasn't a close friend, though she'd thought until this week that they might become good friends. And she certainly had no authority to prod her for information. It wasn't any of her business.

The hell it wasn't. This was her new life, her new friends, her new home. "Dolly, if you ever want to talk about anything . . . Just somebody to listen."

"No, I'm fine. Just fine. It's just—" She looked around and then leaned over the counter. "Joss would never hurt anyone, especially not his own brother, even if Pete was no good. I just don't understand why Bill let that happen. It's not like him."

"I think it was taken out of his hands."

Dolly's voice lowered to a whisper. "He should have arrested the Zoldoskys like everyone told him to do. No, I don't mean that. It's just—I better get back to these sticky buns before they harden." She turned away. "Have a nice day," she said as an afterthought and began to ruthlessly scrape the sticky buns onto a doily-covered platter.

Deep in thought, Liv went next door for coffee.

"Yikes," said BeBe, frowning at Liv and giving her the once-over. "You look like you were up all night. Please tell me you were reading a page-turning thriller or out at a wild party, and not getting involved with Joss's arrest."

Liv shrugged.

"Oh Lord. I knew it. It's the talk of the town, those state cops arresting Joss."

Liv started to tell her that he hadn't been arrested, but maybe that had changed. She'd have to ask Ted.

"Well?"

"It's a long story and I have to get to work. I'll tell you later. When I know more." Liv took her carton of drinks and headed to her office, wondering if Ted would already be there.

He was. And not looking happy. "Where's—"

"I left him at home." Liv's stomach burned. She should probably have gotten decaf. She handed him the bakery box and drinks and went into her office without a word.

Ted came in a few minutes later, put the tray on her desk like every day, but Liv knew that today would be the pivotal point in their relationship.

And where would her loyalties lie?

She jumped in with both feet. "Do they still have Joss?"

"Yes."

"Did Roseanne tell you why she came?"

"No. She fell asleep before we'd gone half a block."

Liv nodded. "Catharsis."

"Possum."

"Maybe. Listen, Ted—"

"I know. She made you promise, and you won't break that promise."

"I can't. I'm sorry."

"Don't be. She'll need a friend she can trust."

Liv was reaching for her coffee, mainly to have something to do, but she stopped, looked at him. Ted, as only Ted could, reached for his tea and took a sip.

"Now more than any other time?"

Ted handed her a fork across the desk. "Use this on the sticky bun. They're a mess to eat, but worth it."

"Ted." She drew out the word and gave him her most intimidating raised eyebrow.

He gave her a half smile, no a quarter smile, in return. "Her father's a suspect in a murder case. The sheriff who has known him for his entire life has been shoved aside by state detectives, and from what Bill told me, the detectives sent here are not happy about it and want it wrapped up yesterday."

"Then why are they here? Is murder their jurisdiction? I thought the county could do that."

"Ordinarily they would handle it first. If it isn't a cut-and-dried case, they'll bring in the state to coordinate with them."

"But according to everyone and their uncle, the state has taken over and pushed Bill out."

Ted shrugged. "Evidently."

"But it's only been a few days."

"Which means they probably got nudged into taking over."

"By whom? Wouldn't it take someone with influence?"

"Probably."

"Any ideas?"

The door to the outer office opened and two men walked in.

"Speak of the devil." Ted stood up, wiping his hands on a napkin, and went out to meet them. "Gentlemen, how can I be of service?"

It had to be the state police. Both were of medium height, middle-aged, and wore dark suits.

One stepped ahead of the other and pulled out an ID card. "I'm Lieutenant Devoti and this is Sergeant Pollack. Are you Theodore Driscoll?"

"Yes, I am," Ted said and shut Liv's door, shutting Liv out of the conversation.

She heard the muffled scrape of chairs, low-pitched voices. She was so tempted to tiptoe to the door and eavesdrop, but she sat there thinking furiously. If they wanted to question Ted, they might want to question her. After all, she was the third person—that she knew of—on the scene.

Unfortunately, she was also the keeper of Roseanne's confidences. Was it withholding information if she kept her promise? Would she be culpable? Was she willing to sic the police on a young and naive girl?

Was that why Ted shut the door? So the detectives wouldn't question her and she wouldn't betray Roseanne? How could he think that? She wouldn't obstruct the law and she wouldn't lie. But she would convince Roseanne to tell Bill everything she knew, and Bill could deal with the information as he saw fit.

She was a resident of Celebration Bay. And it was time she started acting like one.

She pushed herself out of her chair and carefully made her way to the door. She knelt down and stretched her ear to the keyhole.

"And what did you see when . . ." The voice trailed off so that she couldn't hear the end of the question.

"Well, Detective." Ted's voice was not loud but it carried right through the keyhole. "I told him not to touch anything and wait for me by the front door of the store."

"And did . . ."

Liv made a face at the door. Couldn't the man just ask a question without winding down to a whisper?

"Yes. Joss was very upset, as you can imagine. He took me to the back room where the apple press exhibit was set up. And there was the body in the apple press."

"And did you . . ."

"I think any situation in which a murder has been committed an odd one."

Bless you, Ted, Liv thought. He had excluded her from the interview, but he knew she'd be listening and he'd couched each question in his answer. He was unruffled but vague in his answers. He was keeping her up to speed and she'd take the cue to do the same; then she'd insist on calling Roseanne and Bill.

"Can you think of . . ."

"Pete Waterbury has not returned here that I know of for nigh thirty years. No one liked him then, but a lot can be forgotten in thirty years."

The detective pounced. "Like what?"

"Whatever I suppose you would consider motives for murder. I wouldn't know."

"Isn't it true . . ."

Liv was getting really annoyed at the way the detective's sentences invariably trailed off, but at least she was receiving Ted loud and clear.

"Yes, but it was never proven."

They were asking him about Victor's death. Trying to make a case for Ted as the murderer? *Don't get too excited, fellas.* There were plenty of people who might have a motive for murder. Ted was only one of them.

Liv missed the next question.

"I phoned her after I alerted the sheriff, Bill Gunnison." A slight accusatory pause. Ted was good. He must have had speech classes in school. Debate club? *Concentrate, Liv.*

"Because she's the town's event coordinator. Contingency plans had to be put in place immediately before a horde of tourists trampled all over the crime scene."

"And what makes . . ."

"Detective, the man was bleeding from a wound above his ear. And really, no one would climb into an apple press to die."

Liv could swear someone chuckled.

She was sure of it when the detective snapped, "This is hardly funny, Pollack."

A mumbled, "No, sir."

"Thank you, Mr. Driscoll. Now we'd like to ask Ms. Mon—"

Liv hurried away from the door, all those karate lessons making her light on her feet. She was seated at her desk when a strange buzzing sounded in her ear. Not her cell, but the intercom. They never used the intercom. Ted was giving her time to compose herself. She fumbled with the old-fashioned buttons.

"Yes, Ted?"

"Detectives Devoti and Pollack would like to ask you a few questions."

"Certainly. Send them in."

She pushed the tea tray aside and replaced it with her laptop. Her document on Chaz Bristow was open, and she clicked out of it just as the door opened and Ted ushered the two detectives in.

Liv half rose to greet them. "Won't you sit down?"

Ted pulled up an extra chair, catching Liv's eye before he placed it next to the one he'd been sitting in.

"Thank you. That will be all."

Ted gave her a look over the detective's head and left the room.

The detective sat down across from Liv, but the sergeant continued to stand by the door. Probably an intimidation factor. It didn't intimidate Liv. She'd dealt with the housewives of New Jersey.

"You are Olivia Montgomery."

Liv winced. "Yes."

"And you are . . ." He consulted his notes. "Event coordinator for the town of Celebration Bay."

"Yes. For nearly six weeks," she said, anticipating his next question.

"And before that you lived in New York City?"

"Yes."

"On the morning in question, did you receive a call from Theodore Driscoll?"

"Theodore? Oh, you mean Ted. Yes, I did."

"At what time?"

"Five thirty."

"And are you certain about that?"

"Yes."

"Why?"

"Because I was asleep and thought it was my alarm. I reached to shut it off and saw the time, then realized it was my phone."

"And what did Mr. Driscoll say?"

"That there was a problem and could I come out to the Waterbury farm."

"And do you often get called with problems that would cause you to leave your residence in the middle of the night?"

"All the time."

The detective looked taken aback.

"In your occupation as event coordinator."

"Yes."

His expression said he didn't quite believe her.

"For instance, the month before I came here, I had to drive to the Bronx before sunrise to pick up a dozen ice sculptures when the refrigerated truck broke down en route to the Plaza. Once, I had to—"

"Thank you," he said, unimpressed. He continued through his list of questions; the sergeant shifted his weight as if his shoes hurt.

No, she didn't know any of the people at the scene well. No, she'd never heard of Pete Waterbury until that morning. "Sorry, Lieutenant Devoti, that I couldn't be more help."

He got the idea that he was being dismissed, and he didn't even resent it. He had about as much interest in this case as a turtle. He stood up.

"Thank you for your time, Ms. Montgomery, and if you think of anything else, please contact either me or Sergeant Pollack at this number." He handed her his card, dipped his chin, and left, followed by the sergeant, who had not said a word.

She followed them to the door, mainly to calm the flutters in her stomach. And to make sure they didn't sneak back in to catch her and Ted comparing notes. Not that she had anything to be nervous about; she had nothing to hide.

Okay. Maybe she had a little to hide. But mainly she was annoyed at the detectives' obvious lack of interest. Halfway through Devoti's rote questioning, she decided not to mention Roseanne's late-night visit, her Peeping Tom theories, or the altercation between Ted and Pete. If she needed to give information, she would give it to Bill Gunnison.

The detectives had reached the outer door when Devoti turned around. "Oh, does either of you recognize this?" He reached into an inner pocket and pulled out a folded check.

Liv knew even before she looked at it what it was. "May I?" she asked, holding out her hand.

Devoti handed it to her but hovered over her, probably in case she tried to eat it. He was really beginning to make her mad.

She perused the check, not believing what she saw. One thousand dollars made out to Pete Waterbury and signed by both of them, Ted Driscoll and Liv Montgomery. It was Ted's signature, but it wasn't hers. Someone had forged her signature.

She turned to Ted. "Looks like we found our missing check."

Ted moved close to see it.

Devoti moved even closer. "Is that your signature?"

"Of course not," Liv said. "Ted and I noticed there was a check missing a few days ago. I figured I had forgotten to write it down."

"Do you often forget to enter expenses?"

"Never. The town hires an accounting firm to balance the monthly accounts, but I keep a running account of expenses and income."

"You must handle large amounts of income from the various events."

"Yes, Detective, that's one of the reasons we require two signatures on each check."

He turned on Ted. "Is that your signature?"

Ted looked at the check. "Yes."

Devoti looked back at Liv.

"Ted often signs a block of checks for me to sign when he's not here. Obviously someone came in and helped themselves to a check and signed my name themselves."

"Not a very secure system."

"Perhaps not, but it's the way we do things here."

The detective cleared his throat, letting her know what he thought of her business acumen. Behind him, Pollack was practically smirking.

"And do you ever sign the check first and leave it for Mr. Driscoll to sign?"

"Yes." Liv turned the check over. "It hasn't been endorsed or cashed."

"Apparently not."

"Well, that's a relief." She handed it back to him. "Is there anything else?"

"Not at the moment." Devoti nodded minutely and gave Liv a complacent smile that made her want to deliver a snap kick to his groin. "We'll be around."

The sergeant quickly opened the door for him as he made his exit.

Ted and Liv stood unmoving for a long minute after they left; then Liv turned to Ted. "Those were the dullest, most officious policemen I've ever met. And what was with the attitude? How on earth did they get assigned to this case?

"Do you think they were trying to be stupid or are they just pissed to have to be working upstate?"

"The detectives? Both, I imagine," said Ted, and went into Liv's office. Liv followed him in.

"Did they think they were going to catch us off guard by waiting until they were leaving to pull out that check?"

"This tea is cold." Ted picked up the tray and carried everything back to his office.

Liv followed after him. "But it is . . ." She groped for the right word. "Worrisome about the check."

Ted tossed cups and the remains of their sticky buns into the trash. "How about an early lunch."

"Fine," she said, knowing that Ted would discuss this with her in his own time. "I'll have a cup of butternut squash soup and a roast beef and Swiss wrap."

"Worked up an appetite, did you?"

"Yes." Liv sighed. "Answering police questions without volunteering information isn't easy, and I don't feel totally good about it."

"No. I don't feel so innocent myself." But he looked innocent.

"About the check."

"I didn't forge your signature if that's what you're wondering."

"Of course not, but who do you think did?"

"I have no idea, and I can't think on an empty stomach." He picked up the phone.

The outer door flew open and crashed against the wall. Liv jumped. Ted dropped the phone.

Donnie Waterbury rushed in, searching wildly around the room. "Where is she? What did they do with her?"

Chapter Thirteen

....

"Hey, where are your manners?" asked Ted.

"Where is she?" Donnie's fists clenched and he continued to look around the room.

"I'm right behind you, butthead." Roseanne appeared in the doorway, then slipped past Donnie to stand behind Liv.

"Oh, for crying out loud." Ted picked up the phone. "I guess that's four for lunch."

"Where were you?" Donnie asked, trying to see Roseanne, who was using Liv as a buffer.

"Why are you following me?"

"Because I knew you were going to do something stupid." He glared at his sister.

"Who's for roast beef and who wants turkey?" asked Ted over the yelling.

"Well, I didn't."

"They followed you in here."

"Make that two turkeys on wheat with lettuce and mayo, a roast beef and Swiss wrap, a butternut squash soup, and one pastrami on rye, extra pickles," Ted said into the phone.

"Delivery. Better throw in a couple of bags of chips, a couple of Cokes, and could you ask Henry to pick up our regular order from the Buttercup? Thanks, Genny. I'm sure it's going to be fine. Yes, yes. Just the kids being rambunctious. Sure I will. Thanks a lot." He hung up.

"Now, who would like to go first?"

"I told her not to come here. But no-o-o, she had to sneak off and talk to Miz-z-z Montgomery." Donnie glared at Liv, his eyebrows knitted forbiddingly, dark curls tumbling over his forehead; Liv noticed he had the beginnings of a pimple in the crease of his nose.

"Stay away from my sister. She's just a kid and she doesn't know what she's talking about."

"I do, too," Roseanne answered around Liv's shoulder. "So just shut up."

"Both of you," Ted said. "Be quiet. And apologize to Ms. Montgomery for bursting in like you were raised in a stable."

"I apologize, but Rose—"

"He doesn't have any right to—"

"Quiet."

Both of them stopped talking, Roseanne scowling at Donnie, Donnie scowling at Liv.

"Do you think that between you, you could get out a coherent story?"

They both started talking at once.

Ted raised his eyes to the ceiling. "I guess not. Donnie, bring that chair into the other office. Ladies, after you."

Liv smiled in spite of the current of agitation ricocheting around the room. One thing she'd learned in the last few weeks: this job wasn't going to be boring.

They sat around Liv's desk, Liv in her office chair, and Ted between the two siblings.

"Now, Roseanne, why don't you start?"

She shot a worried look to Liv. "You didn't tell them, did you?"

Liv shook her head.

Roseanne slumped with relief.

"And she didn't tell me," Ted said.

"Rosie shouldn't've told anybody," Donnie blurted out.

"You'll get your chance, so stifle yourself."

Donnie shut up and slouched down in his seat.

Roseanne shot Liv a beseeching look. "I've been think-ing about what you said, Ms. Montgomery. About telling the truth and all. I was coming to tell you that I'd decided to talk to Mr. Gunnison. Not those men that were just here. Just the sheriff. I'd just gotten inside and I was kinda stand-ing across the hall deciding, you know. Then I saw those two men come in. They were the same ones that came after Dad, and I was afraid they'd followed me here. So I ducked into the closet right across the hall.

"I knew for sure I was gonna get caught. I was holding my breath, praying that they hadn't seen me. And then I heard them go into your office."

"Why didn't you leave when you had the chance?" Don-nie asked. "I thought for sure they'd arrested you, too."

Roseanne made a face. "I can take care of myself."

"Is that why you didn't even see those two before you came in here?"

She scowled at him but shifted uncomfortably in her chair.

Ted automatically went to the window and looked out.

"Don't worry," Donnie said. "I wasn't so dumb. I parked around the corner and waited until they drove away."

"You think you're so smart."

"Smarter than you."

"Are you two quite through?"

Roseanne shot a quick apologetic look at Ted, then turned to Liv.

"Anyway, I'd been thinking about what you said, and well, I was hoping maybe you'd go with me to tell Mr. Gun-nison about what I did."

"Oh Lord," said Ted.

"Rosie," Donnie snapped.

"I know, I know. I shouldn't have gone there. I shouldn't have talked to him. But I did. I'm sorry, okay?" Roseanne's shoulders slumped and she looked down at her hands. "I've messed everything up. It's all my fault."

Ted stood up. "I think I'll call Bill Gunnison and see if he can meet us here."

"No. You can't," Donnie said. He turned on his sister. "See what you've done. The sheriff will have to tell those state detectives, and they'll keep Dad in jail forever."

Ted's normally pale face turned paler. "What exactly did you do?"

Liv stood up. "Donnie, I don't think anything Roseanne knows, at least what she told me last night, necessarily implicates anyone. Unless there was a witness or some other kind of hard evidence, whatever Roseanne tells them will only be circumstantial."

"How do you know?"

CSI? *Law & Order*? "Well, I don't know for sure."

Donnie groaned. "See, Roseanne. I told you. That's what you get for—"

"But," Liv said, interrupting. "I do know that Rose cannot withhold the information." She mentally crossed her fingers, hoping that she wasn't condemning Joss Waterbury or his son to life in prison. "Ted?"

"Considering I have no idea what this is all about, I can hardly make an informed decision."

"I saw Uncle Pete. I talked to him. He asked me to open the store for him, so he could surprise Dad. I did it. But I told Donnie, and he locked it again. Right, Donnie?"

Donnie looked everywhere but at his sister.

"Didn't you? Donnie?"

"Oh my God. Don't say anything else. I'd better call Bill." Ted pushed out of his chair and left the room.

"I'm in big trouble, aren't I?"

"I don't know, honey. But you do have to tell the truth."
Liv leaned back in her chair, fighting some strange maternal
instinct to put her arms around both teenagers. But she knew
they would both be embarrassed, so the three of them sat
looking into their laps while they listened to Ted talk over
the phone.

Three heads turned to the door when he reentered the
office.

"Is he coming?" Liv asked.

"No, but I brought lunch." Ted deposited two large paper
bags and a carton of drinks on the desk.

"Um, Ted?" Liv looked a question at her less-than-
forthcoming assistant.

"He wasn't at the police station. He didn't answer his
cell."

Roseanne looked a little hopeful. "I don't have to tell?"

"You will eventually," Ted said. "First I want you to tell
me everything that happened and when. Donnie, no com-
menting. If you have something pertinent to add, then do.
But no blaming. Got it."

Donnie huffed out a sigh. "Yeah. Yes, sir."

"Liv . . ."

Liv wondered if he was going to order her out of the
office.

"Do you mind listening to all of this again?"

Liv listened to it all again. Ted passed around the sandwiches and drinks. Liv didn't feel much like eating, but she
thought the kids would feel better if they ate something, so
she lifted the lid off her soup container.

There was a general rustling of wrappers. Donnie dug
into his sandwich, but Roseanne just looked at hers.

"Eat," Ted said.

She unwrapped the paper, took a bite of the pickle, then
took a bite of her sandwich. Slowly, between mouthfuls, she
told Ted what she'd told Liv the night before: how she'd
recognized Pete because of the soccer photo, how she went

to his trailer and was caught spying on him. How she promised to unlock the store for him to surprise her dad. How she'd changed her mind and asked Donnie to go lock the store.

Ted listened intently, expressionless, not interrupting. After she wound down, he asked, "Did anyone see you?"

She shrugged, washed a mouthful of sandwich down with her soda. "I don't think so."

"If nobody saw her, does that mean she doesn't have to tell?"

"Afraid not. Do you want to add anything?"

"Just that she was stupid to go and meet him. Dad's gonna have a fit."

"Donnie," Liv said. "That's not helping. Did you lock the store that night?"

Donnie suddenly became quiet, began folding his sandwich wrapper until it was a little square.

"Donnie?" Liv coaxed.

Roseanne dropped her sandwich. "He didn't. You didn't, did you, Donnie? You said you would and you didn't. I am so screwed."

Two dark slashes suffused Donnie's cheeks. He shook his head, his face averted.

"Donnie-e-e. You said you would."

"I forgot, all right? I was about to do it; then something happened. And I got busy and I forgot. Sorry."

"You went out with Brittany Gorse, didn't you? She texted you, and you went running like the—" She groaned and covered her face with her hands. "I hate you. It's all *your* fault."

"No, it isn't," Ted told her.

"So it's mine." Her shoulders heaved. "I think I'm going to be sick."

Liv bolted out of her chair. "Come on, honey. Can you make it to the ladies' room?"

She hustled a bent-over Roseanne down the hall and held

her head while she lost her sandwich, her soda, and at least
a half bag of chips. Then Liv wet some paper towels and
held them to the girl's forehead.

"Better now?"

Roseanne started to cry. "I'm sorry, I'm sorry, I'm sorry."

"Shh. It's all right. None of this is your fault or Donnie's."

"Not my dad."

"No, of course not. In fact, if the door was left unlocked,
anyone could have gotten in and killed Pete. That could be
better for your dad."

"Really?"

"Really," Liv said, hoping that she was right and not just
giving the girl false hope.

When they returned to the events office, Ted and Donnie
were waiting by the door. Ted looked Roseanne over.

"Okay now?"

Roseanne nodded.

"Donnie's going to take you home. I don't want you to
say anything about any of this until you talk to the sheriff.
Understand?"

She nodded again.

"Not even to each other. Try not to even think about it.
The more you do, the more things will get blurred, and you
want to be very clear when you talk to Bill. You both have
to be strong. Just tell the truth." He glanced at Donnie. "The
whole truth. Now go home."

They left together, Donnie's hand on Roseanne's back as
he led her out of the building. Ted and Liv watched from
the door until they were gone; then both let out their breath.

"What a tangled web," Ted murmured.

And getting more tangled by the minute. "A lot of con-
fessing going on today," Liv said thoughtfully as they began
cleaning up the lunch things.

"Yes."

"Odd that Roseanne would recognize an uncle she had

never seen." She didn't want to do this, but she didn't see any other way to get to the truth.

Ted didn't reply, so she plowed ahead.

"If Roseanne recognized him, other people probably did, too."

Ted lifted an eyebrow. "Do you have someone in mind?"

Liv bit her bottom lip. She liked Ted; he was a great assistant and was becoming a good friend. If he lied to her, things would never be the same. But she had to ask. She had to know.

"Do you have someone in mind?" he repeated.

"Well, Dolly might have."

Ted snorted.

Liv took a deep breath. "Or you."

Ted stopped with a crumpled sandwich wrapper halfway to the paper bag. "Me?"

"I saw you. That day of the fair. In the green. We'd just been watching the jugglers. I teased you about being so interested in them. I thought it was charming. But it wasn't that, was it? You recognized Pete, or at least thought you did."

Ted shrugged and pushed the wrapper into the bag. Tossed the bag into the wastepaper basket.

"You went back, but you still had my clipboard. I called out, but you didn't hear. I ran to catch you. I saw you go behind the stage. I saw you arguing with Pete Waterbury."

Ted gave her a half smile. "Well, that answers your question, doesn't it?"

Liv's knees buckled and she sat down and closed her eyes. Adrenaline and nerves were coursing through her veins, worse than at any opening gala, international business function, or celebrity bat mitzvah. Because, she realized, this was about more than screwed-up events or irate clients. It was about friends, home, and the future. "Please, please tell me you or Joss didn't kill him."

Ted came to stand by the edge of the desk. "You saw Joss

when he rubbed that greasepaint off Pete's face. He had no idea it was Pete until that moment. You can't feign that kind of surprise."

God, she hated this. "But you weren't surprised."

"No. You're right. Something about the way he moved seemed familiar, even though he was in that ridiculous costume and makeup. It's just like something Pete would do. Brazen and foolhardy and just plain malicious. I couldn't place it at first; then, halfway to the market, it hit me."

Ted hit the desk with his fist. Not hard. Barely a tap, but it sent a chill through Liv down to her bones. "So I went back. Confronted him. He didn't even try to hide the fact that it was him."

"You threatened him?"

"You saw. What do you think?"

Liv shrugged. "You didn't threaten to kill him, did you? Because I wasn't the only person who witnessed you push him away. The balloon-making Zoldosky brother was there, too."

"Junior," Ted said. "Since the detectives didn't mention it or take me away in handcuffs, I surmise that neither of you said anything."

"I didn't. They didn't ask. They don't really care who killed the man. They're just putting in the time. How dare they snigger at a situation that is causing so much pain." She paused, thought. "I think I'll have to tell Bill, though."

"Ah hell, Liv. Bill already knows. He's one of us. That's why they took him off the case."

Liv propped her elbows on her desk, chin in her hands. "Really tangled."

"Like I said, but, Liv, here's my truth. I could have killed him. Maybe for a minute I wanted to kill him, but I didn't kill him."

Ted looked at the ceiling and back to Liv. When he continued, he sounded calmer. "Before Pete left town, he and his cronies chased Andy and another boy, Victor Gibson, into the woods. They beat Andy senseless, then went after Victor. It looked like he made it as far as the lake, managed to jump in a boat to try to get away. Or maybe they beat him and threw him in the boat. They found the boat days later at the south end of the lake. Murdered or drowned. Either way, Pete and his cronies killed him. Victor Gibson was my nephew. His mother was my sister. Victor was a sweet kid. Her only child. He didn't deserve to die, especially at the hands of that—"

It was exactly the same thing Miss Edna had said. *Because Pete Waterbury killed him*. "Didn't anything happen to Pete and the others?"

"No. Pete denied it. Andy was unconscious when Victor disappeared. They got reprimanded for fighting, were given a few weeks of community service, and Victor's death was chalked up to 'an unfortunate water accident.' "

"And his body was never found?"

Ted shook his head. "They dragged as much of the lake as they could, but it's a big lake. And it's deep. His mother never got over it. She went down to the lake every day of her life and waited for him to reappear. We even put ads in the papers asking him to come home in case he was still alive. He never did. Because of Pete Waterbury. And quite frankly, Liv, I'm glad Pete's dead."

"What happened to your sister?"

"She got cancer a couple of years after that. Fought it, still hoping Victor would return, but after a while she realized she'd never see her son again. And she gave up. She failed quickly and died. She was forty-eight years old.

"For that alone I could have killed Pete. And I told him as much that morning you saw us arguing. But for what it's worth, I didn't kill him."

"And Joss?"

"I don't think so."

"Andy? He might have a motive."

"Andy's not one to hold a grudge."

"Then who do you think *did* kill him?"

Ted shrugged. "I don't know. I don't want to know. And anybody who knew Pete doesn't want to know. Even if the murderer is discovered, Liv, no one will turn that person in."

Liv leaned back and let out her breath. "What are we going to do? You heard those guys. They just want to wrap this up and get back to 'important' crimes that can further their careers. They'll take whatever they can spin."

"Liv. I'm shocked at your attitude."

"Are you? Look, Ted. I didn't get where I am in my profession by not committing to what I believe in. And I'm totally committed to Celebration Bay. Yes, somebody—maybe somebody we like or love, even—may have to pay up for his crime. But I'll be damned if I'll let these guys railroad somebody in my town just to make it easier for themselves."

Ted smiled and shook his head. "You are something else. We'll have to give you an honorary citizenship when all this is over."

"In the meantime, what do we do?"

A tap sounded on the outer door.

Liv groaned. "Now what?"

"Who?" Ted corrected, and went to answer it.

It was Mayor Worley, looking meek, apologetic, and just a tad nervous.

"Good afternoon, Mayor Worley," Liv said as Ted showed him into her office.

Worley sat down and gave her a sickly smile. "Sorry to bother you, but were those two detectives I saw leaving here a few minutes ago?"

"Yes, indeed," Liv said. "But not to worry. They just wanted information on the Zoldoskys and Pete." But now that she thought about it, they hadn't even asked what she and Ted knew about the Zoldoskys. Didn't want to see the paperwork. Nothing. Because they already had a suspect they planned to railroad through the system.

"They asked a few questions and left."

The mayor cracked his knuckles. Looked at his hands and folded them in his lap. "Ah." He shifted in his seat. Leaned forward. Gripped the edge of Liv's desk with both hands. "This is just awful. They were supposed to find the killer, not accuse one of our finest citizens."

"Well, someone should have thought about that before they had Bill taken off the case."

The mayor's upper lip glistened with sweat. Now, this was an interesting situation. Had the mayor been the one to call in the state? Was he ruing his decision?

She must have been staring, because Worley wiped his lip. "Don't look at me. I thought about it. I thought they would find the killer more expeditiously. But Janine talked me out of it."

"Janine?"

"And it turns out she was right. This is going to be a disaster. There was a camera crew from Plattsburgh here wanting to interview me about the murder. Terrible publicity. We've got to do something."

Liv was only half listening, because one fact had caught her attention. Janine had talked him out of calling in the state. Now, why was that?

It seemed to Liv that Janine would want to catch the murderer so she could take the credit and move forward on her campaign to get rid of Liv. Or was it that she was afraid the state police might catch the real killer? Did she know something about the murder that she wasn't telling?

Chapter Fourteen

Liv and Ted assured the mayor that everything for Haunted October was proceeding as planned, which was a big fat fib. Work had slowed down since Pete Waterbury's body was found. As soon as the mayor left, they hunkered down with tasks for the upcoming festival. As usual, they divided the work and Ted returned to his office to make calls to the tent and catering supply rental services.

Liv opened the Haunted October file and sat perusing the spreadsheet. As festivals went, this one was fairly straightforward and simple in planning. Special activities were presented only on the last two weekends of October, though the Waterburys would run the Haunted Hayride Thursday through Sunday for the next three weeks—if Joss was free, literally, to oversee it. Andy Miller's Maze of Madness was due to open in a few days. She made a note to touch base with him to confirm.

Things had gone very well, traffic-wise, during the Harvest by the Bay Festival, but she'd better call Fred and make sure the traffic volunteers were in place. She added that phone call to her to-do list. Added another couple of calls to Dolly and Genny Parsons, who were co-coordinating the food and drinks.

Liv still had to come up with a prospectus for hiring an additional security service. It should have been done and voted on by now. Liv had researched several nearby security firms, gotten quotes for various services, but she still needed to consult with Bill Gunnison about the number of guards and services she should request.

Liv tattooed her fingers on her laptop. They could pull it off, providing the town council voted to continue. It had been four days since they'd discovered Pete's body. And it didn't seem like they were anywhere near catching the killer.

And, whether they were guilty or not, Liv had really hoped to see the Zoldoskys gone before the tourists started pouring into town in earnest.

Liv looked out the window. Could Roseanne and Donnie's involvement in all of this have any importance? Would telling Bill or the state investigators move this along any faster?

And could you please just concentrate on being ready to hit the ground running when you get the green light?

Pushing speculation from her mind, she turned back to her computer. She pulled up the committee rosters. Scrolled down the names. She and Ted had checked their credentials twice. Every person on it was either a resident or had been used before.

The heads of the committees had been doing this for years. Dolly, Genny, Fred, Andy. Liv narrowed her eyes. Read on. Bill, Joss. All friends for years. All who remembered Pete Waterbury and, from what Liv could tell, disliked him. All working on the last festival. About to work on the next.

Bill's reluctance to investigate. Dolly's agitation. Fred preventing Liv from talking to his wife. Joss leaning over the body of his brother. Ted, the first person he called. Andy beaten senseless by the teenage Pete.

And none of them was talking to the police, or to Liv. As she sat at her desk, planning the town's future—and hers—she felt the full force of what it was to be an outsider in a town where everyone shared the same history.

A chill ran up her spine, because she knew without a doubt that they might turn on her the way they had turned on the Zoldosky brothers.

Liv's mind was running in overdrive, and it had to stop. Timetables, rental fees, and murder motives were running in tandem, tangling into a useless mess of facts and speculation.

It was late when they closed the office for the night. Lunch was a dim memory; her stomach was empty. She bet Whiskey was ready to gnaw on the table legs. She said good night to Ted and walked the four blocks to her carriage house in record time. Her landladies' house was dark. Only the porch light shone from the shadows. It was bingo night at the VFW hall and the sisters would be there.

For a wild moment, Liv thought about joining them. She was sure to pick up on the gossip, and the food was probably delicious. But she'd been neglecting her exercise regimen lately and eating way too many of Dolly's excellent sweets, though it was already too dark to run.

She was met at her door by excited yelps. As soon as she opened the door, Whiskey ran two circles around her feet, jumping and capering and finally ending with his paws on her shins, his tongue hanging out and his tail whipping up a gale wind.

"Hey, buddy. Did you miss me? Did Miss Edna take you for a walk?" He barked, executed a little twist in the air, and shot past her heading for the kitchen.

She stopped to pick the day's mail off the floor, which, instead of resting in a neat pile beneath the mail slot, was scattered from one end of the hallway to the other. Only the corners of a coupon mailer showed evidence of teeth marks.

Evidence. There was a word she didn't want to think about.

She checked the messages on her landline to make sure she hadn't missed a call that informed her that Joss had been cleared of murder and some transient person from way out of town had confessed.

Whiskey returned to sit politely at her feet, giving her his nobody-loves-me-enough-to-feed-me face.

"Come on, you poor, neglected dog." She opened a can of dog food and poured fresh water in his bowl, then searched her fridge for something to feed herself. The fridge was bare, not even a drop of milk for cereal. The cupboard was bare. One lonely can of chicken noodle soup sat on an empty shelf.

Tomorrow she'd have to make a grocery run. She could walk over to the Quickie Mart for milk tonight. She could pretend it was exercise. And it would give her some quality time with the only man in her life, who was greedily scarfing up the last of his gourmet dinner.

Liv ate the soup in front of the nightly news, channel surfed for another few minutes, then turned off the television. Whiskey, who was sleeping beside her, opened one eye, and settled back to sleep.

"Come on, lazy bones. I need milk and you need a treat."

His ears perked up; he propelled himself off the couch and scampered toward the kitchen. "Not so fast. The milk and the treat are at the store."

Whiskey's head appeared around the corner of the kitchen door. Liv lifted his leash and shook it. Whiskey's head disappeared.

"Whiskey! Treat." A streak of white made several passes at her, then nuzzled under the easy chair, until only his rump stuck out.

Liv cooed. "My bad. I guess I forgot to shop this week. So it's no walkies, no treat."

Reluctantly Whiskey shimmied out from under the chair and with a disparaging look, sat down at the door so that she could clip on his least favorite thing. The leash.

"Sorry, bud. But there might be wild animals out there. We're in the country, after all." Not that she'd seen any. She'd smelled a few skunks and heard something rattling in the garbage cans late at night, which she hoped had been raccoons and not Dolly's Peeping Tom.

She set off in the direction of town. She had half a mind to see if BeBe was still at the Buttercup. She needed a sounding board. One that didn't have a history with the deceased. But when she reached the green, the coffee bar was dark. Most of the stores had closed hours ago, though the Scoop de Ville, the local handmade ice cream shop, was still doing a decent business.

She turned in the direction of the Quickie Mart, which was a block south of the square. Whiskey stopped to snuffle at an empty plastic bag.

The front door of the bakery opened, and someone stepped out carrying a large paper bag. Liv stepped into the shadow of a tree. It was purely reflex. The bakery was closed, and she knew Fred wouldn't let Dolly walk home alone. But it wasn't either of the Hunnicutts.

The door closed and the figure crossed the street, his movements almost furtive. He struck off along the path across the green, walking south. Liv waited, watching until he passed beneath the pool of light cast by one of the Victorian lampposts. For a split second his face came into view before he was swallowed by shadows. Junior Zoldosky. The balloon maker. Coming out of the bakery. After hours. What did it mean?

Did it mean anything?

Discovering a new moving object, Whiskey barked and lunged forward. Only Liv's hold on the leash prevented him from taking off after the man—and his bag of treats.

Junior stopped, looked quickly around, then set off again.

"Hush," Liv whispered and struck off through the park after him. It was probably a crazy thing to do, but she was curious to see where he went. Junior crossed the street, then stopped beneath the neon sign of McCready's Pub and reached into the bag.

Whiskey barked and yanked hard at the leash. It snapped out of Liv's hand and Whiskey took off across the street.

"No. Whiskey, come back here." Liv ran after him, praying no cars would suddenly round the corner. Hoping Junior wasn't afraid of dogs or, worse, hated them. Whiskey was a rescue dog, but his early life of neglect hadn't squelched his love of people or his indomitable spirit. If anything, he had too much spirit. Something that not everyone appreciated.

By the time she'd reached the street, Whiskey was jumping at Junior's pant leg. Junior squatted down and scratched him behind the ears. He was about to make a friend for life.

Whiskey nuzzled his way into the bag.

Junior laughed, a melodious tenor. It was so unexpected that Liv slowed as she approached him. He reached into the bag and pulled off a piece of bread, saw Liv, and averted his face.

Whiskey licked Junior's cheek.

"Sorry," Liv said, coming up to him. "He's really friendly, but he can be a pain if there's food involved."

"Is it okay if he has a piece of bread? It's small enough so he won't choke."

"Sure, but don't be surprised if he begs for more."

"I don't mind." He reached in the bag and presented the morsel to Whiskey, who gobbled it down.

Junior laughed again. "He's a great little dog."

The door to McCready's opened, and a blare of jukebox music burst into the night. Three men wove their way onto the sidewalk. One saw Junior and stopped.

"Why, you—you have a lot of nerve showing your face around here. Murderer."

Junior stood up, clutching his bag to his chest.

"Hey, Cliff, leave the guy alone," said one of his companions.

"I don't think so."

"Cliff's right," said the third man. "We oughta teach this scumbag not to mess with good folk."

"You let an innocent man go to jail, you filthy—" Cliff lunged at Junior, who ducked, and Cliff stumbled past him. He whirled around.

"Stop it," Liv ordered. "You're drunk and stupid to boot. Leave us alone." She tried to stare them down long enough for someone in the pub to come to the rescue.

Cliff turned on her. "You're that new girl they hired to take over for Janine Tudor, aren'tcha? Well, if you plan to stay, you better know which side you're playing for. Now, go on home and mind your own business."

At her feet, Whiskey let out a low growl.

Oh crap, she thought. The first rule of fighting was to run like hell. But she didn't know if Junior knew that. She couldn't leave him to fend for himself, but she wasn't at all sure that all those sparring classes actually would be effective in a real-life situation.

"This is my business."

"The hell." This time Cliff's punch clipped Junior on the jaw.

Liv saw red. The poor man's face had seen enough damage. When Cliff went in for a second punch, she was there before him. One quick sweep of her forearm and the punch hit air.

"What the—" He turned on Liv.

Whiskey went wild, jumping and barking, not knowing whether this was a new game or whether he was supposed to protect.

The second man made a grab for Junior. The paper bag split and rolls, muffins, cookies flew everywhere.

"Hell, we just caught us a thief. He was robbing the bakery. Look at that stuff."

That was all the third man needed. He rushed Junior. Liv's foot shot out of its own volition. It caught him on the ankle and he went down. He scrambled to his feet and stepped right into Liv's fist.

"Damn," said Cliff.

"You want more?" Liv threatened. She hoped she was sounding tough. In reality she was shaking in her Nikes and she was afraid her hand was broken.

"Hell, we can't fight a woman." He jabbed a finger at Junior. "You and your brothers better watch yourselves."

The three of them staggered away.

Junior bent down and began picking up his bakery items and stuffing them in his pockets, much to the excitement of one very enthusiastic Westie terrier.

From the doorway, someone clapped. Chaz Bristow leaned against the doorframe, smiling his most obnoxious smile. "Pretty impressive," he said.

"You saw?" Liv gasped. "You saw that and didn't try to help?"

"I thought about it, but I didn't want to spoil your fun."

"If that's your idea of fun, you're an idiot."

He shrugged, moving away from the door. Still the same ole Chaz. Hair that looked like it hadn't seen a comb in a couple of days and no styling gel maybe ever. Out-at-the-knee jeans, probably the same ones he'd been wearing when they first met. And a green canvas jacket that had been through a few wars.

And why was she standing here taking an inventory of the man's clothes?

She leaned over and handed a roll to Junior, who shoved it into the broken bag and stood up, cradling the remains in his arms like a baby. "Are you okay?"

Junior nodded. "Sorry. Really sorry."

"Anton picking you up?" Chaz asked.

"At the intersection south of here."

"Go on, then. He'll be wondering where you are."

Junior nodded. He stretched down to scratch Whiskey. "Good boy." Turning to Liv, this time he didn't bother to hide his face. "Thank you." He tucked his head and took off down the street away from town.

Liv watched him go, felt a stab of pity. "Will he be okay?"

Chaz also watched the man hurry away. "Yeah. They won't bother him again." He faced Liv frowning; then his usual smile broke through. "Damn, you didn't say in your résumé you were a ninja."

Liv sucked in her breath; she was suddenly shaking all over. "I—I can't believe it actually worked."

"What?"

"It really worked."

Chaz's mouth dropped. It made him look like a half-wit. A very handsome half-wit. "You mean you've never tried it out before?"

"Only in class sparring with other students."

"You mean . . . Holy . . ." He shot his fingers through his hair, leaving it even more mussed. "Are you nuts? Why the hell didn't you say so?"

Liv sniffed. "What? So you could rouse yourself to come to the rescue?"

He shrugged. "I'd at least have called for help."

Liv rolled her eyes. "Do you take lessons on how to be obnoxious?"

"It's an art. Come on, I'll be an obnoxious gentleman and walk you home."

"Thanks, but I was on my way to the Quickie Mart for milk."

Chaz flashed his teeth.

"No smarmy double entendres, please. I'll just be on my way. Good night." She snatched the end of Whiskey's leash and strode down the sidewalk, practically dragging a recalcitrant Whiskey, who'd found a piece of sweet roll that had been lost in the shuffle.

She heard footsteps behind her and walked faster.

"What's the hurry?" Chaz asked, catching up to her and shortening his stride to match hers, which was really annoying. She didn't answer, just took larger steps.

Chaz snorted and kept up.

"What? The fight wasn't enough? You have to come along to bad-manner me to death?"

He laughed, a big belly laugh that sent shivers through her nervous system. And she found herself smiling in spite of herself.

She pulled herself together. They'd arrived at the Quickie Mart and she shoved her end of the leash at him. "Make yourself useful and watch my dog while I'm inside."

She didn't wait for an answer but went through the glass door, bought a half gallon of milk and a small box of dog bones.

When she came back outside with her purchases, Chaz was resting on his haunches. Nose to nose with her dog.

"I won't even ask," she said and held out her hand for the leash.

"I'll walk him," he said. "I have to mend my tarnished hero image."

"Oh," she said, letting him keep the leash. "Did you ever have a hero image?"

He looked straight ahead, and she prepared for his next retort.

"No." He kept walking, staring ahead.

That one word left a gaping hole in the air around them. She had inadvertently stumbled onto the dark side of Chaz Bristow. It made him a hundred times more interesting than the superficial clown.

Clown. Jeez. Stay focused, Liv. She had an agenda here. She'd made a decision while in the Quickie Mart. He might be incorrigible, he might be totally lazy, a lothario, and a fashion nightmare, but he had expertise that could help her and the whole town, and it was time he came on board.

"I have a proposition for you."

He slowed down, turned to look at her. His eyes were deep and unreadable. His expression grave. Then he ruined it all by smiling.

"I'm listening, but I gotta warn you, I only accept propositions that include clean sheets and breakfast in bed."

"That's not the kind of proposition I was talking about."

"Too bad . . . for both of us."

"Speak for yourself." She picked up her pace, fuming. If she thought she could get her dog back without participating in a tug-of-war that would make them both appear ridiculous—or more ridiculous than they already were—she'd do it.

He didn't speak. He started whistling an off-key tune she didn't recognize, and she knew he was doing it just to irritate her.

"Don't you care about anything but fishing?" she blurted out, then could have bitten her tongue. She was playing right into his calculated apathy. It had to be faked. He'd had an exciting career. It didn't make sense. "Aren't you the least bit curious as to what the proposition is?"

The whistling petered out in a sigh. "Like I said: sheets and breakfast."

Liv bit back a growl of frustration. "I don't believe you."

"Why?" he asked, turning his blandest expression on her.

"Because this is your town as much as everyone else's. And this murder is about to tear it apart."

"Murder does tend to do that."

"But don't you want to do something about it? Help figure out who really killed Pete Waterbury?"

"Nope. It's a police matter. That's what we pay taxes for." He lifted an eyebrow at her. "In case you're wondering, I do pay taxes."

"You don't know how that relieves my mind."

"You better put some ice on that hand."

"What?"

"Your hand. The one you're holding against your side.

You probably bruised some knuckles. I doubt if you broke anything. Not even Cliff's nose."

"At least I did something." She stopped and frowned at him. Slowly he turned to look at her. "Would you have really stood there and let those three men beat the crap out of that poor man?"

"We'll never know, will we?"

"What happened to you?"

"Well, I was having a beer, and—"

"Stop it." For some reason she felt close to tears. Of rage, probably. "Something must have happened. Because you used to care."

Chapter Fifteen

....

"Look, Liv—you don't mind if I call you Liv?"

"Would it matter if I did?"

"You can call me Chaz."

"So you said." They'd come to the Zimmermans' old Victorian. "Well, thanks for holding the leash. I can make it from here. Good night."

"You live in the carriage house, right?"

"Yes, and I can make it down the driveway without you, but thanks." She reached for Whiskey's leash, but Bristow took off down the drive, while Whiskey, happy to be home, trotted ahead.

Liv had no choice but to follow them.

He was the most infuriating person she'd met since her arrival in Celebration Bay. Janine's antics didn't hold a candle to Chaz Bristow's lack of interest. Janine was just a jealous, vindictive real estate agent with too much time on her hands.

Chaz was doubly infuriating because he had the expertise to help catch the killer, and he refused to help. He knew the town, the people. He hadn't lived here all his life, so he didn't have strong, if any, loyalties. Not like Bill Gunnison, who must be desperately trying to look the other way.

But the simple depressing fact was that Chaz Bristow, ex–investigative reporter and current bum with a newspaper, didn't care.

Her right hand had stiffened up during the walk and she fumbled with the keys. He lifted them out of her hand, chose the correct one, and opened the door. He swung the door open and let go of the leash, and Whiskey bounded inside.

Chaz dropped the keys into Liv's outstretched hand.

"Ice," he said.

"Good night." Liv stepped inside and shut the door on his infuriating smile. For a moment all she could do was lean against the closed door, fuming.

"Good night, Liv," he said through the door.

"Grr." She spun around, made a face at the door, and heard him whistling that same off-kilter tune as he walked away.

"Grr." Liv dropped her keys in the bowl on the entry table and took her groceries to the kitchen. She had to open the dog treats with her left hand. Whiskey sat patiently until she managed to extract one of the pieces and licked her hand before he plucked it from her fingers.

"He's a no-good, self-involved, useless . . . ugh," Liv complained, pacing the kitchen. Whiskey followed her on her first two passes, then lost interest and padded away to the living room where he could enjoy his treat in relative peace.

"Fine." Liv gesticulated to the fridge. "If he won't help and Bill won't act, I'll do it myself." She held up her swollen hand. If she could prevent three hooligans from hurting Junior, she could figure out just what was going on in her new hometown.

She opened the freezer, poured ice cubes into a bowl, and filled it with water. Then she sat down at the kitchen table to soak her bruised knuckles.

Tomorrow morning she was going to have a little chat with Dolly. First about the state of the Halloween food preparations and then about what Junior Zoldosky was doing at the bakery after hours. It probably had nothing to do with the murder, but Liv had to do something. This investigation was going nowhere fast, and time was running out on Haunted October.

She felt a wet nose nudge her ankle, then two paws on her thigh. Whiskey looked up at her with his big questioning eyes and snuffled. She picked him up and returned her hand to the bowl, while he settled himself in her lap.

"We're in big trouble here, buddy," she said, absently pulling his ears with her free hand. "Big trouble. And I don't have a plan."

"Arf."

"I know. I always have a plan. Plan A, plan B, even sometimes a plan C. Best-laid plans, contingency plans . . ." Her hand and her mind were numb. "Let's just worry about it tomorrow."

But worry followed Liv to sleep, and she tossed and turned until daybreak, when she finally gave up and got up. She looked over at Whiskey, curled up on his plaid doggie bed, snoring peacefully in his sleep. He loved it here with a yard and plenty of people who gave him attention. She loved it here, too. And she'd be damned if she'd let some murderer destroy her future in Celebration Bay.

As soon as she got to work, she was going to call Bill and put her plan of hiring a security firm in motion. And then she was going to jump-start Haunted October.

It was only six o'clock when she left the house. BeBe wouldn't be open for another hour, but Dolly would be finishing up the morning baking, and Liv was determined to talk to her even if she had to do it without caffeine.

Liv stepped outside to frost-covered grass and a biting wind. Winter was stampeding toward them. She shoved her

hands in the pockets of her jacket and wondered if she would
have to buy a down coat.

The bakery was dark, but she could see an aura of light
coming through the curtained doorway that led to the back
kitchen.

She knocked on the glass. Listened. Knocked again.
Dolly's head appeared at the edge of the curtain. She saw
Liv and her eyes rounded. Then she pushed the curtain aside
and came to answer the door.

"Liv, you're up early this morning. I was just about to
open." Two creases appeared between her eyebrows. "Nothing else has happened, has it?"

"No. I'm just getting a jump on the day. The first weekend
of Haunted October is barely a week away."

"Oh. Is it still on? Janine said the council had decided to
cancel."

"Janine was premature. They haven't made a final decision, and until I hear otherwise we're proceeding as planned."

"Oh, good. It would be a shame if we had to cancel."

"So to that purpose . . ." Liv stifled a smile, thinking of
what Chaz would say about her stilted language. "How are
food preparations coming along?"

"Oh." Dolly wiped her hands on her ruffled apron, leaving
a wrinkled patch in the middle of the starched fabric. "Genny
and I had made initial plans, but when all this happened we
just sort of let it slide. I mean. It's just so . . . awful. And if
they arrest Joss for the murder, then where will we be?"

Good question, thought Liv. "I wish I knew. We just have
to keep going and hope they'll find the real killer."

Dolly practically levitated off the floor, not an easy feat
for the well-padded baker. She began to rearrange the items
in the display case. "Maybe you and Ted would like a couple
of these carrot raisin muffins. Raisins aren't a favorite of Ted's
but he'll eat them with cream cheese icing. I can put a little
extra on his. I'll just take one back to the kitchen and . . ."

"Dolly?"

The muffin flew out of Dolly's hand. "Oh dear." She leaned over to pick it up.

"Forget the muffin for a second. I need to ask you something."

Dolly froze with the squashed muffin in her hand. "Something about the food committee?"

"No, about Junior Zoldosky."

Dolly's full lips pulled into a straight line. "What about him?"

"I saw him leave the bakery late last night."

"Oh, that," Dolly said, her relief palpable. She leaned over the display case and said in a low voice, "I let him sweep out the back at the end of the day. Pay him a little and give him whatever didn't sell that day to take home. If you can call that trailer 'home.' I feel bad for them, stuck out there at Andy's and not being able to make any money. But I'd appreciate it if you didn't spread it around. Some people aren't feeling very kind toward those men."

"I know. I was out walking last night and saw him leave. I also saw three men come out of the pub and attack him."

"Oh no. Those damn fools. Junior never did harm to anyone. Was he hurt?"

"No. But I had to practice a little persuasion." She held up her hand.

Dolly's eyes widened at the sight of the ridge of red knuckles.

"You got in a fight? You? With a bunch of drunks? Oh my Lord, Liv."

"It wasn't really a fight. One fell over my foot and I gave the other one a bloody nose, but it was pure dumb luck. I've been taking these karate classes for years. It works off stress. And it actually worked."

"I can't believe it. That's amazing."

"Before you get all excited, I don't plan to ever have to use it again. I scared myself."

Dolly smiled briefly. "Did you know them?"

"No. One of them was called Cliff."

"Cliff Chalmers. Useless troublemaker. The other two were probably the Weaver brothers, good boys but completely loyal to Joss. If we're lucky, you scared them into shutting up. We've got trouble enough without them riling up everybody."

"Is everyone riled up?"

"There's been some talk. People are afraid. We don't have too many murders. The last one was one of the hill folks that came into town looking for trouble and shot his cousin by mistake. But not out-and-out murder." She shook her head. "I can't believe you took on that bunch of hotheads."

"I think surprised is more accurate." Liv decided not to tell Dolly about Chaz's noninterference. Everyone seemed to take his blasé attitude in stride. Dolly was looking at her in admiration and Liv hated to destroy this step toward acceptance, but she didn't have a choice.

"Dolly, what's going on?"

"Just some talk; nothing will come of it."

"That's not what I mean." Liv paused, then, choosing her words carefully, said, "I know you're upset about something."

"Who wouldn't be? The Peeping Tom and the murder. Those detectives arresting Joss. It's just got me spooked."

"I think you recognized your Peeping Tom."

"I didn't." Dolly shook her head vigorously and began to knead her hands, then realized what she was doing and dropped them to her side. "Really."

"If you know something, you should tell the detectives, or Bill."

Dolly grabbed Liv's sleeve. "No. No, not Bill."

"But you know something that you're not telling." Liv lifted Dolly's hand from her arm and held it with both of hers, a gesture that both consoled and trapped.

Dolly's gaze slid away.

"Dolly, you know I would never ask for confidences. I'm not being nosey. We need to get to the bottom of this before it kills the town's economy, its reputation. The detectives don't seem to have a clue or care that much. Bill isn't answering his calls."

"That's because he's been taken off the case."

"Officially?"

"Evidently. They said he had a conflict of interest and pulled him right off. And they're throwing their weight around, practically accusing us all of killing Pete."

That was bad news. Now Bill wouldn't even have access to evidence or knowledge of how the case was proceeding. Bill's words rang in her head. *They'll tear this town apart.*

"Dolly, you have to help."

Dolly pulled her hand away, looked at the clock, took a deep breath. "Let me get Mary to mind the cash register."

She disappeared through the curtain, and for a minute Liv was afraid she had bolted. But she returned a couple of minutes later with a young woman whom Liv had seen around town a few times.

"Liv and I will be in back if you need me." Dolly held the curtain for Liv, then led her past huge ovens and mixers and baking racks to a corner office, barely large enough for a battered desk and three hand-me-down chairs.

"Sit down, Liv. I guess I have something you should see."

Liv sat.

Dolly pulled a key from her apron pocket and opened her desk drawer. She rummaged inside, brought out a box, and opened it. When she sat down next to Liv, she was holding a crumpled piece of paper.

She ran her tongue over her lips. "I didn't recognize the Peeping Tom. Well, not until the next morning. Then I knew who it was."

Liv had guessed as much, and if she had guessed, so could anyone else, including the state detectives.

"It was Pete. But I didn't kill him. I swear."

"Of course not. But why did you guess it the next morning?"

"After Fred left for the festival, I took out the trash that I'd been meaning to take out the night before. And there it was."

"What?"

"This." She thrust the paper at Liv with trembling fingers. "He left it on top of the trash can with a rock holding it down."

Liv took the paper and read the print. *Bring ten thousand dollars to the old place just like before. I'm back and I'll tell.*

"Tell what? What old place?"

"In the woods down by the lake. There's a hollow where we all used to hang out. It's also where I was supposed to take the money, like the last time."

Blackmail. Holy cow. Talk about a motive for murder. "Are you saying Pete Waterbury blackmailed you before?"

Dolly nodded slowly. "In high school."

"But you were a teenager then. How could anything he held over your head then possibly matter thirty years later?"

Dolly's face crumpled. "I'm so ashamed."

Oh Lord, Liv thought. *What have I gotten myself into?* "Dolly, if this is really serious, maybe you should tell this to Bill?"

"I can't, not Bill of all people. I'll tell you if you think it will help Joss, but you can't tell anyone."

"Oh, Dolly, I can't promise that." Liv was getting a really bad feeling. She was afraid to hear what Dolly might say and afraid not to hear it and let it seal the fate of the future of Celebration Bay. She tried one last time. "If not Bill, what about the detectives?"

"No. I can't. I won't. If you tell them, I'll deny it."

Liv sighed and plunged ahead. "Then tell me."

Head lowered, Dolly fingered her apron. "Fred and I were sweethearts all of high school. Other guys flirted with me, in a fun way. But not Pete. He used to come on to me, always standing too close, saying really disgusting things. Joss overheard him one day and told him he'd give him the beating of his life if he didn't leave me alone."

"And did he leave you alone?"

"Nothing could stop Pete when he wanted something. Fred fought him a few times. I thought it was really stupid. But that's the way they were brought up. Settle things with your fists." A reminiscent smile played across her face. "You wouldn't think it to look at him now, but Fred was athletic in those days. Played varsity ball and . . .

"Anyway, he was also in the ROTC reserves. They'd go off for maneuvers about four times a year. The last time was when . . ." She heaved a sigh, spread out the creases she'd made in her apron. "He was gone and there was a dance. I was meeting some girls before, but I couldn't decide what to wear. Stupid. If I'd just worn my pink dress like I intended, I would have been on time and none of this would have happened."

"Dolly," Liv said gently, pulling her back on topic.

"When I finally got to Charlene's house, they'd already left for the dance, so I had to walk to the high school by myself. Pete must have been on the lookout, because he stopped me." She shuddered. "He grabbed me and kissed me; his hands were all over me. I tried to get away but he ripped my sleeve and my top fell off and he could see my bra and everything. Then he tried—so I screamed and kneed him; then I ran like crazy."

"And Joss found out?"

Dolly looked bewildered. "Joss? I don't know. No, I don't think so."

"I don't understand. Why did Pete try to blackmail you? You didn't do anything wrong."

Dolly's lip trembled; a tear rolled down her cheek. "Bill."

Liv closed her eyes. If it weren't so tragic, it would be comical. But it *was* tragic.

"I ran; I didn't care where. I felt disgusting. I could still taste the beer he'd been drinking. I stopped by the lake and cried. And Bill found me. And put his arm around me and told me everything would be fine. And he started rubbing my back—"

"I think I'm getting the picture," Liv said.

"It was just that one time. I don't know how it happened. I was just scared and alone and so lonely. It never happened again. Fred and I weren't married yet, but still, I wasn't one of those fast girls. I mean, I know it was old-fashioned, but I was saving myself for Fred, but I—I didn't."

"And Pete found out."

"He followed us and saw. He stopped me in school the next Monday, said he'd seen us and that he'd tell Fred and my father if I didn't pay."

What could a small-town girl of seventeen possibly have to pay?

"I had inherited five thousand dollars from my grandmother. I gave it all to him."

"Oh no, Dolly."

"I know, and of course when the bank statements came, my father saw that it was missing. Bill told my father everything and insisted it was his fault. He promised to pay the money back and he saved all that summer. But Dad wouldn't take the money. He just said the less talked about, the better, which meant not to tell anyone, and we didn't.

"I felt awful and almost told Fred I couldn't marry him, but I loved him so much."

Liv thought about Fred, stocky, round, and bald, and she was just a little envious of that kind of love.

"You never told him?"

Dolly shook her head. "I couldn't stand it if he knew. He would be so hurt."

"So did you take ten thousand to the hollow?"

"That's most of our savings. I couldn't do it. I was sure he would retaliate and tell Fred, but he didn't. I guess because someone killed him."

"I guess." Liv wasn't sure what to believe. She was certain Dolly hadn't killed him; she couldn't have lifted him into the apple press. But Fred? Bill? Joss?

"Liv, please don't tell. I know I should have confessed years ago. But so much time has gone by. I hardly ever thought about it until Pete came back stirring it all up again. Now I feel worse than ever."

"Have you ever considered just telling Fred? I mean, after twenty-five years of marriage, he should know how much you love him. He might be upset, but he'll come around. Then you won't have to worry about it anymore. I think you'll feel better if you do."

"I actually do feel a little better just telling you."

"Then think about telling Fred." Liv hoped she was advising the right thing; she didn't know beans about sustaining a relationship. She should be getting advice from Dolly, not giving it, not that she had a relationship to seek advice about.

"I will, and, Liv, don't worry about the food concessions. I'll get started today. We've done this for years. It'll come together. You'll see."

Liv stood up. "I'd better get going, but I have one more question. Who else got blackmail letters?"

"No one. At least, I don't know of anyone." Dolly's mouth opened. "Do you think he did this to other people in town?"

"Considering how much he made from you, I'd say it's a good bet he was doing the same to a lot of people. A very lucrative after-school job."

Liv reached the office before Ted, which was just as well. She had lots to think about. She left the bag of muffins and Ted's tea on his desk and took her latte into her office.

She spent the next few minutes going over the schedule for the coming weekend and the rest of the month.

Food was way behind, but she was confident that Dolly and Genny could pull it together in plenty of time. Andy

Miller's maze had looked good from the outside when she was out there last, but she hadn't talked to Andy at all. That was something she needed to do.

She'd go today, take a look at the maze, get an update on the hayrides, and if the Zoldoskys were home, she'd check on Junior. The neighborly thing to do.

She called Bill. He didn't answer. She left a message telling him about her plan to hire a security service. Gave him several names she'd researched and asked his advice.

Maybe he'd get back to her. If not, she would hire whichever one she could afford. But first she'd have to clear it with the council and the mayor at the next meeting.

The outer door opened and Ted walked in. "You're early," he said, lifting his eyebrows.

"I'm getting anxious about the weekend."

"Hmm."

"Did you hear about Bill?"

"That he's been taken off the case?"

"Yes. Why didn't you tell me?"

"I just found out last night when I went over there to see if he was okay, since nobody has seen him or heard from him in days."

"Was he okay?"

"No. He looked like—pardon the expression—shit."

"He must be pretty upset."

"That's an understatement. People were giving him a hard time before the state took over; now they're accusing him of not doing anything."

"That sucks."

"It does. But Bill's tough. He'll get through it. What's on the agenda for today?"

"We're going full steam ahead, but if the council is going to balk, we need to get our deposit back on the tents and start triage."

"I don't think there's going to be a problem with that."

"The tents or the council?"

"Neither. I found out who called in the state police."

"Not the mayor or Janine."

"No. Rufus and Roscoe."

"The councilmen?"

"Yes, dimwits that they are, they wanted to help speed things along. Instead, they've helped railroad Joss into jail. They're feeling pretty contrite. I don't think they'll vote against us."

"Good." Liv sat back down. "Ted, come in and close the door."

"Sounds serious."

Liv nodded. "Maybe." She picked up a pen and tapped it on the desk, wondering how she could ask Ted what he knew about the blackmailing attempt without breaking her promise to Dolly.

"Did—What kinds of things did Pete Waterbury do when he was younger that got him into such trouble? Besides what he did to Andy and Victor Gibson?"

"Why this sudden interest in Pete's past?"

"If I'm going to save the festival, I need to understand what I'm dealing with."

Ted perched one hip on her desk and looked down at her. "What do you want to know?"

"What was he involved in? Drinking? Drugs?"

"Check and check. Mainly he was just a conniving snake. The kind of kid who bullied smaller kids on the playground, stole their lunch money, told them he'd beat them up if they told. In high school he turned to bigger things. Stealing. Lying. Extorting money from anybody he could scare."

"Blackmail?"

"Who have you been talking to?"

Tread very careful, Liv. "What do you know?"

"Well, we have muffins and tea and coffee. You've been to Dolly's and BeBe's this morning. Since BeBe didn't even live here when Pete was carrying on, it must be Dolly. What did she tell you?"

Liv shrugged. "Just some stuff about Pete spying on and blackmailing people."

"People? Or Dolly?"

Liv looked away. This was harder than she'd expected. She could lie. Hell, it had been part of the job description back in Manhattan, but she didn't want to lie to Ted.

"Let me make it easy on you. Did she tell you about her and Bill?"

"I'm sworn to secrecy. How did you know?"

"Oh hell, Liv. It's no secret what happened between them."

"Dolly thinks it is. She's afraid it will break Fred's heart if he found out."

Ted chuckled. "Not his heart, but Fred almost broke Bill's jaw."

"When?"

"When he got back from ROTC camp. Bill confessed and apologized. Fred let him have it. Fred was athletic in those days, and I don't think Bill tried very hard. He was feeling pretty guilty."

"And how did you know about it?"

"Oh please, this is Celebration Bay. Even in those days, guys talked. But they did swear me to secrecy. Much ado about nothing, if you ask me."

"Men," Liv said, disgusted. "Dolly's been carrying around this guilt all these years. Why didn't someone tell her?"

"Fred thought it would save Dolly embarrassment. Guess he was wrong."

"Well, since you know that much, I don't suppose it matters if I tell you Pete was up to his old tricks."

Ted raised both eyebrows, which made his eyes pop. "Dolly didn't pay him?"

"No."

"Well, that's a relief."

"But I think it was because she couldn't figure out a way to come up with the money without Fred knowing."

"Dolly, Dolly, Dolly." Ted shook his head.

"She didn't pay him, but I think it's about time someone told her that her secret is no secret."

"I think you're right. What a fool Pete was. Did he actually think anyone would care about what happened thirty years ago?"

"Somebody did."

Chapter Sixteen

··

"What? Are we giving up on the idea that one of the Zoldoskys killed him?"

"What do you think?" Liv said, not able to keep the sarcasm out of her voice.

"I'm afraid that it's looking more and more like a local matter. But, if we must investigate, can we stick to figuring out who stole the check and forged your signature?"

"Okay. If we discount you and me . . ."

"Which we do, in case you're wondering."

"I wasn't wondering." Though she had other questions she did want the answers to. "It had to be someone who had access to the checkbook, and who was savvy enough to take one out of order, so we wouldn't realize it was gone until we got to it, which makes a really big window of opportunity. So who else besides Dolly was Pete blackmailing?"

"Sometimes your mind scares me," Ted said.

Liv shrugged. "The devil is in the details. An event planner's motto. You have to see the pieces without losing the whole picture—ever."

"So you've told me. You didn't mention, however, that they take being proactive to the next level."

"Is that a euphemism for buttinsky?"

"Let's leave it at overly curious."

"Well, if those detectives would light a fire under their butts, or if Chaz Bristow would rouse himself to help, I wouldn't have to do it."

"Chaz?"

"Yes. Did you know that he used to be an investigative reporter?" She held up her hand. "No, don't say it. 'It *is* Celebration Bay, Liv,'" she mimicked.

Ted chuckled. "And you asked him to help?"

"Yes. He turned me down flat."

"I'm sure he has his reasons."

She gave him a tight smile. "And I'm sure you know what they are."

"Leave it alone, Liv."

She rolled her eyes. "I do have more important things to worry about, like who stole the check. And when."

"Well, the checkbook is locked up every night. So it had to be during the day. And it could have been last year, for all we know. That's when we got the new checkbook. We only discovered it this week because we'd finally gotten to it."

"True, but it was made out to Pete and he didn't arrive until last week," she reminded him.

"If he was the impetus for the theft."

"Which seems likely. I wonder . . ." She fanned through the remaining pages but didn't find any more missing checks. "Well, that's a relief, sort of.

"So who had access?"

"The mayor?" Ted guessed. "And wouldn't that just cut it?"

"Actually, anyone could walk right into this office. The mayor, his secretary. Anyone on town business. Anyone just passing through. Committee chairs, vendors. What were we thinking to leave such a temptation out in the open?"

She hadn't been thinking. She'd become enamored by her new life, was enjoying the laid-back, easy lifestyle, and she'd forgotten there were crooks and, unfortunately, murderers, even in the smallest town. She wouldn't make that mistake again.

"It's usually in a desk drawer. Someone would have had to look for it."

"Or know where it was kept," Liv added. "Which brings us to . . ."

"Janine," they said simultaneously.

"You think so, too?" Liv asked.

"Seems crazy. She doesn't need the money. Her ex-husband paid a bundle. But she had access to the checkbook before you came. And probably afterward, too."

"But why? She was just a kid when Pete left town. Why would she be paying him blackmail? Or was she just being spiteful? Trying to derail the festivals?"

"Sounds extreme."

"It does. Even for Janine. But who else could it be?"

"I don't know, but we're not going to confront Janine and risk a lawsuit. I suggest we let the detectives deal with catching the thief, if they are so inclined."

They spent the next hour coordinating the following weekend's activities. Made location grids for the food tents, which would be located in the town green, at the Waterbury farm where the Haunted Hayride was held each year, and at Andy's Maze of Madness. Other farms and households were participating with produce stands, yard sales, u-picks, and yards turned into private parking.

"I'd better run out and make sure the maze is ready and that Andy has taken care of who will be running the hayrides. I should have done it sooner, but with the funeral and Joss's arrest, it just seemed like an insensitive thing to do, not to mention downright rude. Now I feel irresponsible for not having done it."

Ted chuckled. "You could just call."

"I know. But a picture is worth a thousand words."

Ted nodded his agreement. "In that case, I suggest we close the office early. This is not strictly festival business, but I want to talk to Bill and tell him Roseanne's story."

"We promised not to tell."

"You did. But I mean to run it past Bill before I hand Donnie and her over to the detectives."

"I supposed it has to be done."

"Yes. And besides, it might help get Joss out of jail."

"I think I'll come with you if that's okay."

"What about Andy and the Maze of Madness?"

"I'll go tomorrow."

"Vacation?" Ted exclaimed. "Bill hasn't taken a vacation for as long as he's been sheriff."

The desk sergeant quickly looked around and leaned forward. "He's not the only one thinking about taking time off. Since those muckety-mucks from the state came, we haven't had a minute of peace. They don't need our help in the investigation; they just want us to step and fetch. The head guy told Bill to stick to parking tickets." He glanced at Liv. "I won't repeat what Bill said."

Ted blcw out air. "And then he put himself on vacation leave."

"Pretty much," the sergeant agreed.

Liv was speechless. How could he just walk at a time like this when there was a murderer loose in their town, when Joss's freedom was hanging in the balance, when they needed him to keep things running smoothly?

The sheriff's office door opened. Detective Devoti stepped out, saw Ted and Liv, and after a piercing look, began walking toward them.

"So," Liv said loudly to the sergeant. "I just wanted to let you know that my dog has been found, so no worries, but thanks anyway."

The sergeant looked confused, then got it. "Glad to hear it, and you just keep him on the leash when you're out. We do have wild animals that come into town sometimes. Wouldn't want the little fellow getting mauled."

The detective arrived at the desk.

"Good morning, Detective . . . Devoti, isn't it?"

He didn't condescend to answer.

Liv started to turn away, then turned back. "Oh, while we're here. Did you find out who forged the check from my office?"

"It's under investigation."

"Maybe handwriting analysis?"

Devoti gave a slight snort. "This isn't television, Miz Montgomery."

Liv gritted her teeth and smiled. "If only we had their budget." She turned to the desk sergeant. "Thanks again. Have a nice day."

With that, she strode toward the front door, half afraid the detective would call her back and destroy her exit. But she and Ted were on the sidewalk, before she stopped.

"That officious little pr—so-and-so." She took off toward Ted's car, which was parked at the curb.

Ted blipped the locks and opened the door for her. His mouth was going through a series of contortions. Liv glared at him and got in the car.

When he got in the other side, he was laughing. "I'm sure the lieutenant was relieved to know you found your lost dog." He started the car. "Really, Liv. That was awfully close to false reporting."

Liv shrugged. "Just a little stretch of the truth. Whiskey did run out in the garden last night. It took me forever to get him back in."

"You are one cool cookie."

Cool cookie? "Why, thank you, Ted. I think."

"Grace under pressure. You didn't miss a beat."

"I've dealt with brides more outrageous than Detective

Devoti and handled them without breaking a sweat." She paused. "Besides, you don't jerk my town around and expect me to take it lying down."

Ted's smile broadened. "Good."

They drove to the north side of town and stopped in front of a small white cape with green shutters. The yard was immaculately trimmed and mowed. The bushes were shaped into perfect cubes. Liv had learned from BeBe that Bill was divorced, lived alone, and had two grown children who lived on the West Coast. He sure took good care of his home.

Ted rang the bell, waited, rang the bell again. When no one answered, he walked around the side of the house, Liv following on his heels.

The backyard was enclosed in a chain-link fence. At the back of the long yard was a vegetable garden. And sitting on a step stool was the Celebration Bay sheriff weeding a row of bushy green plants.

Ted marched toward the garden. Liv had to make a couple of running steps to catch up to him. "Bill."

Bill looked up, hesitated with a clump of yellowing leaves grasped in his hand. Then he tossed the weed into a woven basket and pulled at another clump.

Ted didn't stop until he was standing right over his friend.

"Of all the stupid, asinine—we've got serious trouble here, and you're weeding your garden."

"Might as well get something useful done."

"You might as well have kept your temper with that arrogant jackass from the state."

"Why bother." Bill yanked another clump of grass from the ground and tossed it toward the basket. "My guess is they're just some screwups that someone higher up sent to get them out of the way. All posturing and not a brain between them."

"Which is why it was even more important for you to stick around."

Bill grunted and heaved himself to his feet. Gardening

was probably not the best activity for a man who suffered from sciatica.

"Parking tickets. That's what he said. Stick to parking tickets."

Ted growled in frustration. "And you got on your high horse over that? He was baiting you. You have more sense than to walk into that kind of manipulation." He stopped. His eyes narrowed. "It wasn't that. Why did you put yourself on vacation leave?"

"Aw, hell, Ted. Don't start surmising. I don't know nothing you don't know. But I've been a cop here for almost twenty years, run folks in that deserved it, helped out a few who needed it. I've even given out my share of parking tickets. I know my job."

Ted nodded slowly. "You're upset that someone felt they needed to call in the state."

Bill picked up the basket of weeds and walked over to the fence where he dumped them into a pile of drying clippings. He carried the basket back, moved his step stool farther down the row, and sat down.

Liv was pretty sure she was about to see Ted lose his temper for the first time. He was vibrating with suppressed frustration.

"And you call Devoti a jackass. You're the one that needs a swift kick."

"Your opinion."

Liv couldn't stand the tension. "Bill, we need you to find this killer."

Bill looked up, smiled a half smile, and shook his head. She knew just how Ted felt; she felt like giving the sheriff a swift kick herself.

"Liv, when you've been around awhile longer, you'll see that folks usually end up doing the right thing."

"What does that mean?"

"Nobody's gonna let Joss go to jail for something he didn't do."

"And if it's an outsider?"

"We'll just have to hope that Mutt and Jeff can figure it out."

"I don't get it," Liv said. "I don't know what you're up to, but I don't believe you're just going to weed beans or whatever those things are and let your good friend rot in jail."

Bill flinched. "It's out of my hands, and if I act on my own, there will be hell to pay, not to mention that anything I find will not hold up in court."

Ted snorted. "Then I guess you don't want to know that Roseanne recognized Pete from pictures of her dad. She sought him out and he convinced her to unlock the store for him."

Bill straightened up, suddenly interested. "And you know this how?"

"She told Liv."

"Liv?" Bill turned to Liv. "She came to you?"

Liv sighed. "She thought that since I was from Manhattan, I could solve the murder."

"Of all the—" Bill said fondly. "Maybe you better tell me the whole story. I've got some cider in the house. Something tells me this is gonna take a while."

They followed him through a back porch crammed with cast-off machinery, old bicycles, and piles of newspapers and into an old-fashioned kitchen as clean and well kept as his yard.

While Bill poured out three glasses of Waterbury Farms cider, Liv and Ted told him about Roseanne's midnight visit and the second visit at the office.

"So, the door was unlocked. Donnie never relocked it. Anybody could have walked right in."

"Huh," Bill said.

"Which," Liv continued, "has to be good for Joss. Right?"

"They have until tonight. Forty-eight hours or they have to charge him. I wasn't privy to much of the investigation even before they pulled the plug, but I did get a chance to talk to Joss before then. He swears he didn't know Pete was back. And he swears he didn't kill him. That's all anybody needs to know."

He looked at Liv to make sure she was getting it. As if he were speaking a foreign language, and maybe he thought he was. To him, Liv was still an outsider.

And she'd had enough. "Maybe you should take a page from Roseanne Waterbury."

Both men looked confused.

"She came to *me*. Not just because I'm from the city, but because she trusted me. It's about time the rest of you did, too."

"Beg pardon?"

"Don't give me that innocent look, Bill, and don't you, either, Ted. The whole town is depending on me to keep the festivals going. Yet you're all talking to each other all over town but not talking to me."

"Now, Liv."

"You both clammed up and skulked away the other night after the committee meeting. Fred tried to keep me from talking to Dolly. Ted keeps telling me to stay out of it."

"I didn't," Ted began.

Liv quelled him with a look. "And now you've decided that's all I need to know."

Ted sighed. "Only because we don't want you to get hurt."

Liv narrowed her eyes at him. "By whom? You think someone out there is planning to kill again?"

"Aw, hell," Bill said. "Ted doesn't know nothing. And neither do I. But someone is a murderer. Anyone who discovers him—or her—might get more than they bargained for. That's all Ted means."

"So you guys really don't know who killed Pete Waterbury?"

"Of course not," said Ted in an offended voice. "What kind of folks do you think we are?"

"Ones who are very loyal and care deeply about your town and friends."

"But not enough to protect a murderer from the justice he deserves," Bill said.

Liv looked from Bill to Ted. She believed them, strangely enough. "And if you learn something, you won't hold out on me?"

Ted rolled his eyes to the top of his head.

Bill crossed his arms. "Liv, if I learn something in the course of the investigation, I can't tell anyone. Not you, not Ted, or anybody else."

"But you're not part of the official investigation."

"True."

"Ergo."

Bill looked blank.

"Since you're not part of the official investigation, anything you find out wouldn't be confidential."

"I'm still the sheriff."

Liv smiled at him.

"Aw hell, I guess I better get out to Joss's and talk to Rosie. Remember what I told you that night at town hall? This business is gonna tear this town apart."

Liv hoped he was wrong, but it was already taking its toll on her, and she didn't even have a deep-seated interest in the outcome, though it would be horrible if Joss was convicted, and even worse if the killer was never caught.

"I suppose the two of you want to come along."

Ted smiled. "Roseanne did ask Liv to be there when she told you."

"Aw hell," Bill said. "I'll drive."

"I'll drive," Ted countered. "That's all Amanda needs. To see you driving up her driveway. She'll think you've come to arrest them all."

"I didn't arrest Joss. I wish everybody would remember that."

Ted placed his hand on Bill's shoulder. "They know that. They're just frustrated. People take out those frustrations on people they trust. Don't know why. Guess they figure when the dust clears you'll forgive them."

"I guess. Let's get going."

No one spoke on the way out to the Waterbury farm. None of them was looking forward to what was waiting for them.

As they turned into the parking lot at the front of the Waterbury farm store, Roseanne came out the door and checked. Her face drained of color when she saw Bill. She took a hesitant step, then froze altogether.

"Stop, Ted."

Ted stopped the car, and Liv slid out of the backseat. Roseanne's countenance didn't change, but she didn't run.

"Bill just wants to hear your story. Is that okay?"

Roseanne nodded jerkily. "I told Mom. She said it was okay, but she was pretty mad at me." Her eyes filled with tears and her mouth quivered.

"It's just because she's scared," Liv said and hoped that was all it was.

Liv and Roseanne followed Ted's SUV up to the house. Ted and Bill had already gone inside when they reached the kitchen door.

Roseanne stopped. "I can't."

"Yes, you can. Actually, you have to."

"But what if it makes it worse for Dad?"

Liv didn't know how it could make things worse, but she had to admit that she was worried about that, too. "I—I don't know." She opened the door and nudged Roseanne inside.

Amanda Waterbury stood at the sink, looking almost as pale as her daughter. Bill and Ted stood uncomfortably at the far side of the table. When Liv and Roseanne came in, Amanda grabbed hold of the sink edge, looked at her daughter, and then at Liv.

"I don't know if Joss would want her involved."

"She's not involved," Bill said reassuringly. "But she does need to tell me what's what. I can't help if I don't know all the facts."

Amanda chewed at her bottom lip, frowning as if she were carrying on a silent argument with herself, or her husband. Finally she said, "All right."

"Thank you, Amanda. Maybe Roseanne would be more comfortable in the parlor."

Amanda started. "Oh, yes. Do you want Donnie, too? He's in the fields, doing a dry run of the hayride. He's determined to carry on with it. Ed Fenway offered to take over, but Donnie's just like his father. Stubborn and . . . Go on inside. I'll just get Donnie on his cell and tell him to come home." She fumbled in her apron pocket and extracted a phone. "It will take him a few minutes to get the tractor turned around and get back."

"That's fine," Bill said. "Tell him to take his time."

But before she could phone Donnie, a car drove up to the back door. Two car doors slammed. Bill took a step toward the door and looked out, though Liv noticed he stood to one side and looked out at an angle. Police training, she decided.

He suddenly let out a huge sigh and opened the door. Joss Waterbury, looking tired and disheveled, walked into the kitchen.

"Joss," Amanda cried and ran to her husband. "Joss? Joss, honey, are you okay? Did they let you go? Oh, thank the good Lord."

Rose sprinted across the floor and threw herself at her father, sobbing.

Another man had entered behind Joss and he skirted the reunion to shake hands with Bill, then Ted. Bill introduced him to Liv as Silas Lark, a local attorney. He was about the same height as Liv, small-boned with dark, thinning hair and dark-rimmed glasses.

"What's the word?" Bill asked him.

He gave a dismissive shrug, "He's still a person of

interest," he said, putting air quotes around the words. "They don't have anything on Joss. But they also don't have any options. We're not out of the woods yet."

Bill nodded.

"Why don't we leave the family alone to celebrate." The attorney gestured toward the door.

"What now?" Bill said, when they were standing outside.

"You're the sheriff," Mr. Lark said.

"And it's about time you started acting like one," Ted added.

"But in a purely unofficial capacity," suggested Liv.

The three men stared at her.

She shrugged innocently. "Since he's still on vacation, I mean."

Bill broke into a grin. "You're absolutely right, Liv. Silas, mind giving me a ride back to town?"

Chapter Seventeen

···

"Does this mean Bill is going to continue keeping us out of the loop?" Liv asked as she and Ted drove back to town.

"No. He's riding with Silas so he could get the details on what's been going on at the station."

"Are you going to share them with me after he tells you?" Liv asked.

Ted made a face. "Liv, I do believe you're becoming a real Celebration Bay resident."

Liv puffed out air. "I keep telling you this . . . Wait. You mean because I'm getting too nosey?"

"I don't think you're too nosey, and yes, of course I'll keep you informed. Since you were the one to convince Bill to fly under the radar, so to speak."

"Thanks, but I don't believe it's what I said that convinced him."

"Maybe not. Want to stop for lunch?"

"Better do takeout. I've been sorely neglecting Haunted October."

They ate at their desks, making phone calls and checking

orders between bites. A call to Dolly revealed that she had risen to the occasion and everything was good to go for the food preparation. The traffic committee was organized. Everything seemed to be falling into place.

"TGIF. You planning to come in tomorrow?" Ted asked as he put on his coat.

"No. We're in decent shape. God knows why with all this crazy stuff going on. I think we can manage a Saturday off. I'll drive out to see Andy, though, then maybe stop by to ask Joss if he still wants to do the hayride."

"Uh-huh."

"Unless you want to call."

"No, you go ahead. I know how you like to do the hands-on thing."

"I do, but if you're worried that I'll ask Joss a whole bunch of embarrassing questions, I won't." She grinned. "I do, however, expect to hear everything once you talk to him—and to Bill."

Ted saluted and lifted her coat out of the closet. "Then go home."

He helped her on with her coat and she waited for him while he locked up the office. Outside they parted like they did most days, only today Liv felt just a little lonely as she walked home. Maybe from seeing Joss's welcome from his wife and daughter, or maybe Dolly's not wanting to hurt Fred.

And here she was eating alone on a Friday night. She took out her cell, called BeBe, and invited her for Chinese.

"Sorry, I have a date. A guy who works down at the marina. Don't think he's Mr. Right, but you never know. How about next week?"

Liv hung up and tried to think what she had in the fridge. Nothing that added up to a meal. By the time she reached home, she was feeling pretty down and just a little homesick for the nonstop pace and social scene of Manhattan. Then she opened the door and Whiskey bounded out, dancing at her feet. Her little house was cozy and quiet and welcoming.

Actually, she didn't miss anything about her old life. She'd never even had time for friends or dates there. She'd barely had time for her dog. Still . . .

"I guess it's just me and you, buddy. What do you say to Chinese?"

The next morning Liv decided to kill two birds with one stone, though she wasn't sure how politically correct the phrase was, considering recent events.

She fed Whiskey, donned layers of running gear, and zipped her cell and a few dollars into the back pocket of her interval jacket. The jacket was hot pink, bought originally to ward off speeding taxis, and would hopefully work just as well with the local deer hunters.

The morning was cold and brisk, and if she didn't know better, she'd think it was about to snow. But AccuWeather was her home page. Success in the event-planning business depended on accurate forecasting. An opportune appearance of complimentary umbrellas or the sudden raising of water-proof tents had saved more than a few events in the nick of time.

She ran south toward the county road, her breath making puffs of clouds in the air. Gradually the compact neighborhoods fell away into clumps of trees, an occasional billboard, some scattered businesses, insurance, antiques, bicycle repair, marine supplies, and finally settled into farmland.

At first cars and trucks passed by in each direction, then only the occasional truck. She had to run in place while a tractor turned onto the road in front of her; she kept pace with it for a few strides before sprinting ahead. The farmer waved as she passed by.

Soon she was alone on the road; fields stretched out in rolling golden waves, some closely shorn, others knee high. Some were marked by rows of straggling trees, others by barbed-wire fences. Round bales of what Liv guessed was hay dotted the landscape.

All was quiet except for the rhythmic pounding of her feet on the pavement, the in and out of her breath, the wind as it rustled the grasses and trees, and the far-off cry of a bird of prey.

Now, this was a little piece of heaven. Relaxing nature and clean air, complete with a smooth running surface. No one to bother her. No one whistling at her from a manhole as she dodged traffic on her way to Central Park.

Liv realized she was pretty darn content, even with a murderer in their midst. One, she reminded herself, they had to catch so their lives and her job could get back to normal. Though for someone, life would never be normal again.

If Joss had really killed his brother, what would happen to his family? She didn't think they would be shunned; more likely the town would fete them for killing the man whom everybody seemed to hate. But all the condolences in the world wouldn't make up for a missing father, husband, employer.

She didn't think Joss was guilty, but what did she really know? She'd only met him a few short weeks ago, had dealt with him only over the cider press exhibit.

Liv slowed her breathing as she powered up a hill. Some people in her business would spin the fact that a murder had taken place at the mill into a real tourist attraction. And people would come. But the idea disgusted Liv. Besides, Pete wasn't killed in the cider press. His body had to have been dropped there after he was dead. Convenience? Or a symbol?

Anyone could have done it. Anybody who had a key or knew the door would be unlocked.

Joss would never have left the body in his own store. But if not Joss, then who?

Dolly or Fred? Dolly *and* Fred? Liv couldn't see them hitting Pete over the head, stuffing him in the trunk of their car, and driving out to Joss's to dump the body. And wouldn't someone have heard a car and wondered who it was?

Bill could have done it. He was big enough. Except not with his sciatica. Unless that was an act. But he didn't seem to have a motive, though she might not even know what all the motives were. She tried to think back to the morning Ted called her to come out to the store. The scene she walked in on. Joss staring down at the body.

He had seemed genuinely surprised, and Liv was pretty good at recognizing fakes. She'd had enough practice with the excuses clients used to try to get out of paying. She was sure Joss's horror and disbelief had been real.

But Ted had had advance warning. He'd admitted that he'd recognized Pete. Had he told anyone else?

He might have told Bill. Being the sheriff, he would naturally take an interest in Pete's return. But he'd seemed more angry that they had tampered with the body than he was concerned over the death.

Because they had interfered with the investigation? Or because they'd messed up clues he'd carefully planted to implicate someone else?

A sudden stitch in Liv's side told her she hadn't been paying attention to her pace or her breathing. She'd been indulging in too much speculation.

Then again, if she didn't speculate, who would? It was becoming more and more obvious that the detectives weren't searching too far afield. They'd be content to arrest Joss, and since they hadn't arrested him, they must not have enough evidence to make a case.

And where did that leave Celebration Bay? Stuck in the quagmire with its livelihood put on hold.

She slowed her pace as she ran downhill, keeping her stride steady, though her step stuttered when a gray pickup rattled past going toward town. She ran in place and turned to watch its retreat. Two of the brothers were sitting on the truck bed, which meant there were probably two sitting up front.

Fine with her, though she'd meant to stop and inquire about Junior. It was just as well they weren't at home. She wasn't exactly afraid of them, and she actually liked Junior. He'd been nice to Whiskey, and Whiskey had taken to him. Of course, Whiskey was friendly to everyone, especially if they had food. But the others, she could live without.

She'd run about two miles when she heard a car coming up fast behind her. She veered onto the shoulder, felt the prickles of sticks and dirt on her legs as a beige Cadillac sped past her.

Janine. Now, where was she going in such a hurry?

Liv ran back onto the pavement and picked up her pace. She was only a few hundred feet behind the Cadillac when it made a left turn into Andy Miller's farm.

Interesting. It seemed a little early for a social call. Liv was on her way there only because she knew Andy would be working on the maze this morning.

But Janine didn't stop at the maze or the house. Instead, she cut off to the left and followed the tire tracks across the field to the Zoldosky trailer.

Liv sprinted across the highway and stopped to watch as Janine got out of her car and looked quickly around before she climbed up the steps to the trailer door. Liv had seen the Zoldoskys drive by. Surely Janine had seen them, too. So whom was she meeting?

Liv's appointment with Andy could wait. She eased through the wire fence and headed across the field. She circumvented the car and hid in the shadow of the trailer, listening for voices. But the only thing she heard was someone moving around inside.

Searching for something. And Liv bet she knew what. What she didn't understand was why.

Checking over her shoulder to make sure no one was coming, Liv edged around the side of the trailer and crept up the two steps. The door was ajar. Janine was leaning over an open drawer. Liv watched as she grabbed a notebook and shook it out. Dropped it back into the drawer and rifled through a stack of bills. Threw them back.

"Fingerprints," Liv said from the doorway.

Janine jumped, and a handful of papers fell to the floor. She glanced at Liv but knelt down and began gathering them up. She stuffed them back into the drawer and pushed it shut.

"I don't know what you're talking about."

"When the Zoldoskys realize that someone has been burgling their trailer, they'll have the police dust for prints."

"I'm not burg—stealing anything."

"No? Probably because you couldn't find it."

"I was just looking for a piece of paper to leave a note."

Liv just shook her head. "Try again."

Janine's eyes darted past Liv to the open door. Then around the room. Calculating and frantic. And so readable. It was amazing how well you learned to read people in her business. She could tell exactly what Janine was thinking. She was weighing escape against the need to keep searching.

"The police already have it."

Janine reeled back. Grabbed the edge of the built-in dresser, scattering more papers.

"I don't know what you're talking about."

"So you keep saying. So let me help." *And do it fast before we're both caught trespassing.* "The check you stole from the festival checkbook and wrote out to Pete Waterbury for a thousand dollars."

Janine feinted toward the door.

Liv stepped in front of it.

"I didn't."

"Sure you did. You're the only one besides Ted and me who had access to the checks." Not totally true, but she knew how to wheedle payment out of a recalcitrant client. She figured it would work on getting the truth out of Janine. "Did you think you could really get away with something like that? Even if Pete had cashed it, we check the bank statement every day just as a precaution and would have caught it. But

Pete never got a chance to cash it. Did you have anything to do with that?"

Janine's expression was blank; then slowly, as Liv's words sank in, it changed to horror. "You think I killed him? I didn't."

"Was he blackmailing you, too?"

"Too?"

"I guess that answers my question." Liv sighed. She was way out of her league and trying not to show it. She kept an ear out for the sound of a truck.

"I have nothing to hide."

"Everyone has something to hide."

Janine's mouth worked and Liv was afraid she might burst into tears, which wouldn't help at all.

"Look, I'm just trying to help."

"No, you're not. You'll tell everybody."

Jeez, the woman was stubborn. Liv reached in her pocket for her cell, though she had no intention of calling the police.

"Okay, okay, don't shoot."

It was everything Liv could do not to burst out laughing. She bit the inside of her cheeks to keep her composure, and slowly she dropped her hand. Took a breath.

"Then tell me."

"Can we go someplace else?"

There was nothing Liv would like more, but she might lose her advantage if she gave Janine time to relax. She shook her head. Glanced at the door to drive her point home. The Zoldoskys could come back any moment. *And we'll both be in big trouble if they do.*

"All right, but you have to swear."

Liv deliberated. What was it with this town and their secrets? First Roseanne, then Dolly, now Janine all begging Liv to swear. "If you didn't kill him, I'll keep mum on why you wrote the check."

Janine hugged herself. "It's nothing I did. It's not my fault."

Liv glanced toward the door. "Janine, I think you should hurry up."

"Pete knew my brother, Joey. They used to hang out together in high school. I didn't know him; they were much older than me."

She swallowed, looked toward the door, then hurried on. "Pete left a note in my mailbox that Joey killed that boy, and he said he'd spread it all over town if I didn't pay." Janine shivered. "I'm not responsible for what Joey did—it's not my fault—but if people found out, I'd never be able to show my face in town again. Can we leave now?"

"Excuse me, but why steal the town's money? Don't you have a savings account? I mean, you sell real estate, and I have it on good authority that you get beaucoup bucks from your ex-husband."

"They're going to be back any minute. Let me go."

Liv gave her a look.

"I thought I could make you look bad and keep Pete off my back. Nothing is working out the way it should."

"Did you kill him?"

"No!"

"Can you prove it?"

"Yes." Janine's lip curled. "I have an alibi for that night."

"All night?"

The smile became smug. "All night. Do you want to know who with?"

"Not really." Liv *really* didn't want to know that part. She just hoped whomever she was spending the night with didn't turn out to be Chaz. Not that it was any of her business. Not that she cared what or whom he did. But still. Ick.

"I'm leaving now, no matter what you do." Janine fled past Liv to the door, and Liv didn't try to stop her. She heard Janine's car start up and speed away.

Liv quickly looked around the trailer. It was a mess. But she wasn't about to try to clean up after Janine. Then she heard another car coming closer. Janine couldn't be coming back. Which meant only one thing. The Zoldoskys had returned.

Liv ran for the door, slammed it shut, and jumped to the ground just as the gray pickup stopped at the side of the trailer.

It was too late to run; she'd just have to brazen it out. Hoping that Junior would stand up for her since she'd helped him out, she turned to face the four Zoldosky brothers.

There were only three.

Anton climbed out of the driver's side and scowled at her. Serge, of the broken arm, came to stand beside him, looking ominous. The third brother hopped down from the back of the truck and stood with his hands on his hips. Junior was nowhere in sight.

Anton frowned until his eyebrows met above his nose. "What were you doing in our trailer."

Drat. Surely they hadn't seen her close the door? She'd already been on the ground when they drove up. She could outrun them, make it to Andy's. . . . *Liv, you're being ridiculous.* She tried another tactic.

"Good morning. I was out for a run. I had to see Andy about Halloween and thought I'd stop by to see Junior while I was out here." *TMI, Liv. Just stay calm.*

"He is in town."

"Oh, well. I'm sorry I missed him. Tell him I said hi. Gotta run." Literally. She took off over the field. She saw Andy coming out of his barn, and thankfully he saw her, too, though he was probably wondering why she was running across his field like a madwoman.

"Look like you just saw the ghost of Henry Galantine," he said as she skidded to a stop in front of him.

Liv sucked in breath. "I won't ask who Henry is." She sucked in more air. It really didn't pay to run in a panic. She was sure she must have sprinted across that field without taking a breath.

Andy waited patiently until she caught her breath and took a few hits off her water bottle. "Actually, I was planning to check on the maze and the hayride today, so I figured I might as well get my exercise in." She wondered if Andy had seen Janine's Cadillac speeding over the field.

If he did, he didn't ask, just looked toward the trailer.

Feeling that he might expect an explanation, she said, "I wanted to see if Junior was okay. He had a run-in with the Weaver brothers the other night."

"Did they hurt him?"

"Just trash talk mostly." Except her knuckles were still bruised. "But I thought he might be upset about it. He wasn't home. So how about that maze?"

"It's ready," Andy said. "Would you like a tour?"

"Sure."

They walked around back of the barn. "This here's the kiddie maze." He pointed to a configuration of rectangular hay bales about four feet high. "Fun but not scary. Most of them can see out over the bales. They can have fun getting lost without really getting lost."

"Fun getting lost," Liv said. Mainly it just made Liv want to sneeze.

"Yeah." He kept walking and she followed him into a field of cornstalks. A sign with ragged black letters dripping in bright red blood marked the entrance to the Maze of Madness.

"This is the big one. A quarter of an acre of maze."

"That sounds really enormous."

"We have guides and an observation tower in case anyone panics. You want to see inside?"

"Love to."

He led the way, walking along a narrow path cut through the rows of corn higher than their heads. It was a good thing she wasn't claustrophobic, Liv thought. Because she felt really enclosed.

"There's not much to scare you in the daylight," Andy said over his shoulder. He rounded the first corner. A skeleton sprang out of the stalks, swung across the opening, and disappeared again. "See what I mean. Kinda hokey in the daylight, but at night with the lights popping on and off, and the spooky sounds, we get some good thrills and chills."

Liv sidestepped the skeleton and hurried to catch up.

They came to a wall of cornstalks so thick Liv couldn't begin to see through it.

"Right or left?" Andy asked.

"Left."

He turned to the left. Nothing happened for a while; then the stalks began rattling and strange noises echoed around them. Okay, that was pretty scary even in the daylight.

"It's not like a regular maze," Andy explained, as they turned left and right and Liv became thoroughly lost. "Normally, there's only one entrance, but in the spirit of commerce, we have two. That way we get 'em in one way and keep 'em moving to the exit. More or less. That way we don't get bogged down with slowpokes."

Something dropped behind them and Liv whirled around. A mass of black material writhed on the ground. She moved a little closer to Andy.

"Good, huh?" he said proudly.

"Great," said Liv.

Another turn and they stepped into sunlight. "There's more, but you get the idea."

She did and she'd seen enough.

"Is it all automated?" she asked, brushing dried stems and dust from her interval jacket.

"A lot of it is." Andy pulled off his John Deere cap, slapped it on his knee, pushed his hair back, and replaced the cap on his head. "Some of the simpler effects are spring-loaded. It takes about five guys to run the more complicated ones. If anybody seems to be getting freaked-out"—he flashed a quick half smile—"the grim reaper leads them out. Though I'm thinking about something less gruesome, considering the current situation."

"Well, hopefully that will be cleared up before too long."

"Yeah."

"I guess you know they let Joss come home."

Andy nodded slowly. "About time, too."

"Do you know what he's going to do about the hayride? I would go up there but I hate to bother the family."

"Donnie's planning on doing it, and I guess Joss will help. Work is a good way to forget your troubles."

Liv nodded and wondered if he was speaking from experience. "There is one other thing. I'm worried about the Zoldoskys."

"They won't cause trouble."

"I was thinking more that they might have trouble with some of the rowdier locals. I know people are upset, and Halloween and Mischief Night are good excuses for troublemaking."

"That's what the run-in with Junior and the Weavers was about?"

"They were upset that Joss was arrested."

"He wasn't arrested. Nobody would let him be arrested." Two dark red flags had broken out on Andy's fair skin.

"Bad choice of words. Let's just hope it doesn't come to that."

"It won't come to that." Andy seemed certain of the fact. Liv hoped he was right.

"I hope not. Do you think one of the Zoldoskys did it?"

"I don't know what to think. I'll tell Joss that you came by. If there is any change of plans, he'll call you."

There was a sudden chill in the sunshine. And it was coming from Andy.

"Thanks. You guys have been doing this a lot longer than I have. You've got it all under control."

"Yeah . . . we do."

"Well, I'd better be running. The maze looks great." She headed toward the road at a slow lope, picking up speed by the time she hit the tarmac. She turned right at the gate and waved back at Andy, but he didn't see her. He was moving pretty fast himself. And he was headed right toward the Zoldoskys' trailer.

Chapter Eighteen

....

Liv was sweating by the time she reached her carriage house. Physically because she'd pushed herself on the run back from the Miller farm, and mentally because even though she'd turned the murder over and over in her mind, she'd came no closer to finding a suspect. Except Janine.

But she couldn't see Janine hauling Pete's body into the apple press. Which meant someone had helped her. The someone she'd spent the night with. Which brought her to Charles Bristow. She shuddered. She really hoped he wasn't her accomplice.

She was jolted from that thought first by the smell and then by the sight of a thin curl of smoke coming from the Zimmermans' backyard. A month ago she would have panicked and called the fire department. But she was an old hand at country ways now and knew Miss Edna must be burning leaves.

This was confirmed a moment later when a flying ball of white fur ran down the drive and launched himself at Liv. She leaned over to brush pieces of leaves and dirt from his whiskers and fur. "Are you helping with the fall cleanup?"

Edna Zimmerman, wearing a battered canvas hat, overalls, a fisherman's sweater, and work gloves, came around the side of the house. "I thought that must be you. Whiskey never takes off like that."

Ida was a few steps behind. She was wearing her green car coat over her tweed skirt; her flowered gardening gloves and sneakers were her only nod to manual labor.

"So don't you worry with him being out with us. He's a good doggie. Aren't you?"

Whiskey lifted his head and barked in agreement, then pranced by Liv's side as she went over to say hello to her landladies.

"You heard that Joss is back home," said Miss Ida.

"Yes," Liv said. "That's wonderful."

"I knew they couldn't keep him." Edna sniffed. "There's no way they had enough evidence to arrest him. I don't know what Bill Gunnison is about. Letting those two morons from the state police take over."

"Bill was always such a fine, polite boy." Ida sighed. "I never saw him as a police officer, though. Still waters run deep, you know."

"Still waters?" asked Liv.

"Never saw him get angry like some of the boys. Never got into fights."

Except over Dolly.

"I guess he was just waiting to have the law behind him."

"Lacked gumption, I always said."

Ida pursed her lips. "Well, Sister, he's the sheriff now, and that takes some gumption, and he was never afraid to stand up for what he believed in."

Edna snorted. "Well, he oughta stop hobbling around like an old man and grow some—" Edna caught herself.

"Sister!"

"Well, he oughta."

Liv smiled at the sisters. They were always a storehouse

of information. Now, if they could just give her some insight into who might have killed Pete Waterbury.

She realized that both sisters and Whiskey were all looking at her. "I just hope somebody solves this case."

"Indeed," said Ida. "What you need, dear, is a lesson plan."

"Pardon?"

"A lesson plan. Figure out what you need to do in what order to catch the miscreant. That'll do the trick." Ida turned to her sister. "Edna, you know it's dangerous to leave a fire unattended."

"I was just about to say so. If you'll excuse us, Liv."

"Of course. Oh, one more thing."

"Yes, dear?"

"Is the library open on Saturdays?"

"No," Ida said. "Unfortunately it had to start closing weekends because of the budget cuts."

Edna shook her head. "I don't know why those men in Albany think the way they do. People need libraries more than ever these days, what with the economy and all. Not everybody has their own computer, and people looking for work need their resources just as much as schoolchildren and the rest of us."

"Sister, if you get started on politics, you'll let the house burn down."

"I'm not talking politics. I'm talking common sense."

"You can't teach common sense."

"I realize that, but, Liv, if you're looking for back issues of the *Clarion*, the library doesn't keep them."

Liv opened her mouth in astonishment. "How did you know what I wanted?"

"Stands to reason," Edna said.

Ida nodded. "We just happened to be there the other day, and Lola Bangs, the head librarian, said that old man Bristow was kind of batty and insisted on keeping all the back issues at the *Clarion* office. Such a fire hazard."

"Off his rocker toward the end," Edna said. "Sniffed too much print ink."

"Sister, you'll give Liv the wrong impression," Ida admonished. "Don't worry, dear. It wasn't Chaz's father. His great-uncle."

"If you want to see back issues, say around nineteen eighty-two, you'll have to ask Chaz," Edna added with a sparkle in her eye.

"You two are something else," Liv said.

"Anything we can do to help," Ida said. "Even if it means going through a bunch of musty old newspapers. Is there anything else, dear?"

"Yes. Would you mind if I came with you to church tomorrow?"

Both sisters beamed at her.

"We'd love to have you," said Ida. "We would have invited you before but we didn't want to appear pushy."

Edna raised her eyebrows at her sister, and Liv had to concentrate not to laugh. She was already completely attached to the two retired teachers.

"We drive over at eight forty-five."

"I'll be ready. Thanks." *Lesson plan*, thought Liv. Why hadn't she thought of that?

When Liv's alarm woke her Sunday morning, she had second thoughts. She'd sat at her computer long into the night, charting out suspects, means, motives, and opportunity. It just served to show her how much she didn't know.

Outside her window, the day was gray and windy. There was rain in the air. She was so tempted to snuggle back under her new down comforter and sleep all day. But the social hour after church would be gossip central, and besides, she could use some divine intervention to catch this killer.

Liv pushed the covers away and went to stare into her closet. Whiskey opened one eye, then went back to sleep.

What did one wear to a country church? *Besides a raincoat,* Liv thought as thunder sounded overhead. She settled on a charcoal suit with a soft, cream silk blouse. She considered her four-inch heels for a millisecond before she tossed them back into the closet and chose a conservative two-and-a-half-inch pump. Very demure, she thought, twirling for the mirror. Maybe she'd just throw those stilettos away and be done with them.

She pushed a recalcitrant Whiskey outside for a quick pit stop, then put on her raincoat and went to wait for the sisters. They were just coming out their back door, wrapped up in raincoats and bonnets and carrying umbrellas. Edna opened the garage door to reveal a twenty-year-old dark green Buick.

"We keep thinking about buying a new car," said Edna. "But we never really need it, and in summer we have our Vespas."

Sure enough, two scooters, one bright red and the other royal blue, were parked in the corner of the two-car garage.

"We can take my car," Liv said. "I should have offered."

"No, no. Our pleasure," said Ida. "You get up front with Edna."

They drove the four blocks to the Presbyterian church and parked in the lot across the street before joining the others fighting the wind to get to the door. They met BeBe coming up the steps. She looked surprised. "I didn't know you were Presbyterian," she said to Liv as they climbed the steps.

She wasn't. She used to be Episcopalian.

Pastor Schorr was standing on the steps, his cassock and hair blowing with each gust.

"Good morning, ladies. I believe winter is knocking at the door," he declared as the four of them hurried inside.

"But the place is packed," Liv said to BeBe as the usher guided them to a pew.

BeBe went in first, followed by Liv, then Edna and Ida.

"It always is. People take their religion seriously around here."

The choir filed into the chancery, and Liv saw Dolly and Fred among the singers.

"Does everybody we know go here?"

BeBe shook her head. "Bill's a Baptist. Ted doesn't go at all. Andy's just about as bad. Let's see. . . . Who else?"

Pastor Schorr climbed to the pulpit. He must have come in a side door because his hair was neatly combed. Ida leaned over Edna. "Such a lovely young man."

BeBe and Liv exchanged looks. Though now that Liv thought about it, the pastor would make BeBe a better boyfriend than the marina guy or Chaz Bristow. For herself, she had no intention of ever dating a preacher no matter how "eligible" he was.

The organ started up, hymnals opened, and the congregation stood to sing "Rock of Ages."

Liv kind of liked the old hymn and thought it was particularly apt for the current mood in Celebration Bay. They were on the second verse when the back door opened and the Waterburys entered the church. People stopped singing to greet Joss and Amanda, then doubled their voices as the family moved down the aisle.

When the hymn ended, Pastor Schorr raised his hands. "Hallelujah, what a day to have all of us together again. Take a minute to welcome your neighbor."

People leaned over their seats to pat Joss on the back or shake his hand. There was a general migration toward the Waterbury pew. And above it all Phillip Schorr beamed beatifically at his flock.

When the commotion began to die back, the pastor said in his full-bodied voice, "We're all glad to see you back, Joss. And I hope your whole family will stay after for our social hour so folks can say hello."

Joss Waterbury nodded. His face was flushed with embarrassment or some other strong emotion. It couldn't have been easy for him to walk into that church not knowing how he'd be received. But then again, he probably did know.

Liv hadn't heard one person in town even hint at thinking he was guilty.

Schorr was a dramatic speaker, and Liv was swept away on his story of the prodigal son, which he must have chosen with Pete Waterbury in mind. Especially when he talked about the most recent prodigal son and made some pretty astute comparisons about both. Several times Liv glanced over at Joss, who sat bolt upright, his gaze focused on the preacher.

After the service they all retired to the basement for coffee and cookies. Joss and Amanda were mobbed by well-wishers, but Donnie and Roseanne managed to stand to the side chatting with several kids their own ages. Roseanne saw Liv and skirted the room to see her.

"Is it over?" she asked in a quiet voice.

"I sure hope so; just don't say anything unless Bill asks you to."

"No gossiping. I got it." She looked more at ease when she went back to join her friends.

Liv had just accepted a cup of coffee when Roscoe Jackson and Rufus Cobb came to a stop in front of her. "We just want to apologize for calling in the state. Jeremiah was sure that they could clear things up faster than Bill, but we never expected them to arrest Joss. We're on our way to apologize to him."

"Very altruistic of you," Liv said. "But maybe you should wait until a more private time."

"You're right," Roscoe said. "Folks will be ready to draw and quarter us."

Rufus pulled on his mustache. "I told Jeremiah we should stay out of it, but everybody was so worried about Janine and the mayor closing down the festivals, we just sort of panicked."

"We're awful sorry."

"Well, thank you, but you can show your goodwill by voting to continue the festivals when the board meets tomorrow morning."

"We definitely will, and so will Jeremiah."

They nodded and disappeared into the crowd.

The Waterburys had already left, and Liv hadn't even gotten a chance to add her well wishes. Liv and BeBe wandered from group to group saying hello and listening for news. Across the way a woman with a shrill voice had cornered Dolly. "I just hope you know what you're doing, Dolly Hunnicutt."

"Now, you listen here, Ruth. I'm just doing my Christian duty, letting that boy earn a little money."

"Don't blame me if they find you dead on the floor."

"Don't be ridiculous; he's a poor, disfigured man, harmless. They're stuck here without a source of income and it's the least I can do."

"Oh dear," BeBe whispered to Liv. "The natives are getting nasty. Let's go help Dolly out."

They crossed the floor and met the Zimmerman sisters on the same mission. Just as they reached Dolly, the woman said, "People might get the wrong idea about where your loyalties lie. You mark my words." And huffed away.

"Awful woman," Dolly said. "And talking like that right here in church."

"That Ruth Benedict never had an ounce of sense," Edna said.

"And those are the kind who always have something to say when they ought to keep their mouths shut," Ida said.

Dolly smiled fleetingly at the sisters. "I don't pay her any mind. But there have been others."

"Others?" Liv asked. "Have you been getting a lot of that?"

"Some. People don't know what to think, so they make up for it by minding everyone else's business."

Liv wondered if Dolly was counting her among those who were minding everyone else's business, but her next words erased her doubt.

"You shouldn't hold it against them, Liv. They're good

people for the most part. They just don't like to have their way of life threatened. So they get fractious."

"Fractious? I've got another word for it," said Edna. "But I won't use it in church."

"At least Janine Tudor isn't here today," BeBe said.

"She goes to church here?" Liv asked.

"Regularly."

Edna snorted. "Keeping up appearances. It's good for business."

"Sister, for shame."

"It is a shame," Edna agreed, turning her words.

"She should be here asking for forgiveness," BeBe said. "After what she said to you the other day, Dolly, I could have strangled her."

"What did she say?" asked Liv, Ida, and Edna in chorus.

Dolly frowned. "Oh, she was just being Janine. Told me I was aiding and abetting a possible murderer. Just because I did what any good Christian would do and gave some day-old bread to that poor man and his brothers."

"She didn't," the sisters exclaimed.

"I heard her," BeBe said.

Edna shook her head. "I bet she started talking about property values."

BeBe guffawed. "Of course she did. Everything in life circles back to property values for Janine." She touched Dolly's sleeve. "I'm sorry. I shouldn't make fun. It was a nasty, vicious thing to say, but that woman should get a life."

"Well, she was certainly trying to at that scoundrel's funeral," said Edna.

"The way she chases poor Charles around," agreed Ida.

"Charles?" asked Liv.

"Chaz Bristow," BeBe said. "You saw him run when he saw her making a beeline for him."

Edna chuckled. "Poor man."

"Indeed," Ida agreed. "And he's such a lovely boy with such nice manners."

"Chaz?" Liv said.

"Charles Bristow, the editor of the *Clarion*," Ida said as if she were explaining to a slow student.

"Oh," Liv said, and cut her eyes toward BeBe, who was fighting to keep a straight face.

"It's about time he was getting married, but not to someone like Janine Tudor. But to someone to be a helpmate, like our BeBe here."

"Don't look at me," BeBe said.

"Or Liv," Ida said.

"Don't look at me, either," Liv said. She wasn't interested in Chaz. But it did bring up an interesting question. Janine had to be in her forties regardless of what she did to fight it, but she might be able to persuade a single man to do things he wouldn't normally do. Like kill Pete Waterbury? Or at least help her dump the body.

"Liv, hon? Are you ready to go?"

"Oh, yes. See you later BeBe, Dolly." Liv followed the sisters out of the church and across the street to the car.

"So how is the investigation going?" Edna asked when she stopped at the corner of Main Street.

"Investigation? I don't have an inside track."

"Well, everyone knows that you and Ted went to see Bill Gunnison, and don't say it was on another matter. Because Thelma Jenkins saw you all leave together, and Earl Weaver saw you at the Waterburys'. And his brother saw you and Ted leave and Bill leave with Joss's lawyer a few minutes later."

Liv stared at Edna. Amazing what the sisters had learned in less than twenty-four hours, and to Liv's knowledge they hadn't even left home.

"So who saw Pete Waterbury being killed?" Liv asked, only half facetiously.

"Exactly what we've been asking ourselves," said Edna.

"Except he was probably killed when everyone was at home in bed," Ida said.

"He was," Liv said without thinking.

"Do tell."

"That's all I know. I saw the brothers at ten o'clock when they closed up for the night. And he was dead when I saw him at six the next morning."

Ida shuddered. "You might have been the last person to see him alive."

"Oh no," said Liv. "He drove away with the Zoldoskys." At least, she supposed he did; she hadn't really noticed him.

"Everyone will be happy if one of them killed him," Edna said.

"Indeed," Ida said. "But only if they're guilty."

They turned into the drive and returned the car to the garage.

"Would you like to come for lunch?"

"Thank you, but I think I'll go over to the *Clarion* office. See if Chaz Bristow has a few decades of *Clarions* lying around."

She changed into jeans, dropped Whiskey off with the sisters, and casting a look at the sky, set off at a brisk pace toward the center of town. She felt the first raindrop as she passed the Woofery; by the time she passed the now-empty First Presbyterian Church and graveyard, a light drizzle had begun to fall.

She sprinted the last block and a half to the *Clarion* office and jumped onto the porch just as the sky fell.

And saw the sign. Gone Fishing.

Fishing? It was raining. Though he might have been out all night. And now she was stuck on his porch in a monsoon. Grr. She kicked the door in pure frustration and turned to go.

A gray pickup passed by, and Liv took an involuntary step back against the door. Were the Zoldoskys following her? They'd probably realized by now that someone had been rifling through their trailer. Their suspicions would naturally fall on Liv. She should have explained to them when they'd caught her, but at the time her only thought was escape. She would make a point to explain to them as soon as possible.

A figure was sprinting down the sidewalk cuddling a brown grocery bag. Chaz Bristow was back from fishing. He ran up the short walk to the house and leapt onto the porch. He shoved the grocery bag at her and shook the rain off.

"I hope these aren't fish," Liv said, holding the bag away from her.

"Fish? No, it's breakfast. Oh, the sign. Nah. I just use that when I don't want to be bothered."

"It's afternoon. A little late for breakfast."

"I was up late."

Liv lifted both eyebrows. Not fishing and hopefully not doing the after-dark tango with Janine.

"You're cold. Come on in. I'll make you some coffee."

"I'm not cold."

"Then why did you shiver?"

The thought of you and Janine? The thought of Janine and anybody.

"I was just remembering your coffee."

Ignoring the Gone Fishing sign, he opened the door, which Liv noticed was unlocked. She followed him to the kitchen, which was as bare as the office was cluttered. Chaz Bristow must eat a lot of takeout.

Then Liv had a horrible thought. What if whomever he was buying all those bagels for was still there? How embarrassing. She listened for sounds of someone else in the house.

Chaz nudged her with a bagel.

"No, thanks."

"Don't tell me you're one of those women who only eats lettuce."

"I'm not. It's just that I came here on business."

"I didn't think I'd gotten lucky." He sliced a bagel and spread a glob of cream cheese over one half. "They're still hot. Not New York, but pretty damn good." He passed the bagel half under her nose and her stomach growled.

"Oh, all right. Thank you." She took the bagel half.

He spread another half for himself and perched one hip on the kitchen table. "Okay, shoot."

She wiped a smear of cream cheese off the corner of her mouth.

He smiled. She frowned. "I was hoping to see some back issues of the paper."

"Checking up on whether I ran your ads or not?"

"No. Much further back."

His eyes narrowed. "How much further?"

She shrugged. She didn't think she could fool him for a minute. After all, he was—had been—a world-class investigative reporter. "Say the eighties?"

His mouth tightened.

She jumped in before he could say no. "I was hoping you had computer files, microfilm, microfiche?"

"I got boxes."

"Boxes?"

"In the basement. Years and years of them."

Good grief. Boxes of newspapers. A dirty and tiring afternoon awaited. "Do you mind if I take a look?"

He shrugged, walked past her to the hallway, and opened a door. "After you."

She stepped into the doorway. Below her was a pitch-black hole.

Chaz leaned over her to flick on a wall switch. Yellow light dimly lit a forest of cardboard boxes stacked almost to the ceiling.

"Go for it. Just don't leave a mess."

Jackass, Liv thought as she carefully made her way down the stairs. There was barely room to stand up at the bottom and only a few narrow alleys between the cardboard towers. There were probably bugs and no telling what else down here.

Dates were handwritten on the side of each box. The latest ones were the closest to her, naturally, which meant she could spend hours just getting to the eighties.

Which she did. Two hours later, she found 1990, and

twenty minutes after that, the eighties. At the very top of the stack was 1989. She read down until she got to the bottom box—1985. She was going to have to move all these out of the way to get to 1982, the year Pete Waterbury had left home.

She sneezed for at least the fortieth time that afternoon. She was covered in dust just like the boxes; her hands were filthy, her throat was parched, but she'd be damned if she'd ask Chaz for a glass of water. He could have offered to help. Though she really hadn't expected him to.

She wondered how he could stand looking through archives. Because someone *had* been looking. A number of the boxes showed less dust than the others.

She stretched her aching back and pulled the box from off the top of the stack. Dust and dirt particles fell on her head; she dropped the box to the floor, and another cloud of dust assaulted her nose.

She pulled the second box down and a third. There was an open space behind it, just large enough for someone to stand in to search through the files. She pulled the third box away and climbed over the rest. There were the remaining eighties and—hallelujah—this stack was shorter than the others and less dusty.

She wanted to crow with success. 1984, '83, '79. What? She wiped her eyes on her sleeve and looked again. The first three years of the eighties were not there. She turned around in her little column of space, checked the stack behind her: '78, '77 . . . She pulled those boxes away and found a stone wall. The three boxes she needed were missing.

Missing. And she bet dollars to doughnuts where they'd gone.

She climbed back over the boxes and stomped up the stairs. And found Chaz Bristow right where she knew she'd find him. Asleep on the couch.

Her fingers itched to grab him by his faded, torn shirt and throw him on the floor. But being a rational person, she jabbed him in the ribs.

"Wha-a?" He bolted upright and blinked at her. "Oh, it's you. Find what you're looking for?"

"No. I did not," she said, her teeth clenched so tightly she could hardly form the words. "Where are they?"

"Where are what?" With his hair sticking up and that surfer smile, he was darned charming, and she wanted to slap him.

"Nineteen eighty through 'eighty two."

"You didn't find them?"

"You know I didn't. You sent me down there knowing I wouldn't find them. You jerk. You let me waste a whole afternoon looking for information you knew I wouldn't find."

Chaz shrugged. "You're kind of cute when you get all riled up."

"You haven't seen riled. I'm just getting started. You think you're so clever? Well, let me tell you, you lazy, conniving, unmitigated chauvinist throwback—"

"Even cuter when you use all those big words." He grinned unrepentantly at her.

"Ugh. Thanks . . . for nothing. I'll see myself out." She stormed toward the front of the house, knowing full well he was following her.

She reached for the doorknob, but his hand enclosed around hers. "Maybe you should give this up."

Liv stilled, her anger gone. His statement, his tone of voice. Was that a warning or was he threatening her? Even though she'd flirted with the idea of him and Janine as a Bonnie and Clyde duo, she hadn't really thought that either of them would actually murder someone. Now suddenly it seemed all too possible.

"Fine. Whatever you say." She tried to turn the knob, but he held it fast.

And being a New Yorker with a black belt in karate, she did what she was trained to do. She stomped on his bare foot, clipped his chin, and ran like hell.

Chapter Nineteen

....

She'd run two blocks before she realized that one, no one was following her, and two, the rain had stopped. She slowed down to a fast walk. It was getting pretty dark, and she fought the urge to look behind her.

But Chaz wouldn't be chasing after her. He wasn't a killer, and she doubted that Janine was, either. A wave of contrition swept over her. She really hoped she hadn't broken his foot. She'd *way* overreacted.

She was such a dope. Now she'd have to apologize. She started trotting toward home, where she would take a hot shower, wash her hair, and pull the covers over her head until she could pretend she hadn't just made a fool of herself.

She hadn't left the outside light on, but the Zimmermans' back porch light was on and it was just enough to see by. She reached in her pocket for her house keys. A shadow stepped out of the bushes. Liv let out a screech.

"Jeez," she exclaimed. "What do you want?"

But it wasn't Chaz. As the figure stepped into the semi-light, she recognized Anton Zoldosky.

"I have been waiting for you," he said ominously.

"Me?" she squeaked.

"I want to ask you why you were searching our trailer yesterday. What was it that you hoped to find? You are not a thief."

"I can explain."

Anton grunted and crossed his arms. She wondered if her landladies were watching from their window. If they would call Bill. Because Liv couldn't run; there was nowhere to go but home.

Whiskey began to bark on the other side of the door.

"I am waiting."

Liv took a calming breath. "I wasn't."

"You were."

"No, actually, I was stopping . . . someone who was searching your trailer."

"Who was doing that?"

"It doesn't matter. I was on my way to talk to Andy Miller. I saw a car at your trailer, but I had seen your truck in town, so I went to check it out."

"Who?"

"It doesn't matter, truly. They were looking for a check they had written to Pete Waterbury. Pete was blackmailing he—them. But the police had already confiscated it."

"Who is this person?"

"I can't tell you. But, perhaps, can you tell me who Pete was blackmailing?"

"I know nothing about blackmail. He was a hired hand. Kept to himself."

"Did you see him talking to anybody in town?"

Anton's brows dipped. Liv hoped that meant he was thinking. "No. No one. Ah. To a young girl. I told him none of that."

Roseanne, thought Liv.

"And one other. A man with silver hair."

Ted. She had seen the fight, but she hadn't seen Anton watching. Had Pete and Ted met a second time?

"Do you remember when he talked with this man?"

"The evening before he died. We were waiting to pack our things. In the parking lot for the workers."

The vendors' parking lot. So Ted must have gone back to continue his argument with Pete. Something he hadn't bothered to share with her.

"And you are sure this person took nothing else?"

Liv thought back. She hadn't searched Janine; that would have been ridiculous. But what else could she have been looking for? "I don't think so. I didn't see anything. I made her—them—leave. Are you missing something?"

Anton scowled but didn't answer. Then he slowly shook his head. "You stayed behind."

"To make sure the person left. I was leaving when you came."

"This is true?"

Sort of. "Yes."

"Anton?" A brother stepped out of the shadows. He was followed by Serge.

"You were to wait in the truck."

"We were worried." Serge glared at Liv. "Why did you break into our home?"

"We don't appreciate thieves," the other brother said, and curled his lip.

In a moment of sheer insanity, Liv wondered what his name was. "I'm not a thief. I was explaining this to your brother."

"Hey!"

They all turned to see Chaz Bristow running up the driveway.

Liv groaned and slapped her forehead. This whole day was becoming a farce. She might even laugh if she hadn't been scared out of her wits several times in the last few hours.

"Chaz," Liv warned.

He sprinted the last few yards, shoved an accordion file at Liv, and pushed her behind him.

"Chaz, wait."

Chaz landed the first punch.

"Stop it," Liv demanded.

Serge surged forward and threw his body weight and cast into Chaz's chest. Chaz staggered back, and the third brother punched him in the face. After a stunned moment, Chaz rebounded. Anton grabbed him by the shoulders and pushed him aside.

"Serge, Georgi. Go back to the truck."

The two brothers stopped fighting, but stood fists clenched and scowling. Then they turned as one and disappeared into the growing darkness.

Anton glanced over at Chaz, who was nursing his eye. "You are not hurt much. I apologize for my brothers, but you are much too impetuous, my friend." And he, too, slipped into the night.

"No shit," Chaz said, fingering his cheek.

"Come inside. I'll get some ice." Liv unlocked the door.

Whiskey shot out the door, looked back at Liv and Chaz, then jumped into the bushes where the Zoldoskys had disappeared.

"Whiskey, come back here. There are bears in the woods."

"Are not," said Chaz, holding his face. "Well, maybe, sometimes."

"Whiskey!"

The Westie's head appeared out of the bushes, then the rest of him. He shot past them and back into the house.

"That bear threat really worked," Chaz said.

"He knows it's dinnertime."

They followed Whiskey to the kitchen. Liv dropped the file on the table, opened the freezer, and got out an ice tray. Whiskey barked and sat down, looking up expectantly.

"You'll have to wait your turn, buddy. We have an emergency on our hands." She dumped ice cubes into a dish towel, twisted it into a bundle, and handed it to Chaz. Then she went back to the fridge and fed her dog.

"Do I get fed, too?" Chaz asked from behind the red plaid towel.

"Only if you want half a can of chicken bits in sauce."

"I'll pass."

"Thought so. What's in the file?"

Chaz pulled the file toward him and clutched it in his free hand. "First there have to be some ground rules."

"Which are?"

"No more hitting, stomping, or slapping."

"I apologize, but I didn't slap you."

"You would have gotten around to it."

"Possibly. Now, I take it you came all the way over here, not to save me from the Zoldoskys, but to show me what you probably could have shown me before I wasted a whole afternoon looking for something that you knew wasn't there."

"Party of the third part." Chaz grinned, which was a bit lopsided. Hopefully he wouldn't have a fat lip as well as a black eye.

"You are so annoying."

"Then how come you're trying not to smile?"

Liv shook her head. "Because you're that kind of annoying."

Chaz gave her a look but opened the file and dumped a pile of newspaper articles on the table. "But I'll expect dinner."

"It's only five thirty."

"This might take a while."

She pulled a chair next to him and watched while he arranged the yellowing, brittle papers with one hand. But she knew what they were about long before he had finished. Clippings from 1982. Articles on miscellaneous acts of violence and theft perpetrated on the citizens of Celebration Bay. Others reporting on the disappearance and subsequent search for Victor Gibson.

"Why are you showing me these now?"

"Because you're not going to give up. And I'd rather know what you're up to than find you, like tonight, standing up to three crazy Romanians. Jeez. You could have been seriously hurt or killed."

Liv shook her head. "They were angry because they caught me in their trailer yesterday."

"Are you crazy? Do you have some death wish issue?"

"Put that ice pack back on your cheek. If you'll calm down, I'll tell you."

Chaz jammed the towel against his eye. "Ouch."

Liv rolled her eyes to the ceiling and explained to him about Janine and the forged check. "She said Pete accused her brother of killing Victor Gibson."

"According to the police reports, Joe Tudor and several others were questioned about Victor's disappearance. But since the others were minors, their names were not given."

"You read the police reports."

Chaz looked at the ceiling.

"You've been investigating this all along, haven't you. Of all the disingenuous—"

"Now, don't start using those hundred-dollar words again."

"Ugh. You stop acting like some deadbeat hillbilly."

Chaz stood up and tossed the ice pack in the sink. "Look. I don't want to get involved in this. But more than that, I don't want you or anyone else to get involved in this."

"I know how to take care of myself."

"So you've said. But it's more than just you. You know Pandora?"

"No. Oh, you mean the goddess who opened the box and set all the ills on the world?"

"Yeah, that one."

"And you think that's what can happen here?"

"I know it can. And once it starts, there's no telling where it will end."

"Are you trying to scare me?"

"Yes. I just . . . Oh hell, go on and read to your heart's content."

Liv picked up the first article. An incident report of break-ins and thefts. Stereo equipment, jewelry, electronics. What you'd expect from petty thieves.

"Did you clip these?"

Chaz shook his head. "Not me. Must have been my dad or uncle."

"Investigative reporting must be a family trait."

"Curse."

"But you found these because you were . . ." She trailed off, hoping he would finish the sentence.

"Because they were there. Are you going to read the rest or are we going to dinner?"

She gave him a look and carefully slid the second group of papers closer.

Local Boy Missing Near Lake. A local boy, Victor Gibson, 12, was listed as missing today by the county police department. Sheriff Leslie Dorin told reporters that Victor and a friend had been out digging for earthworms for fishing when they were set upon by four youths and chased through the woods near Lakeside Road.

The name of Victor's companion, a boy of 14, is being withheld because he is a minor.

There was a notation in the margin, *Andy Miller.* It looked like an old entry. It seemed the *Clarion* had done a bit of investigating on its own.

According to the testimony of this young man, they came upon the other youths digging a hole in the earth near the shore. There was a large crate nearby and the two boys were afraid they were witnessing a burial. They were spotted by the group and pursued, at which time the companion tried to hold them off while the younger Victor made his escape. The companion was badly

beaten and was treated at County General Hospital
before being released to the custody of his parents.

When Victor Gibson did not return home, his mother,
Eleanor Gibson, widow of the late Ron Gibson, called
the police. The police immediately began searching the
area, fearing that he might be injured. Smears of blood
were found on the town boat landing. A rowboat, belong-
ing to a local fisherman, was missing. The boy is still
missing. Ted Driscoll, the boy's uncle, is offering a
reward to anyone who has information that will lead to
the whereabouts of the missing boy. The police ask that
anyone having information call . . ."

Pete had killed Ted's nephew. Ted had offered a reward.
But except for that one outburst of temper, he'd taken Pete's
return with unnatural calm. Liv reached for the next article.
"Local Boy Still Missing." The police had exhumed the box,
but what it contained proved to be not a body but stolen
goods belonging to several local stores and nearby farms.

The next item was a piece of notepaper torn off a small
spiral notebook with handwritten notes, ostensibly from the
editor of the paper.

Millers allowed me to speak to Andy. No new evidence.
Still no missing boy. Bad. Did learn that the ringleader
was Pete Waterbury. Andy says they threatened to kill
him and Victor if they told. Have talked to Joss. He is
distraught and angry. Vows to do something about Pete's
behavior.

Liv cast a sideways glance at Chaz.
"It was thirty years ago."
"Still, it wouldn't look good for Joss if—"
"Not gonna happen. Those are the ramblings of some guy
decades ago. Hearsay, even then. And unsubstantiated."
"Except everyone knows that Joss sent Pete away after

that. He could have been pretty mad if he suddenly showed up and was back to his old tricks."

Silence from Chaz.

The next article. "Dinghy Found at South End of Lake."

"Oh God," Liv exclaimed as she read through the details of finding the boat. "That poor kid."

"Yeah. So now are you satisfied?"

"I think that is a poor choice of words. I understand better what happened."

She read through the last two articles and slipped them all into the folder.

"Thanks for showing these to me."

Chaz shrugged. For someone with such a glib tongue, he was being stubbornly quiet.

"Do you know more that you're not sharing?"

"Not me."

"Where are the boxes from these years?"

"Aw hell, Liv. They're in the hall closet. Yeah, I got them out. It's like an addiction, okay? I took one little peek inside, and that thing was sitting on top." He lifted his chin toward the accordion file. "The rest is history."

He sighed, and she heard him mumble under his breath, "And history repeats itself."

Was he talking about Pete or something more personal? Liv just didn't get him, and she was usually pretty good at reading people.

"It didn't say anything about Pete's blackmailing propensities. Of course, it wouldn't. Blackmail is paid to prevent public knowledge."

"Pete was blackmailing, too? He couldn't have been more than eighteen or nineteen then."

"Well, he was, and as you said, history repeats itself."

For the first time that evening, Chaz looked interested. "Since he came back?"

Liv nodded.

"Want to share?"

"I promised not to, but everyone seems to know anyway." She told him about Dolly and about catching Janine in the Zoldoskys' trailer.

"That it?"

"That's as far as I've gotten. No one has come forward saying, 'Guess what—Pete's blackmailing me.' "

"But if he was and Joss found out about it . . ."

"But Joss didn't know he was back," Liv reminded him

"So he said. Now can we eat?"

The restaurant in the inn was closed, but they were serving in the bar. A smiling hostess led them to a booth at the back where they were met by a smiling waitress. It seemed that Chaz was a favorite of all the staff.

"So Janine's brother was one of the gang," Chaz said, digging into a rare T-bone steak.

"That's what she said."

"So we know two of the culprits. I wonder who the other two were?"

"We could ask Joe Tudor," Liv suggested.

"He lives in Detroit or someplace."

"I think you should call him."

"He might not be too anxious to recall those days, especially if Pete's accusations are true. And if he thinks he might be incriminated, he might tip off the other two. One of whom might just be Pete's murderer. Forewarned. Besides, they're probably long gone."

Liv sighed. "Okay, scratch that idea. I just hope the murderer isn't someone we know and like."

"Tough. You get what you get. And once you start, you can't turn back. I learned that the hard way." Chaz signaled the waitress, who hurried over and flashed him another toothy smile. "I'll have another beer. Liv?"

Her wineglass was still half full. "No, thanks." She played with a julienned zucchini strip. "So we have the Dolly, Fred, Bill, and Pete situation. Janine and Pete. Joss and Pete."

"And it looks like you've questioned them all."

"Not Joss, and I wouldn't have to if somebody else in this town would lift a finger."

"Don't look at me."

"I gave up on that days ago." She was disappointed that he wouldn't help, but she was no longer angry. There was more to Chaz's reasons for leaving journalism than met the eye.

"I wonder if the police talked to Andy."

"Liv, leave it. If they don't catch someone soon, it will become a cold case and quietly fade away."

"But that would mean the killer would go free."

"Pretty much."

"But there would be no closure. No one would feel safe."

"Oh, give it a rest, Liv. Any one of us is capable of murder. Even so, just because it happened once doesn't mean it will happen again."

She stared at him, incredulous. "You don't care if he's caught."

"Not really."

"But—"

"Let me give you some advice. This was not a random psychopathic act. Pete was targeted. I think it's over."

"How can you be sure?"

"I can't." He finished his beer. "Don't listen to me. Are you finished? Then let's go."

Chaz insisted on paying for dinner, but Liv thought it was more about impressing the waitresses than it was about treating Liv. They certainly were appreciative, though Chaz didn't seem to notice. Liv just couldn't get a handle on the man. Infuriating and intelligent, though he spent most of the time acting like a rube.

They walked out into the night. Only a few of the inn's lights shone in the dark, but the moon was full and it cast a shimmer of iridescence over the lake. It would have been romantic, and she was certainly beginning to like Chaz a little better, but the solitary pier at the far side of the parking lot put a damper on any romantic inclinations.

Without speaking, they walked toward the pier and looked out at the lake. Trying to see into the past and wondering if that was the reason Pete had finally met a violent end. A boy running for his life, bleeding and hurt. Did he make it to the boat? Or was he caught and beaten, left to drown? Or did they throw him into the boat and push it away from shore? Had he fallen overboard? Were his remains out there still?

Liv shuddered. Chaz's arm went around her shoulder, then dropped again.

He took a step out onto the old wood plank and she followed him.

He didn't stop until they reached the end of the pier. "It was October. A night like this, maybe. A good night for finding wrigglers."

His voice sounded hollow in the eerie stillness. Then he barked out a bitter laugh. "How many lives were destroyed or altered, how many people suffered because of one nasty, amoral boy. It's always the sad, pitiful, weak ones who get the shaft, who do the suffering. And there's not a damned thing any of us can do about it."

Liv stared at him, stunned. "Is that why you quit reporting? The futility of it all?"

"It's why I fish. We'd better get back."

He walked her home and by tacit agreement they didn't discuss the murder or Chaz's former profession. He didn't linger but waited for Whiskey to make his round of the garden and for Liv to go inside and lock her door. She watched through a slit in the curtains as he walked away.

"Strange man, buddy. What do you think? Shall we give him the benefit of the doubt? Maybe he's not such a deadbeat, after all."

Whiskey barked.

"I know. It's hard to tell. But one thing I do know. It's time someone talked to Andy Miller. And I think that someone would be me."

Chapter Twenty

....

Liv wrapped her scarf more closely around her neck as she hurried toward work the next morning. The rain had stopped, the sun was shining, but the temperature had dropped a good ten degrees. The nip of winter was in the air; frost coated the ground. Ted had said winter was coming, Liv had hoped it would wait until next month. Would people be inclined to go on hayrides in forty-degree weather? She shivered just thinking about it.

What if the pumpkins froze?

No one else seemed concerned, she noticed, as she walked across the green toward the bakery and the Buttercup. When she'd left work on Friday, they were eking out the last few days of the harvest festival. This morning the town was transformed.

Hay bales that for the last month had been used as benches for the weary were now populated by scarecrows and skeletons. Store windows no longer displayed the golds, browns, and oranges of fall leaves, but the bright orange and black of Halloween.

The Apple of My Eye Bakery was festooned with orange and black crepe paper. Liv stopped outside. It would be the first time she'd seen Dolly alone since their talk and Dolly's confession about Pete's blackmail attempt. She wasn't sure of the reception that she'd get, but the sooner it was over, the sooner they could get back to normal.

Just inside the door a pyramid of pumpkins was topped by a plate of samples of pumpkin bread. Wonderful smells wafted in from the kitchen. Dolly came through the doorway carrying a heavy tray of sliced brown bread. She hesitated when she saw Liv, but only for a second.

"Morning, Dolly," Liv said hopefully.

"Morning." Dolly pushed the tray onto the top of the counter and looked around. "I was hoping you'd come in today." She motioned Liv closer. "I thought about what you said and told Fred . . . everything." Her mouth worked.

Oh no, thought Liv. *I've broken up their marriage.* "Dolly, Fred—"

"Has known all this time. He and Bill fought it out years ago."

"It wasn't fair for him to keep you in the dark, but—"

"He didn't tell me because he didn't want me to feel bad. Wasn't that just the sweetest thing you ever heard of?"

Letting Dolly feel guilty all these years?

"It just cleared the air and we had the best weekend."

TMI, thought Liv, and she hastily said, "That's wonderful, Dolly. I'm so glad."

"Thank *you,* Liv. I just feel like I have a new lease on life."

"Great."

"Now, what will you have this morning? I've been making orange frosting all morning. It's good but not for breakfast, unless you're in kindergarten. Now, let's see. . . ." Dolly chatted on while Liv got her equilibrium back.

All's well that ends well might be good for Fred and

Dolly, but there was still a murderer at large, and even though Liv had stopped worrying about him striking again, she still wanted him caught. She sighed. Even if it was someone she liked.

"Is something wrong, Liv?"

"What? Oh no. I just was trying to decide between the brown bread and the caramel pecan rolls."

"I'll give you two of both. On the house. A little thank-you."

Liv smiled, thanked Dolly, took her bread, and walked next door.

There was a short line at BeBe's. Liv looked around while she waited her turn, wondering what decorations BeBe had come up with. She laughed when she saw a grim reaper sitting at one of the little tables, his scythe balanced against the wall and a cup and saucer in front of him.

The customers left, and Liv stepped up to the counter and read the blackboard specials: Kandy Apple Kona and Devil-Mint Chai. She made a face.

"You're such a snob," BeBe said, reaching for the milk jug.

"A purist," Liv amended.

"No, a purist drinks their coffee black. You're a snob." She poured Liv's latte and handed it to her, leaning forward as she did. "Did you notice anything different about Dolly this morning?"

Liv shrugged.

"I think she . . . um . . . had a *nice* weekend."

Liv bobbled her cup. "BeBe," she said, not able to suppress a laugh.

"I think they're so cute."

"They are that."

"Well, fifty is the new thirty." BeBe slid Ted's tea in a cardboard carrier across the counter.

"I thought sixty was the new forty."

"Both. Good luck with the board meeting this morning."

"Right," said Liv. "I'd better get going." Balancing bags, drinks, and briefcase, she hurried past the bookstore where cutouts of black cats and witches grinned from the window, while mobiles of Day-Glo skeletons danced above their heads. The windows of A Stitch in Time were swagged in black and orange fabric.

Everyone was going about their business getting ready for Halloween, just like their future wasn't hanging in the balance of the town council vote. Liv was determined not to let them down. Now, if she could just trust Rufus, Roscoe, and Jeremiah to keep their word and vote for continuing the festivals instead of being cowed by Janine, the town would get its celebration.

Liv jogged up the steps of the town hall and lucked out as Andy Miller came out the front door. He held it open for her to go through.

"Thanks, Andy."

Andy nodded and hurried down the steps.

Now, what kind of business did he have here this morning?

"I just saw Andy Miller leave the building," Liv said as she set the drinks tray down on Ted's desk.

"Did you?"

"Yes. The question is, did you?"

"Just some festival business."

"Anything I should know?"

"Nothing important. It's taken care of."

Liv gave him a look and went into her office. *More secrets*, she thought as she opened her briefcase and took out the folder holding her security firm background checks and fee charts.

"Dolly must think we're starving," Ted said, bringing the tea tray into the room.

"She was feeling generous."

"Yep, the cat's out of the bag and all is right with the world."

"How do you know these things?"

"An ear to the ground, my dear."

"So what did you hear from Bill? And don't say it's privileged information."

"Well, it is, and we're not supposed to know. Bill isn't even supposed to know. But that's how things work here."

"So?"

"Bill made a call to the commissioner to tell him what a hash those detectives are making of this case. Seems they were both on probation, and this was their last chance to make good. Didn't happen. With any luck we should see the back of them in a few days." Ted took a sip of tea, his eyes sparkling, and Liv knew there had to be more.

"And?"

Ted chuckled so long and hard that he had to put down his tea to keep from spilling it. "They arrested Janine this weekend."

"Get out."

Ted burst into a full laugh.

"For murder?"

"No. For forging checks." Ted wiped his eyes with a white handkerchief he pulled from his vest pocket. "Mayor Worley bailed her out. And spent all weekend pulling strings to hush it up."

"What's going to happen to her? That's a serious offense."

"It is, but Janine insists that the festival owed Pete for services rendered. We won't even go there." He shuddered dramatically. "She said that since you weren't in your office, she took the check and signed your name. Something we do all the time in the festival offices."

"What? We'd never do that. And she doesn't even work here."

"True. And true. We won't quibble about the check writing. And Pete's not alive to explain that he was blackmailing her. Ergo . . ."

"She broke the law."

"Yes, and it's reprehensible. But she's not really a criminal, just a pain in the butt. If we don't pursue it, she'll get a slap on the wrist, we'll be chastised for questionable practices, and life will go on."

"But we didn't."

"Of course we didn't, and everyone will know we didn't. No one will mention it, but everyone will know."

"That's crazy."

"That's Celebration Bay. Look on the bright side. It may keep Janine off our backs."

"Or make her twice as bad."

"Let's go find out, shall we. It's almost ten."

They were not the first to arrive. Rufus, Roscoe, and Jeremiah sat together. Nodded together as Liv and Ted walked in. A study in solidarity. Liv just hoped they remembered their promise. A few minutes later the door opened and Liv was surprised to see Chaz. He looked like he'd rather be anyplace but here, and Liv wondered why he had even come. Because of the vote? She hadn't asked him how he would vote. They still had the majority even if he voted no, unless the mayor opted to override the board's decision. Would he be able to stand up to Janine?

Chaz sat down and Liv frowned at him, trying to get his attention, but he just leaned back in his chair and closed his eyes.

She caught herself drumming her fingers on the folder. Ted shot her a sideways glance, and she dropped her hands to her lap.

Finally the door opened and Liv held her breath until the door swung shut and the mayor called the meeting to order. The mayor. Alone. No Janine.

The meeting went like clockwork. Ted presented the harvest festival's profit and loss figures. Mostly profit and little loss, which made the council very happy.

Liv shared the specs on the three security firms she was considering. Rufus, Roscoe, and Jeremiah voted to continue the festivals, contingent on hiring extra security. When the time came for Chaz's vote, he opened one eye, and said, "Why not?" which made four votes for and none against.

The mayor banged his gavel. "Well, that's settled. This meeting is adjourned. Now, let's get ready for Halloween."

Anton Zoldosky was standing outside the locked events office door, a Tyrolean hat in his hand.

"What's he doing here?" Ted asked, and Liv realized that she hadn't had time to tell him what had happened over the weekend. Though knowing Ted, he already had all the details.

"Mr. Zoldosky," Liv said. "What can we do for you today?"

Anton glowered at Ted.

Ted unlocked the door and showed Anton inside, shooting a look at Liv as he did.

"I'll see Mr. Zoldosky in my office, Ted."

Ted pursed his lips in a parody of a pout. "Don't mind me. I'll just be filing some papers."

Translate: listening at the keyhole.

Liv shut the door and gestured to a chair. "Won't you sit down, Mr. Zoldosky?"

"No. I thank you. I came to apologize for my brothers' behavior. We are very private people. And they are a little hotheaded."

An understatement, thought Liv, but she didn't say so.

"I hope they did not hurt Chaz. He has been good to Junior."

"Just a little bruise. And he did rush in without thinking."

Anton nodded slowly. "He wished to protect you."

Liv nodded, too, but she couldn't help but smile.

And strangely, Anton smiled, too. It was the first time she'd seen him smile, and it looked odd on the angular face.

"Junior told me what happened with those men. I want to thank you for helping him. Not many in this town are so kind."

"They're just frightened."

"And blame us."

"It's easier than blaming one of their own."

"He said you were like a ninja."

"Hardly. Just a few self-defense techniques."

"He was ashamed that he had a woman protect him."

"Oh, not at all." She smiled, this time genuinely. "I'm a bit of a hothead myself."

"Very good. Still, I thank you." He reached across the table and tentatively held out his hand. Liv stood, took it and her hand practically disappeared in his.

He walked to the door but stopped when he reached it. "I'm sorry that we have brought this awful thing upon you. Hopefully, we will be leaving soon. I think we won't be back this way again."

Liv selfishly hoped they wouldn't, either. "It hasn't been easy for you, either. I wish you the best." And she meant it.

"What was that all about?" Ted asked the minute the outer door closed behind Anton.

"He came to thank me."

"For taking out the Weaver brothers?"

"Do you know everything that happens in this town?"

"This was rather newsworthy. Half the guys in the bar were watching."

"Were you there?"

"No. I would have come to your rescue and spoiled all the fun."

"But I would have appreciated it."

"Good to know. Now let's get to work. We have a festival to organize."

They spent the rest of the day jump-starting Haunted October, calling committee heads, confirming rentals. Liv hired the security firm and faxed them a schedule of the weekend events. They ate lunch at their respective desks. They were in festival mode.

It was growing dark when Liv finally looked up from her

desk. Five thirty. She jumped up. "I have to pick Whiskey up from the groomer's. Edna took him over this morning, but it's potluck night at the Elks Club. Can you close up?"

Ted looked over the rim of his reading glasses. "Sure. Go ahead. I'm almost finished."

Liv was bundled up and out the door in five minutes. "See you tomorrow."

She struck off across the green, bypassing McCready's Pub to the Woofery.

The proprietor, Sharise Lee, put down the phone when Liv came in.

"Sorry, Sharise. Halloween is on and I got immersed in work."

"No worries. I was just calling you. I need to get home and make my three-layer dip for the potluck tonight."

"Doubly sorry." Liv wrote out a check while Sharise went to get Whiskey.

He pranced out, white as the snow and his outer coat brushed soft as a baby bunny.

"He was some dirty dog," Sharise said. "Let me get his leash." Whiskey bumped Liv's leg and she knelt down to give him a pet.

"Okay, let's get out of here so Sharise can go home."

Sharise was just coming back with his leash when the front door opened. "Thank goodness you're still open," said a woman wearing a fur-trimmed all-weather coat.

Whiskey shot past her.

"Whiskey!" shouted Liv.

Sharise started for the door. "I'm so sorry. I'll find him."

Both of them rushed outside and stood on the sidewalk searching the streets.

"He just started doing this," Liv said. "I guess it's time for a refresher course in obedience."

"My fault. I should have leashed him first. But you were my last client. I don't know why Mrs. Stucky is here."

"You go deal with Mrs. Stucky," Liv said, catching a

glimpse of white streaking down the sidewalk. "I see him."
She took the leash from Sharise. "Don't you dare roll in
anything nasty!"

Whiskey bounded through the open gate of the Presbyterian cemetery just as Liv crossed the street.

By the time she reached the cemetery, Whiskey had disappeared among the gravestones. She slowed down, strain-
ing her eyes in the dimming light. It was a good thing she
wasn't superstitious, or the graves at dusk might be a little
spooky. She caught sight of a wagging white tail.

Please don't let him be digging up somebody's grave, Liv
prayed as she ran down the path.

And came to a sudden stop when a figure rose from the
ground. Her heart, when it started up again, pounded hard
enough to hurt until she realized it was a man, not a ghost,
and that Whiskey was jumping up to his hand.

As she drew nearer, the man saw her and began walking
toward her while Whiskey gamboled about his feet. Those
in the know said that dogs can always tell whether a person
is friendly or not, but Mr. Congeniality liked just about
everybody.

And then she recognized Junior Zoldosky. No wonder
Whiskey was so happy to see him. He might have more
food.

He automatically shaded the bad side of his face as he
drew nearer. "I wondered what he was doing out here alone."

"He escaped from the groomer's while I was paying the
bill. Thanks for waylaying him." She grabbed Whiskey's col-
lar and clipped the leash on. "Gotcha, you little vagabond."

"Well, I'd better be going. Are you going toward town?"

She had been. But there was something strange about
finding Junior in the cemetery.

"No, I'm headed home. Thanks again."

"Sure." They separated at the gate. Liv going south and
Junior going north toward the green.

Liv guessed that he must have been visiting Pete's grave.

Even though Pete was hated by everyone in town, and he'd brought the Zoldoskys a whole lot of trouble, he might have been Junior's friend. It couldn't be easy for Junior to make friends. But Pete didn't seem to be the kind of guy that would befriend a shy, disfigured man. More likely, he would have tormented Junior.

She started to cross the street toward home, hesitated, then turned the opposite way and walked the half block to the south entrance of the cemetery.

"I know this is crazy," she told Whiskey. "But it won't kill us to take a little look." She headed down the path, slowed by Whiskey's insistence to smell every possible disgusting article.

She came to a gravestone, still surrounded by colorful arrangements. She could make out the name Waterbury on the family marker. Nothing looked out of place. None of the flowers were disturbed. Junior hadn't been defiling the grave. She turned to go, and a single bit of color from a nearby site caught her eye.

A bouquet of fall wildflowers tied with a piece of string lay at the simple headstone. Liv shortened Whiskey's leash and went to see who was honored by such a simple homage. It was an older grave, the earth had settled years before, and the grass was thick. Liv bent down to read the name of the deceased.

Eleanor Driscoll Gibson, 1951–1999.

Eleanor Gibson. Ted's sister. Victor's mother.

The grave was well kept, though the leaves around it had been disturbed. By a little dog happy to see his friend.

She didn't know a lot about flowers that didn't come from a florist, but she knew that wildflowers wilted quickly once picked. These had been picked recently, and the only other person in the cemetery had been Junior.

Could it be possible? Liv wondered as she stared down at the grave. He was about the right age. His disfigured face. An accident? Or from a beating?

Victor chased and beaten so badly that it crushed his facial bones, his boat found at the south end of the lake, but no body ever recovered. Because the Zoldoskys had found him and taken him with them? But why wouldn't Victor come home and relieve his mother's grief?

Liv remembered the newspaper articles and Andy saying, *We thought it was a body. They said they'd kill us if we told.*

Had Victor been hiding all these years, afraid that Pete would kill him or hurt his mother? Had he been afraid to come home? And then to see Pete after all these years? It was so far-fetched that it might be true.

Liv stood up. It might also be a motive for murder. She needed to be absolutely sure. And she needed advice on how to proceed. She could ask Ted, but what if she were wrong? To open those old wounds and be wrong, she didn't have the heart to do it. She could just ask Junior outright but that seemed cruel. At least until she did some research.

She had her laptop but was too anxious to go all the way home. The closest place with an Internet connection was the *Clarion* office. And Chaz would know what to do if her information proved right.

"Come on, Whiskey. We're going to pay a call on the recalcitrant reporter."

Chapter Twenty-one

··

The Gone Fishing sign was on the door at the *Clarion* office, which could mean anything or nothing. She knocked. No one answered. No surprise there. She tried the knob. It turned and the door opened.

"Chaz?"

Nothing. There were no lights on. "Chaz?" she called again.

Hearing nothing, she flipped the switch and made her way back to the office. She called again and turned on the light. Whiskey darted into the room. A stack of papers went flying.

"Whiskey. Come here."

An innocent white face appeared out of the pile of promising rubbish. "Sit right here next to me. Don't eat anything. Don't roll in newsprint."

Whiskey cocked an ear as if to say, "What newsprint?"

"I know. I'm stressed. I'll make it up to you. Now, stay."

With a snuffle, Whiskey lay down at her feet.

She booted up her computer. Pulled up the file she'd

made on the Zoldoskys. Perused the articles starting back
to when the parents were members of Ringling Brothers.
Anton, the eldest, joining the act. Their demotion to a family
circus that toured the East Coast. Their retirement. And
after that the occasional mention of the Zoldosky Brothers
as members of fairs and carnivals. She opened the picture
file, already knowing she wouldn't find anything new. She'd
studied each of the few grainy photos she'd collected when
she first discovered that Pete wasn't a Zoldosky. But they
were mainly of the parents back when they were a big act.

She didn't learn anything new today. She leaned back in
the chair and sighed.

"Where the hell are you, Chaz? I need advice." If he
really were out fishing, he might not be back until the morning. And she needed to know today.

No, you don't, she told herself. *You don't need to know at
all. You should call Bill and let him deal with it. You could
be totally wrong.*

If she was right, she might be responsible for sending
Junior or one of the other Zoldoskys to jail. At least that
would clear Joss. And any others whom Pete had blackmailed or injured and who would be glad to see him dead.

*Yes, but not kill, Liv. Don't surmise. Stick to the spread-
sheet and don't get distracted by nonessentials.* Liv smiled
ruefully. The first rule of planning a perfect party. Or the
perfect lesson plan. She wouldn't go to Bill yet. Not until
she knew for sure that Junior was Victor Gibson. And the
most efficient way to find out was to ask Junior himself.

She closed her laptop and stood up. Whiskey rolled away
and looked up at her.

"Yes, you can get up now," she said with a sigh. "We have
some not very nice business to take care of."

Whiskey wanted to stop and sniff at everything on the
way to Dolly's, and it took all Liv's patience not to pick him
up and carry him across the green. But that might look odd,
and she really didn't want to attract any attention.

The town was fairly quiet. The weekend tourists had gone and the weather was a bit crisp for lingering in the green.

She stopped outside the door to the Apple of My Eye and looked down at Whiskey, whose tongue was hanging out in anticipation of all the treats he imagined coming his way.

"Behave," Liv said, and opened the door.

"Liv, what a surprise." Dolly seemed a little wary. "I was just putting these samples away before I close." She indicated a stainless steel tray of bite-size sweets on top of the display case. "Have one. They're my cinnamon crunch muffins." She pushed the tray closer to Liv.

"Thanks, but actually . . . Is Junior here?"

Dolly darted a look toward the curtained door behind her. "He's sweeping up in back." She hesitated. "He isn't in any trouble, is he?"

"Not that I know of. I just wanted to ask him a question."

"What kind of question?" Dolly didn't move to let Liv through.

"Dolly, I need to ask him something before the police do."

Dolly's hand went to her chest. She shook her head, already denying what she might hear next.

"Please." Liv's heart was thudding in her chest. She just prayed that Chaz wasn't right about her being Pandora. She wanted to get things right, not make them worse.

Finally Dolly pulled the curtain aside and Liv stepped through, aware that Dolly was following her. Did Dolly already know, or was it just her generous nature that made her protective of the man?

Junior was standing in the far corner, bent over while he swept dirt into a dustpan.

Liv took a breath. "Victor?"

Junior looked up, saw Liv. Then his eyes widened as he realized what he'd done. He dropped the broom and stood up.

"What are you saying? What's going on?" Dolly looked from Liv to Victor, her eyes filled with worry.

Junior's eyes darted toward the back door.

"Don't run. It's all right. No one else knows."

"Liv, what's this about? You're scaring me."

"I think Junior is Victor Gibson, the boy who disappeared all those years ago. You didn't die, did you, Victor?"

He didn't answer. Just stood, body tense, ready to bolt.

"Don't be afraid. I just want to help you."

He stayed silent.

"If I figured it out, so will everyone else."

"Victor?" Dolly said. "Is it really you?"

Junior slowly turned to look at her. His lips tightened and the scars on his face looked white against the suddenly livid skin.

"Oh my God." Dolly leaned on the cook island, one hand going to her mouth, as she studied the disfigured face. "It's really you?"

Junior shrugged.

"Oh, honey. Why didn't you come home? We all looked and looked for you."

"I couldn't."

"Why?"

"Look at me."

"Jun—Victor. You need to tell Bill Gunnison right away before—" Liv stopped. "Or does he already know?"

Victor shook his head.

"Does anyone know?"

Victor hesitated.

"It's important."

A loud clatter made them all jump.

"That was from out front." Dolly rushed to the store, but Liv was there first. The platter of samples lay on the floor, bits of muffin scattered in every direction

"I must have pushed it too close to the edge," Dolly said, and began cleaning up the mess.

"I don't think so," Liv said as she noticed a squished piece of muffin and the skid mark where a shoe must have slipped. "Keep Whiskey inside. I'll be right back."

She slipped out the front door and stood, looking up and down the street. Two middle-aged women were getting into a car in front of A Stitch in Time. She saw several people at the far side of the square, but no one making a quick escape from the bakery.

Whoever it was had either ducked into one of the stores or made a really quick getaway. And she couldn't really go around checking the bottoms of everyone's shoes for muffin residue.

Damn. Maybe she had been wrong to confront Junior in the bakery. To confront him at all. It was time to call in Bill, whether Victor was willing or not.

When she returned to the bakery, Dolly was dumping the remains into the trash basket behind the counter, and Whiskey was licking muffin off his fur.

Liv rolled her eyes at him and went back to the kitchen. It was empty; the back door was open.

Victor was gone. And unless Liv was really wrong, someone besides her and Dolly knew his secret. She looked out the back door; the alley that ran behind the buildings was empty. She turned to go back inside and ran into Dolly.

"Oh dear, I had no idea. Why didn't he—Do you think someone overheard?"

"Yes. I thought it would be safe to talk to Junior at the bakery."

"You have to do something. They might think he killed Pete. You have to find him before the police do. Oh my Lord, do you think Pete did that to his face?"

"I don't know. I have to go. Don't say anything until I can straighten this out."

Liv started for the door, had to snap at Whiskey's leash to pull him from a muffin square. But as soon as they were out the door, he seemed to sense her urgency, and he set a brisk pace for home.

It was dark by the time Liv reached the driveway to her carriage house. The Zimmermans' porch light was on, and as she stood trying to catch her breath, the front door opened and Edna ran out onto her front porch. "Thank God you've come home. The police just put out an APB on that poor Zoldosky boy. I heard it not two minutes ago on my police scanner. Do you think he was the murderer?"

"I don't . . . know," huffed Liv. "But I'm on my way out to Andy Miller's. Can you watch Whiskey?"

"Of course, dear."

But Whiskey refused to be left behind. As Liv opened her car door, he scrambled off the porch and jumped inside.

"You're right. You can probably help," she told him. "But sit down."

She took the long way through town, slowing at corners and looking down streets, hoping to catch a glimpse of Junior. Hoping to catch up to him before the police did. In the back of her mind a little twinge of guilt told her she might be aiding and abetting a murderer, but her instinct said Junior was no killer.

She sped up as soon as she reached the county road. If he cut through the fields, he might be back at the trailer already. Or he might be too afraid to go back to the trailer. He could be anywhere. They may all have packed up and fled. Fugitives instead of itinerants, and that would be her fault.

She turned into the Miller field and was relieved to see that the trailer was still parked near the far trees, outlined by a waning moon. There were two small rectangles of light coming through the windows and the flicker of a campfire nearby.

The car bumped over the uneven ground as Liv sped across the field. Her headlights bounced wildly in the dark. She slammed on the brakes and her car rocked to a stop.

Anton Zoldosky was sitting by the campfire. He stood up and took a step toward Liv, large, formidable, and angry, silhouetted by the flames behind him.

"The police are looking for Junior," she gasped. "Is he here?"

Anton shook his head. "Why are they looking for my boy? He has done nothing."

"It's all my fault. I found out that he's really Victor Gibson. Someone must have overheard us talking, and now the police are looking for him."

Anton roared, a sound so primitive that Liv quaked.

"Serge. Georgi."

The two brothers appeared from inside the trailer.

"We must find Junior. The police know who he is and are looking for him."

The two brothers jumped to the ground.

"Take the truck. I will stay here."

They ran for the truck without questions.

"I'll look, too," Liv said and got in her car. She backed up and left skid marks in the grass as she turned around. Whiskey fell to the floor with a yelp.

"Sorry, buddy." She followed the gray truck almost to the road, then stopped. Andy's truck was gone, but Victor might have gone to him for protection. Because how could Andy not know who he was?

She turned into the drive up to Andy's house. Drove around to the back of the house to hide her car, knowing she was probably breaking the law, but at the moment she didn't care. It was her fault they'd found out about Victor. She couldn't just feed him to the dogs.

Casting a quick glance toward the road and finding it dark, she ran up to Andy's front porch. She knocked, called out, and finally, getting no answer, put her hands to the window and peered in. His house looked totally deserted. Had he already found Victor and was helping him escape?

"Oh Andy, that's not the way."

Whiskey was scratching at the car window, feeling her anxiety. "It's all right, boy," she called, and ran back to her car. But when she opened the door, Whiskey shot past her and raced to the barn and scratched frantically at the wide metal door.

Liv ran to the barn and pulled at the door, but it was heavy and her palms were beginning to sweat. She wiped them on her jacket, grabbed the handle, and pulled again.

One side of the door opened a few inches and Whiskey squeezed through. Liv followed and found herself in darkness. She was surrounded by empty space and weird shapes that her rational mind said must be farm equipment. She groped her way to the first one. Felt the cold metal of the machine.

"Victor?" she called quietly, holding on to the machine for balance. "Victor. You have to come out."

She heard a whimper and followed the sound, squeezing between two machines, then almost tripped on a metal shaft that lay across the floor. She reached for the next machine to steady herself and found that it was covered by a rough canvas tarp. She inched her way past it.

"Victor. Where are you?"

Another whimper. This time from Whiskey.

Ears pricked, listening for any sound, Liv shuffled forward in the darkness. And found man and dog huddled beside the corncrib.

"Victor, you have to come out. The police are looking for you. We'll help you but you can't run. It will—"

He moved faster than Liv thought possible and ran past her, knocking against her. Disoriented in the dark, she fell backward, grabbed at the tarp cover trying to break her fall, but the tarp fell with her and she landed hard onto a row of metal teeth. Fortunately they were pointing toward each other and not her.

Whiskey stopped long enough to sniff her, then took off after his new friend.

"Whiskey. Come back here." Liv wrestled out from under the tarp and grabbed hold of a lever that stuck out right above her head. She hauled herself to her feet.

She ran to the door and saw them headed for the trailer. She saw something else, too. Flashing lights coming over the hill, getting closer. She didn't stop to get her car but took off across the field as fast as she'd ever run.

The gray truck passed her before she got there. Serge and Georgi jumped out. "It's the police. We must run. Get in the truck."

"It is too late," Anton said, thrusting Victor behind him.

Three police cars turned into the field and sped toward them.

Victor looked up, his eyes wild, and a choked animal cry escaped his throat.

"You must run," Georgi said. "Run, Junior. To the lake."

Liv's hand flew to her mouth as she pushed back tears. Not the lake. Not like all those years ago.

Junior hesitated, shot a fearful look at Anton, shook his head no.

"You must," Anton told him. "I will take care of things."

The first car slammed to a stop and the two state detectives got out.

Junior took off toward the water, Whiskey at his heels.

"Whiskey!" Liv cried, but they were already too far away, Junior a mere shadow and Whiskey a phantom cloud of white.

The Zoldosky brothers formed a shield in front of the detectives. But two other squad cars had stopped and four uniformed men were getting out.

"Stop him," cried Detective Devoti. "He's gone to the lake."

The four new arrivals hesitated. Local men, Liv guessed. They wouldn't care to be ordered around by some arrogant state detective.

"After him," Devoti bellowed.

They took off toward the water.

"Leave him alone," Anton shouted. "You want me. Not him."

Devoti shot him a derisive look. "Keep it to yourself, old man. We know the whole story."

Serge and Georgi surged forward, but Anton managed to hold them off the detective.

Devoti stepped back, reaching for his side.

"Don't shoot," Liv said. "And tell your men not to shoot. I mean it. He's unarmed, and if you hurt him . . ."

Devoti huffed out a disgusted sigh and nodded to his subordinate, Pollack, who took off after the others, running as fast as his crepe-soled shoes would carry him.

Liv watched him go, helpless and guilty. He'd just reached the trees when a shot was fired.

"No!" she cried.

Anton broke for the lake. Serge, Georgi, and Liv followed right behind him, leaving the detective alone.

"Stop. I won't be responsible for civilian casualties," he yelled, and trotted after them.

Serge and Georgi easily passed Anton, and Liv had no trouble keeping up. The three of them reached the shore at the same time.

The surface of the lake reflected moonlight, but two feet into the trees was pitch-dark. Liv saw the random motion of flashlights bouncing through the trees as the policeman spread out. Searching for Victor.

Liv just kept looking for a little patch of white. She knew Whiskey would never desert his new friend. She prayed she wouldn't find either one of them lying bleeding on the ground. She struck off along the shoreline, heard a rustle in the trees to her left, tripped, and nearly went down on all fours.

She peered down at what had tripped her. Just a gnarled tree root sticking out of the ground. She heard shouts down lake and she began to run, heedless of rocks and roots, trying to keep close to the water until it was impossible and she was forced to venture into the trees. Still she ran, not slowing down as leaves slapped at her face and vines grabbed at her ankles.

There were shouts ahead of her and answering shouts

behind her. She could hear the men slashing through the woods and hoped it was Serge and Georgi and not that despicable detective. She kept running until her lungs burned and her legs shook, though she knew it was as much from fear as from fatigue.

She stumbled upon a narrow path, followed it, her ears alert, her eyes focused on the ground, and burst out onto an open rocky beach. The policemen faced Victor, his back to the water. Whiskey stood guard at his feet, his coat bristling, the sweet little canine's teeth flashing menacingly in the moonlight.

Liv stopped, slid on the pebbles beneath her feet.

One of the officers turned. "Can you please call off your dog, ma'am?"

Liv deliberated. She was so out of her realm of expertise. Would Whiskey even come if she called him? And if he didn't, would they hurt him to get to Victor?

She slowly stepped forward. Caught Victor's eye, hoping he could see how much she hated having to do this. And instead saw only his fear. Fear of the police, fear of jail. Fear locked inside him for thirty years. Liv saw it. The fight, the chase, the escape. But mainly the fear.

And she saw the moment when he made the decision to flee no matter what the cost. He stepped away and then plunged into the shallow water, splashing and groping for balance. A split second later, Whiskey jumped in, too, paddling alongside him.

Liv cut back a sob as Detective Devoti ordered the men into the water. Serge and Georgi came up behind her just as Victor fell headlong into the lake and the officers grabbed him by the coat and pulled him back to shore.

Beside her, Serge clenched his fist and muttered something she didn't understand.

Georgi growled in her ear. "See what your meddling has done?"

Held by two policemen, Victor stumbled onto the pebbled

beach, hair and clothes dripping, shivering in the night air. The officers were shivering, too, and for a selfish moment Liv hoped they all got nasty colds.

Whiskey reached the shore and shook himself energetically. It was small consolation that Detective Devoti had to jump out of range of the spray.

"Take him away, Pollack."

The tone of his voice sent Whiskey back to Victor's feet.

"Now."

"The dog, sir."

"To hell with the dog. If he tries to bite you, shoot it."

"No!" Liv yelled and jumped in front of Whiskey. It was probably the dumbest thing she'd ever done in her life. Half her life flashed before her before a new voice said, "I wouldn't do that, Detective Pollack."

Bill Gunnison walked out of the dark and onto the bank. Liv could practically hear the sighs of relief from the four local officers.

"Thank God," Liv said. "How did you find us?"

"I was monitoring the police band. Looks like I made it just in the nick of time."

"Stay out of this, Gunnison. You are no longer on this case."

"We'll see about that. In the meantime, if you want to take this man in, do it."

Devoti tried to brush past him, but Bill crowded him back.

"One misstep, one shove, and I'll nail your ass to the nearest billboard."

Liv heard a stifled chuckle from one of the men.

"I'll have you brought up on charges of insubordination."

"Really? On whose authority?"

There was a brief standoff; then Devoti lifted his chin toward the officers, who were now all shivering with cold and suppressed laughter. "Get him out of here."

Behind him, Bill nodded and the officers walked right

past Whiskey to take Victor. One of them even leaned over to let Whiskey smell his hand, then patted him before taking Victor by the elbow.

"Sorry, Mr. Gibson, but you'll have to come with us."

Liv marveled at the young officer's civility. He wasn't even born when Victor had disappeared and yet he treated him with respect. Because he was one of them. She really loved this town and its inhabitants, even the cranky ones.

They led Victor past the little group congregated on the shore.

Victor held back when they reached Anton, who was still breathing heavily from the run. "I didn't kill him, Anton." His teeth were chattering so hard he could barely form the words.

"And get him some dry clothes," Bill ordered.

"I swear I didn't."

"I know. I will fix it."

They escorted Victor away from the lake.

Liv grabbed Whiskey as he tried to follow and held him tight. He shivered against her.

Anton turned on Liv. "Your fault," he said and hurried to catch up to the detectives, Serge and Georgi following close behind him.

"What did he mean, your fault?" Bill asked.

"Someone overheard me ask Junior if he was Victor Gibson."

"So that's how they found out."

Liv nodded, the enormity of what she'd done tightening her throat. "Did you know? You could have prevented this if you had just trusted me."

"I didn't know. Dammit. The Zoldoskys have been coming here for several years and I never recognized him. I don't think anyone did."

"People didn't really look at him; they didn't want to stare. You could see them avert their eyes when he was around. I did it, too."

Bill shook his head. "He was here in plain sight every year and he never said anything. Why?"

"I don't know. You'll have to ask him that. Dolly asked him and he just said that he couldn't."

"He didn't say why?"

"No. But I don't think he killed Pete, even though he had every right to."

"Liv, no one has the right to exact that kind of vengeance, even if it's deserved."

He was right. But she was still glad Pete Waterbury had gotten his just deserts, no matter who had been the hand of justice.

"Well, let's get up the hill. I'd better accompany them and make sure nothing untoward occurs."

The police cars were driving away when they reached the trailer. The two detectives were standing by the campfire while Anton gestured wildly in the firelight. Georgi and Serge stood directly behind him. A united front.

"Enough, old man. We'll get to you later."

"Junior did not kill that man. I did."

"Sure you did. Nice try, but you're in enough trouble. Harboring a felon. Aiding his escape. Don't worry. We'll be back for you. So don't think about leaving town."

Ignoring Bill and the others, he walked back to his car. Detective Pollack made an apologetic grimace before following him.

"Ugh," Liv said. "He's been watching too many bad cop shows."

"He's an egomaniac and his partner is an imbecile. This was their last case to see if they could redeem themselves after a long line of mishandled cases. Pollack might get a desk job if he's lucky, but that so-and-so Devoti is about to get drummed out."

"Good. He's awful."

Another truck was making its way toward them.

"Andy," Bill said, and turned to wait for him.

The cab door swung open; Andy Miller jumped down and ran toward them. "What's the commotion? What were those police cars doing here?"

"They have arrested Junior," Anton said.

"What? No. They can't." He looked at Bill. "He's innocent."

"I hope so," Bill said. "Did you know he was Victor Gibson?"

Andy's eyes slid away.

"For how long?"

"A few days. A week, maybe."

"You never recognized him all the years they camped out here?"

Andy's mouth trembled. "He never got close enough for me to see. I guess he was afraid. And he was my friend." He scrubbed his hand over his eyes. "All those years." He drew himself up. "I think I should—"

From the corner of her eye, Liv saw Anton give one, barely perceptible shake of his head.

Bill had seen it, too. Maybe he wasn't as slow as Liv thought. But what did it mean?

"I think I'd better get back to town and oversee the arraignment."

"We will raise the money for bail," Anton said.

Bill shook his head. "If the judge grants bail at all, it will be more than you probably have."

"I'll see to it," Andy said. "And we can count on Joss, too, if need be."

"I don't think they have enough to hold him. They were a bit too quick on the trigger. Let's just wait and see."

"I do not want him locked up," said Anton. "He will be afraid away from the family."

Bill's mouth tightened. "I'll see what I can do. But . . ." He looked around the group, his eyes resting on each one of the men. "Do not interfere. Understand?"

Anton and Andy nodded. Even Liv nodded. Serge and Georgi just looked on and scowled.

Bill pointed at the two of them, then said to Anton, "Don't let these two hotheads do anything rash. Come on, Liv. Where's your car?"

He dropped her and a very dirty, wet Whiskey off at her car. Waited for her to start the engine, then drove away.

She jacked up the car's heater, but couldn't move any farther, just sat there, close to tears as the enormity of what she'd unleashed took hold. Fought a losing battle against tears. Brushed them away with an impatient hand. Noticed the residue of rust across her palm. Damn machine. Damn detectives. Damn everything.

She rubbed her hands on her jacket and drove back to town.

Everyone had already left and she was alone on the road. A metaphor for her life in Celebration Bay. She brushed away another tear. She had caused a whole lot of trouble for nothing. Unless Victor really was guilty. It didn't make her feel better that she might have helped catch a killer.

Chapter Twenty-two

· ·

Liv drove right up to her door, grabbed Whiskey, and hurried inside before the Zimmerman sisters could stop her to ask what was going on. She ran into the little bathroom to get towels to dry him off, but Whiskey disappeared under the bed.

She didn't blame him; she felt like crawling under there with him. She went back into the bathroom. Turned on the water and filled the little lavatory with warm water.

She pulled a clean washcloth from the bar and saturated it with water, then pressed it to her swollen eyes. Stood there breathing and letting the warmth seep into her skin. She dropped it back into the water and stopped.

Looked. Looked again. The rust, which had been dark orange on her hands, had turned to splotches of red on the cloth and had tinted the water pink. She looked down at her hand. A rusty red streak spread across her palm. Disbelieving, she slowly looked into the mirror, a smear of red across her cheek.

Blood. It had to be. She must have cut herself when she

fell over that stupid farm machine. She inspected her hand, then her face, but found nothing.

Whiskey must have cut himself in the woods. She grabbed a towel and hurried into the bedroom, dropped to her knees by the bed, and peered beneath it. Whiskey was curled up in the far corner.

"Come here, boy," she coaxed. Whiskey just looked at her. "I've got a treat."

Slowly, Whiskey crawled out. She grabbed him by the front paws and pulled him out from under the bed. Sensing betrayal and no treat, he wriggled to get away, but Liv held fast, inspected his ears, his muzzle, legs, body, and found nothing but a brush of pink where she had held him and a lot of burrs and mud.

She sat back on the floor. After a poor-me look, Whiskey skulked away to the kitchen. Liv made a note to call the groomer in the morning and went back to look at the stained washcloth.

Junior? But she hadn't touched him, or anyone else for that matter. What else had she touched besides the farm equipment in Andy's barn? An idea was pushing at her brain but she didn't want to go there. Didn't want to be any more involved in this whole mess than she already was. But it wouldn't go away.

Blood. She forced herself to go back into the bathroom. She lifted the washcloth out of the water and wrapped it in her shower cap. Then she carried it to the kitchen and removed it to a freezer bag, sealing it tight.

Looking at it long and hard, she tried to make that niggling suspicion go away. So what if the blood was on the machine? Farming was a physical business. The farmhands were bound to get cut and scraped. She was probably blowing this all out of proportion.

Like you've been doing ever since they found Pete Waterbury's body.

Hey, she argued with herself. *I haven't blown this up. If anything, I've sped along the investigation.* Much to her chagrin and guilty conscience. And she couldn't ignore the stains on the washcloth. Or the pink-tinged water. Or the blood across her face.

But she also couldn't go running to Bill or anybody else with the information. She was also responsible for Victor's arrest; she wasn't going to endanger anyone else.

At least not until she had more information. And until then she was just going to pray that one of Andy's employees would be sporting a big, big Band-Aid.

"Emergency," Liv said when Sharise Lee opened the door to the Woofery the next morning.

"Good heavens, what happened?"

"He went for a dip in the lake."

"Well, we'll fix you right up, won't we, sweetie," Sharise cooed and took Whiskey from Liv.

"Thanks. I hope it doesn't put too much work on you today."

"I never have too much work," Sharise said. "I'll have him finished and smelling sweet as a Westie terrier by six."

"Thanks." Liv speed walked across the green. She considered going straight to work and letting Ted pick up their morning drinks. She was sure everyone had heard the news of Victor's arrest, and she wasn't looking forward to taking the fallout.

Suck it up, Liv. The sooner you face it . . . She went into the bakery.

Dolly didn't mention the arrest. She barely exchanged a word with Liv while she bagged two sour cream pecan muffins.

BeBe was more sympathetic. "I know you had to do it, but I hope he's not guilty. From what everyone has said, that Pete was a snake."

Ted just gave her a look and took the drinks tray and bakery bag from her.

"It's not like I set off to entrap him," Liv said as soon as Ted carried the tea tray into her office.

"No one said you did."

"Dolly hardly said a word to me this morning."

"Dolly has a soft spot for the underdog. And people are already asking her if she knew he was Victor and that's why she let him sweep out the bakery."

"So what if she did?"

Ted shrugged. "Doesn't matter in the least. Just something to talk about. You're the only person in town who's upset about Dolly. We're good at putting on events, but what we're really good at is making something out of nothing and talking about it to everyone. It's what we do. Now, drink your coffee before it gets cold."

"Ted, he's your nephew."

Ted put down the muffin he'd been about to take a bite of. "I am well aware of that. And I'll do anything I can to help him. But no, I didn't recognize him, either. He was probably ten when I saw him last. I was away most of those years." He paused, gave her a considering look. "We all have a lot to answer for."

"Especially me. If I had made sure we were alone when I confronted him. If I hadn't made the connection at all. If I had minded my own business. I didn't intend to tell the police—at least not until I was sure—Why are you smiling?"

"You're an organizer, a planner, a problem solver. That's what makes you a good event planner. No one expects you to turn that off when you step out of your professional mode. The people to blame for Victor's arrest are those two dingbat detectives and the person who spied and told. Actually, we should thank you for seeing things we were too dense to see."

"Thanks, but it doesn't make me feel better." Liv leaned forward on her desk. "Do you know who overheard us and called the police?"

"No, and I wouldn't tell if I did. I wouldn't want to be responsible for what might happen to that person now that Junior's true identity is known."

"Can we blame this on Janine, too?"

"Sorry. She's spending a few days with friends in New York." He suppressed a grin. "She doesn't know that the buzz about her arrest has been supplanted by something much more interesting. And nobody seems to be in a hurry to tell her."

"Have you talked to Bill?"

"Actually, I did. Last night at the station and again this morning. He called to let me know that he made a few calls. Bill may be slow and a bit stuck in his ways, but he gets the job done and he has friends. I don't think those two detectives will be bothering us for much longer."

"But the damage is done."

"Listen to you. What if Victor is guilty? That would make you a hero."

"That would make it worse."

Ted chuckled. "Well, I guess that makes you one of us, then."

That should make her feel better, being accepted as one of them, but it just made her feel worse, like it doubled her betrayal of Victor Gibson.

She had considered telling Ted about the blood and the washcloth that she'd placed in her refrigerator. But after that affirmation, she decided she'd better keep it to herself. She forced herself to work all morning, but she went out at lunchtime. Straight to the *Clarion* office.

"Nice bit of investigation," Chaz said, when she finally woke him up.

"I feel awful."

"Good. You should."

"Thanks a lot," she said miserably, and sat down on the ancient couch beside him.

"And you banged on my door and woke me up because . . ."

To tell you that I've got a bloody washcloth in my fridge at home? The old Chaz might be intrigued, but the Chaz she knew would just scoff at her. "I don't know. Misery loves company? I thought you might have some words of advice."

"That would make you feel better? Well, I don't." Chaz heaved off the couch, yanked up the coffeepot, and disappeared into the bathroom. Liv listened as he emptied the pot and filled it up again.

He was taking his time. Waiting for her to leave? She should. She didn't even know why she'd come. If she thought he would be sympathetic, she was dead wrong.

He returned with the filled carafe and poured it into the coffeemaker. Measured grounds while Liv watched.

When the coffeemaker began to make popping noises, he turned on her. "Didn't I tell you to stay out of this?"

"I don't recall those exact words."

"And you, of course, would."

"I'm meticulous and I wasn't trying to investigate. I was picking up my dog from the groomer's. He got out when another customer came in, and he took off for the cemetery I followed him right to Junior—Victor—who was standing near a grave. We walked out together, and okay, I'm guilty of doubling back and taking a look at the grave."

"And it belonged to Eleanor Gibson." Chaz blew out a long hiss of breath.

"There was a bouquet of wildflowers on it. It was so—" Liv's voice cracked.

"Oh God, don't lose it. I haven't had my coffee."

Liv sniffed. "I never lose it."

"No, of course not. You probably never have a moment's lack of emotional control."

Ouch. "Oh shut up."

"Look. Here's the deal. If you play in scum, you get dirty." The coffeemaker beeped. "You want coffee?"

"No. Thanks."

"Liv, shit happens. Sometimes it's better not to look too close."

He turned back to the coffeemaker and Liv slipped away.

She walked back to her office, wondering if that was what had happened to Chaz. If shit had happened and he couldn't or didn't want to face it anymore. It would be totally understandable. But even though he was blatantly uninterested in anything but fishing, she thought the reason went deeper than just being fed up with the slime.

And Liv was beginning to sympathize.

Ted had left a note that he would be out for the rest of the afternoon. A water pipe had burst at the VFW hall where the jack-o'-lantern contest was being held, and he had to confirm an alternate location.

Ordinarily Liv would have joined him and checked it out for herself. But it was time she got used to delegating responsibility. Hard for a control freak like her. But it was time to step back, not try to fix everything herself. Almost time. She had one more thing to do before she washed her hands of the whole mess.

She got in her car and drove out to Andy Miller's farm.

The Zoldoskys' truck was gone and so was Andy's. They were probably at the police station and she'd made the trip for nothing. If she were honest, she was a little relieved; she hadn't fully figured out how she was going to ask Andy about the blood without accusing him of murder or appearing ridiculous for asking.

She started to turn around, then thought of the barn and the equipment stored there. No one at home.

Don't do it, Liv. Leave it alone.

But problems didn't get solved by leaving them alone.

Liv resolutely turned off the engine and got out of the car. Just a quick look around. She walked over to the barn, trying not to look furtive, and slid the door open. A shaft of sunlight spilled onto the floor. In the daylight it was easy to make out the contents of the barn. She saw the thresher with its big teeth, but the machine she had grabbed onto had been covered again.

She swallowed and gingerly pulled the tarp back. Peered closely at the handle she had grabbed in the dark. She couldn't really see anything. But she did hear a sound that sent her adrenaline racing.

A truck.

She quickly lowered the tarp and retraced her steps to the door just as Andy's truck stopped and Serge, Georgi, and Andy got out. They stopped, staring at her as she walked out of the barn.

"Liv?"

Liv forced a smile. "Hi, I was just looking for you."

Andy came toward her, his expression puzzled. He looked so tired and pale Liv felt sorry for him. She really hoped he hadn't killed Pete Waterbury. Where was the good of acquitting Junior only to accuse Andy?

"What did you want?"

"What? Oh, I was just out this way and wanted to see how things were going."

"The maze is ready to open, but you know that."

"See you later," Serge said, and he and Georgi left Liv and Andy alone.

"I really came by to see how you were. And to apologize for . . ."

"I'm fine," Andy said without conviction. "If that's all, I have some things I have to do."

"Okay, sure."

Liv got back in her car feeling like she had been slapped. She drove back to town, relieved and disappointed. That had been stupid, a wasted opportunity. She knew no more now than she did before; she'd chickened out just when she might have learned the truth. She needed to call Bill.

She reached for her cell; the call went to voice mail. She

considered just hanging up, but asked Bill to call her. At least he could tell her to butt out and she wouldn't have to be involved any longer.

She worked late but Ted didn't return. Liv picked up Whiskey, paid Sharise for the second time in two days, and took him straight home. As soon as she opened the door, Whiskey shot inside.

Liv heard something behind her. She turned around. At the same time, her front door slammed shut and something was yanked over her head, cutting out the light from the porch. The bag was scratchy, and it was hard to breathe. And the smell, sickly sweet.

She was seized by strong, large hands. She tried to fight but her arms and legs seemed out of her control. They dragged her into the bushes, and she became disoriented. *So hard to breathe.*

Another arm grabbed her feet; three arms. Two assailants. They carried her, then dropped her on a hard metal surface, a truck. Her hands and feet were tied. One man dragged her farther into the truck bed and the other slammed the gate.

After the initial shock, Liv began to think. Not a random act of violence. Someone had been waiting for her.

The truck picked up speed; the metal vibrated beneath her, jarring her bones and her teeth. It hit a bump, and Liv's shoulder came down hard on the metal. She tried to move, and that was when she realized one of her captors was in the back with her.

Think, Liv. Think. But it was hard to think with the burlap tickling her nose and the dust clogging her windpipe. And that smell. *Truck, dust, burlap, farm.* Zoldoskys. Andy, Joss, the Weavers, a dozen other people she knew.

Liv made strangling noises and got no response from her captor.

"I can't breathe," she yelled over the rattle of the truck.

Still no response.

Where were they taking her? On the highway somewhere.

What were they going to do with her? Kill her? Why? Revenge? One of the Zoldoskys? All of them? Two of them. Three arms. Georgi and Serge and his one good arm. What could they possibly be thinking? Surely they wouldn't kill her, would they?

But if they killed Pete . . . No. She needed to stay calm.

Maybe they would hold her for ransom. Good luck with that. She didn't think she was anybody's favorite person right now. They might just think good riddance and get on with things without her.

The truck turned again, bumped violently. They'd left the road; they were riding over dirt now. The truck stopped. Liv slammed up against the cab. For a second she thought she was going to pass out. She heard the gate as it was let down; then she was lifted out of the truck. Her feet fell to the ground.

"Let me—" A hand slapped over her nose, pushing the burlap into her face. She tried to suck in breath but she couldn't take in air. Then nothing.

The rain woke her up. At least, she thought it must be rain. She lay on the ground, stunned.

When she finally tried to move, she couldn't. Her head was still covered; her hands and feet were tied. She'd been kidnapped. It was coming back to her.

She tried to wriggle out of the bag, using her bound hands to push it off her head. Sucked in cold air when it finally fell away. Let the rain fall on her face. Rain. She was outside.

She looked around. It was dark. Above her, the sky was dark. The rain clouds must be blocking out the moon. And she had no idea where she was or how long her kidnappers would be gone.

She twisted at the ropes that bound her wrists and succeeded only in making the knots tighter. Shivering, she brought her wrists to her mouth, using her teeth to work the knot loose, but it wouldn't budge.

She gave up and pulled her feet to her chest. That knot

was looser. Painfully, she began to work the wet rope out of the loop. It seemed to take forever, but at last the first loop fell away only to reveal another. With a cry of frustration, she began again. She had to keep brushing her face against her shoulder to get the hair out of her eyes.

She needed to hurry; they might be back any minute.

She worked the last knot out and yanked the rope from her feet. The violence of the movement catapulted her back and she fell into dried stalks of . . . corn. She was in a cornfield.

No, not a cornfield. The maze. Andy's maze. She breathed a sigh of relief. Freedom was just a few turns away. She remembered Andy saying there was an entrance and an exit, two ways to get out if she lost her way.

She rolled to her knees. Using her bound hands, she pushed to her feet and immediately fell to her knees. Her feet didn't seem to have any feeling. It must have been the ropes, because even though she was freezing, it wasn't cold enough for frostbite. She hoped.

Her second attempt was more successful. She managed to get upright but was struck with a wave of nausea. They must have given her something to knock her out. She stood with her face lifted to the stinging rain, willing her body to be strong, for her mind to clear.

After a few minutes she felt better. She had to move, but which way? She tried to get her bearings, but it was no use. *That's why they call it a maze; just move.* Using the wall of stalks as her guide, she started forward, the dry stalks scratching and slapping at her hands. She moved as fast as she could and smacked into an impenetrable wall. She reached out to her right, more wall. To her left and groped empty space.

She turned left. She had no idea how far she was into the maze, but there was only one direction to take. There wasn't even a star in the sky to guide by. Just black, thick clouds as impenetrable as the cornstalks.

She came to another turn. Lightning split the sky. For the briefest moment she saw corn higher than her head; she was standing at an intersection of paths that disappeared into darkness on all four sides of her. A crack of thunder and the light was gone, leaving her more disoriented than before.

She turned left. A scream split the air; Liv screamed in response. Something flew at her in a another flash of light, not lightning, but something wild, jumping and flashing. A hideous face rushed at her and she screamed again.

She ran, a purely reflexive reaction. Fell headlong into cold, wet vines that slapped against her face and settled on her shoulders and back, trapping her. She flailed wildly to free herself, but her hands were still tied and she succeeded only in getting tangled in the folds.

All around her, lights were still flashing. *Strobe*, she told herself. This was just an effect.

She freed herself just as the octopus retreated into the wall of stalks. She followed it, hoping it would lead her out, but it was just a cavity cut out in the wall to house the mechanism.

She backed out. Listened for the sound of someone running to save her—or her captors returning.

And heard a low chuckle. Another effect, she told herself. Just fun and games for fearless teenagers. Something thrashed among the stalks, and she jumped even though she knew it was just more of the Maze of Madness.

"Aptly named, Andy," she said aloud and felt better for it.

The chuckling started up again, only in a different place. The same thrashing sound. Another laugh slightly louder. Andy couldn't have made this effect move like that. Someone was out there. And they hadn't come to help her.

And Liv did something the veteran Manhattan event planner would never do. She panicked. Began to run. Head-on into another dead end. She fought off the prickly leaves. Twisted around. Lost her orientation. Blind in the dark, she couldn't tell where she had come from or where she should go.

She stumbled back, crashed against another wall of corn that lit up with hundreds of blinking lights showing stalks infested with crawling spiders. Liv turned and began to run.

The laughter followed her this time. Joined by another ghoul. They were beating on the branches around her. How close were they? It was impossible to tell in the dark surrounded by drying stalks.

She thought she saw a light ahead. And raced toward it. It winked out and Liv fell to the ground.

It knocked the breath out of her and for a few seconds she could only lie there and listen to her own ragged breathing. The rain had stopped; she didn't know when. But the air was utterly still. And the breathing, she realized, was not just hers.

Chapter Twenty-three

···

She lay still, holding her breath, while the other continued slow and heavy. Was it a recording? Was there somebody on the other side of the wall?

She couldn't stop the whimper that bounced against her throat.

Do not lose control, she told herself. This isn't some back alley in a bad section of town.

No, you idiot, it's worse. And suddenly all the horror stories of murders in small towns came back in one fell swoop. Right about the same time as the footsteps came nearer.

If she didn't move . . . If he didn't have a light, he might miss her completely. Walk past her. Turn the wrong way. Give up.

The footsteps were getting closer. She drew herself into a tight ball and scooted back against the wall. And fell into empty space. Touched something clammy and nearly screamed. Pulled herself together. She had fallen into one of the cavities carved out for the horror machines. She wasn't alone, but she would rather take her chances with the slithery thing hanging alongside her than with whoever was out there in the maze.

She drew her knees up, breathing into them to keep from being heard. Closer. He was coming closer. She pressed against the back of the cavity, held her breath. The footsteps stopped. She thought she could make out two booted feet right in front of her. Was sure of it when they turned to face her.

Please just keep going, she prayed. *Just keep going.*

He took a step away.

Liv started to breath again. Her cell phone rang.

She'd forgotten about her cell phone.

She heard voices. The other kidnappers. She struggled to unzip the pocket of her jacket. Got her fingers on the phone. Didn't even stop to think whether she should silence it or answer it.

She pressed send.

"Hey, I know I was a bit hard on you this—"

"Chaz, listen to me. I'm in Andy's maze."

"What?"

"They've put me in the maze and they're going to find me because of your dumb call. Help me."

"Liv, are you—"

She was yanked out of her hiding place. Her phone went flying.

Two strong and callous hands grabbed her arms and yanked her to her feet.

Liv lashed out with her bound hands. "Leave me alone. You're going to pay for that, whoever you are."

"Liv."

She knew that voice. Not the Zoldoskys, as she'd suspected. Not Andy.

"Joss?"

No. Not this kind, decent man . . . whose brother had

come close to destroying his life. And strangely she couldn't even blame him.

"Yes. Can you walk?"

"Yes." Mutely, Liv let him lead her though the dark, the small round circle of his flashlight leading them to the exit.

They made a turn and Liv saw light ahead. She'd been so close. Like that guy in the dungeon who after years of digging a tunnel was met by the inquisitors as he finally climbed to freedom.

She had one last flare of hope that Andy had finally come to see what was going on.

Andy had come. He was waiting at the entrance of the maze. And he was holding a shotgun. The uneven light carved deep lines in his face.

Joss, Andy. Were they alone? Had others plotted to kill Pete Waterbury? Bill? Ted? Had they all conspired together?

Chaz had been right when he said that so many lives would be destroyed by one amoral boy, the same boy who grew into an immoral man.

And now she remembered all those furtive looks between the men, shutting up whenever she came near, shutting her out. Not because she was an outsider. It was because they were planning to cover up a murder.

"Andy," she said, weariness in her voice. She didn't even have the spirit to run. It was just too tragic.

She wondered if Chaz had gotten it through his thick head that she was trapped in the maze. Would he arrive just in time to find her body or would her body never be found? She didn't even feel the cold anymore. Just disappointment and a bone-deep sadness.

"Liv? What happened? How did you get here?"

"Andy, don't."

"I don't understand."

"Andy, I saw the blood on the thresher. It was totally an accident. I was looking for Victor, and Whiskey led me to the barn. I tripped over the tarp in the dark. It fell off the machine and I grabbed the handle for support. I . . . I got blood on my jacket."

Liv caught sight of a truck speeding up the driveway. A gray truck. Her spirits sank even lower. The truck stopped and Anton jumped out and rushed toward them; Serge and Georgi followed close behind.

Andy turned to them. "It can't go on like this. We have to end it now."

Anton sighed. "You are right, my friend. It has gone on long enough. No matter what the consequences. Do you agree, Joss?"

Joss sighed heavily and nodded.

A shuddered wracked Liv's body.

The shotgun wavered in Andy's hand. "Oh God." Andy thrust the shotgun into Anton's hands.

They were going to kill her. And she'd only been trying to help.

Andy stripped off his hunting jacket and threw it around Liv's shoulders; pulled it tight over her quaking body.

"Andy?"

"We'd better get her into the house where it's warm. I think she's going into shock." He gathered her close and steered her to his house.

None of it was making sense to Liv.

"Do you know how this happened, Anton?"

"Unfortunately, yes." Anton's voice seemed to echo from the bottom of a deep well. "Serge and Georgi. They thought to teach her a lesson."

He was talking about her, Liv realized, and she fought to pay attention. It was hard. It seemed like her brain was as frozen as her fingers and toes.

She stumbled up the steps to Andy's house, vaguely aware of the others following behind. Andy pushed her into a chair in front of the stove and turned it on. "This will get you warm quick."

"Anton, untie her wrists and help her get that wet jacket off. I'll get a blanket." He passed out of her sight; Liv didn't care. He'd opened the oven door; the image of Hansel and Gretel flashed before her, before she stretched out her hands to the warmth of the gas flames.

Andy returned and exchanged his jacket with a heavy woolen blanket, and Liv began to grow warmer.

He poured tap water into a saucepan and put it on the stovetop.

"I've only got instant coffee."

"I'm fine," Liv said as her brain began to work again. If they were going to kill her, surely they wouldn't be offering her coffee.

"My brothers, they are hotheads. They would not hurt you; they wanted to scare you. For you to see the fear of Victor the night we found him half dead by the water. And again last night when those policemen tracked him down no better than a dog.

"He and Serge are the same age. They are very close. You would take that away from us."

"No. I didn't tell the police about Victor. Someone heard us talking. I tried to catch them but they slipped away. I should have been more careful about where I talked to Junior, but I didn't want any harm to come to him. He's had enough bad in his life."

"You should have left it alone."

"I—" Suddenly she was sick of being the brunt of everyone's anger. Tired of being on the outside. "Don't you think it's time to stop the lies? Which one of you killed Pete? Or was it all of you? How many people did you enlist for that night's work?

"I thought the detectives were stupid when they took Joss in for questioning. But maybe I was the stupid one. Tell me, Joss. Were you in on the kill?"

"No!" Andy practically shouted the word. He slumped, cradled his face in his hands. "No more."

"Oh, no." Not Andy. Liv was hit with a sharp stab of pity. To see his friend after thinking he was dead for thirty years and to have Pete Waterbury return at the same time. It must have been more than Andy could take. And Liv couldn't blame him. She'd feel the same way. But would she have resorted to murder? She hoped not.

"Andy, did you kill Pete?"

"It was an accident," Anton said. "It was my fault."

"No," Andy said. "It *was* an accident, but because of me."

An accident. Could it be true?

"Why didn't you just tell the police?" Liv asked, relieved and exasperated in equal parts.

Anton snorted. "You said it yourself. The detectives, the town. All were willing to to sacrifice us. I would be sent to jail. And who would take care of my family?"

Liv thought that maybe three adult men could take care of themselves.

"Serge and Georgi could make do. But Victor . . . We are the only family Victor has known since his boyhood. He would be lost without us. Without me."

"But you said it was an accident."

"It was. But who would believe me? An itinerant circus man."

"No one, after you put him in the apple press. That made it look like cold-blooded murder."

Serge and Georgi erupted in angry denials. Anton hung his head.

"And what about you, Andy? How could you let them suspect Joss?"

"Because I told him to." Joss's voice sliced through the charged air of the kitchen.

"So you knew about this all along?"

Joss cleared his throat as if it hurt him to breathe. "Afterwards. I didn't know Pete was back until I found him that morning."

"But if you didn't know—"

Andy stood and went to the window and looked out. "I think we should wait until Bill gets here and tell the whole story."

It seemed like they were always waiting on Bill. Then Liv heard it, too. The sound of cars coming up the drive.

Moments later, Bill Gunnison came through the back door. He took one look at the group positioned around the table and went back outside again.

"She's in here," he called, and came back inside with Ted and Chaz.

"Jeez, Liv. Would you like to explain?" Chaz said, glaring at Andy and Anton.

"Yes, we would," Andy said. "Let me bring in a few more chairs."

They all crowded around Andy's table while Andy and Anton brought the newcomers up to speed. Bill lectured Serge and Georgi about taking the law into their own hands.

Then he took out his tape recorder. "This is just for information. Unofficial. I'll take your formal statements later. First tell me, Anton, how it came about that Pete Waterbury was travelling with your company."

"Serge had just broken his arm and I needed a replacement to help with the setup and driving. He showed up and I hired him. I didn't realize at first that he had chosen us on purpose in order to return to this town incognito. I thought it was just circumstance."

"He knew we were on this circuit," Serge said. "He was going to use us as a cover while he gouged people for money."

"Serge, I will tell it. I didn't learn that until later. When Pete began bragging about the money he would make and the revenge he would take for what the town had done to him."

"To him?" Andy blurted out.

"Of all the bald-faced—" Bill shook his head. Rewound the tape. "Go on."

Anton nodded brusquely. "Victor recognized him right away. At first he was afraid to tell even me. His brother. But I could see something was bothering him and at last he told me. Afraid of Pete after all those years. I should have killed him then."

"Anton," everyone shouted at once. Bill rewound the tape recorder. "I'm just recording interviews. I haven't read anyone their rights, but please don't make any statements like that."

Which probably wasn't police procedure, thought Liv. But since Bill wasn't officially back on the case, maybe he didn't have to go by the book.

"So Victor recognized Pete, but Pete didn't recognize Victor?"

"You see his face. We have come here for three fall festivals and no one recognized him, not even Andy."

Andy looked like he might cry. "If he'd only come to me. Let me get close enough to see him, even . . ."

"Do not blame yourself. It was his choice."

"And what occurred on the night of Pete Waterbury's death?"

Anton sat straighter in his chair. "We came home after the park closed. Pete always wore his whiteface so no one would recognize him. But someone did."

"I did," Ted said.

Anton nodded. "But so did Joss's daughter. That night at the show he bragged to Victor about how he was going to pay his brother back for kicking him out of the house. I thought he meant to hurt the girl, and I could not let that happen.

"I would not let him use the truck to go to Joss's, so he said he would take Andy's truck. It was late. Andy would be asleep and he would never know."

"I keep the keys in it," Andy admitted. "Though I won't anymore."

"I followed him and tried to stop him. We fought."

"I heard the ruckus," Andy said. "I grabbed my shotgun

and went out to investigate. They were in the barn. Pete had Anton on the ground—"

"I am not so young anymore," Anton explained.

"You could have taken him," Serge said.

"I would have fought him if you had told me," Georgi added.

Bill held up his hand, silencing them. "You found Anton on the ground. . . ."

"Pete had him by the throat. I yelled at him to stop. I didn't know it was Pete. I just saw this maniac clown trying to kill Anton. I yelled that I had a gun. But he just kept choking him." Andy's voice wavered. He swallowed. "So I hit him on the back with the butt of the shotgun. It didn't faze him. So I hit him harder, this time on the head."

Andy stopped, seemed to be reliving that awful night. "Even then it only stunned him. It was enough for Anton to push him away, but still Pete didn't let go, and he pulled Anton to his knees."

Bill cut a look toward Anton, who nodded. "I grabbed him and pulled myself to my feet; then I pushed him. Hard."

"He fell backward." Andy made a sound between a laugh and a sob. "He tripped over my foot and fell into the thresher. His head hit the shaft. It must have hit something vital because he was dead.

"You'll probably find his blood somewhere on the shotgun. It's over there in the corner. And I kept the thresher covered with a tarp because I knew there might come a time when I'd have to own up to what I did."

"Not you," roared Anton. "It was my doing."

Andy shook his head. "It was an accident. I just wanted to stop him from killing Anton. Then when Anton told me that he was Pete—I was—"

"Andy," Bill warned. "Clearly a case of self-defense," he added, shaking his hand. "Why in the devil's name didn't you call it in?"

Andy hung his head.

"Andy wanted to call the police," Anton said. "But I knew how it would be. They would say I murdered him. Send me to jail. So I told Andy that Serge and Georgi and I would take care of it. Dump the body on the side of the road so someone would find him and think he had been hit by a car."

"So how did he end up in the apple press?" Liv asked.

All eyes turned to Liv.

"Sorry."

"How *did* he turn up in the apple press?" Bill asked.

"We put him in the truck, drove him farther out from town. But as we passed Joss's farm, I began to think. If we left him by the side of the road, everyone would think it was an accident and feel sorry for him. I couldn't stand that. He was a bad man.

"He was so anxious to get to his brother, I took him there. To his family to do with him as they would. I knew the door to the shop would be open because he told us so."

"It was my idea to leave him in the apple press," Serge said proudly. "See no evil, speak no evil, and never do evil ever again." He nodded sharply.

Beside him, Georgi gave an echoing nod.

Anton leaned in and looked intently at Bill. "Fate brought Pete Waterbury to us; fate took him to his grave. He hurt Junior; he will never hurt again."

Liv wasn't sure, but she thought she wasn't the only person at that table whose eyes misted over during that speech.

Anton stood up and held out his hands, wrists together. "I will go willingly."

"Sit down, Mr. Zoldosky. So you left Pete in the apple press." Bill paused to shake his head. Liv thought he might be suppressing a desire to laugh. It sounded so absurd. "And then what did you do?"

"We returned to the farm and told Andy it had been taken care of."

"Andy?"

"He did. I didn't sleep all that night. Just listened to the police scanner waiting to hear that his body had been discovered. But there was nothing. Not until I heard the call to send units over to Joss's. I went over to see. I thought maybe I'd dozed off and missed the discovery. But I hadn't." Andy shot his fingers through his corn-silk hair. "When I saw Pete in the apple press, I didn't know whether to laugh or be sick."

Liv remembered Andy's face that morning. As ashen as his hair. If he'd just called the police, he would have spared them all this trouble and anxiety.

"Where do you fit into all this, Joss?"

"Andy came to me that night and told me what had happened. I told him to sit tight and wait. So we did."

"I wanted to confess right then and there, but Anton said to trust Joss. They would have no evidence against him. And he was right. They let him go. I would never have let him go to jail."

"Is that all?"

The three men nodded. Bill looked at Ted, then Liv. "Nothing more to add?"

"Nothing."

"Do you want to press charges, Liv?"

Serge and Georgi tensed.

Wearily, she shook her head. "It was just a practical joke." She looked at Andy and smiled. "The maze is going to be a huge success."

Bill stood and looked at Anton and Andy. "I'll have to take you both into the station. Just to confirm your statements."

"And then?" Serge asked apprehensively.

"I suspect the judge will let them both out on their own recognizance. He didn't like Pete Waterbury, either."

"Bill," Liv said, shocked.

"Relax, Liv. It'll all be by the book. And the timing is perfect. Those two numbskull detectives are probably back in Albany by now. And if Victor isn't free and waiting for us in the station canteen, I'll be a monkey's uncle."

"The detectives were recalled?"

"Yep. And you can thank Mayor Worley for that."

"And Victor will go free?" Anton asked.

Bill nodded. "Yep. Now, let's get going."

"We are coming, too," Serge said.

"I think I'll go along in case there's a question of bail," Joss said. He followed the others out. Ted took a few minutes to lock up Andy's house; then he and Chaz walked Liv outside. There was a brief scuffle over who would drive Liv back to town.

Ted finally bowed out, saying that he would get all the details from Liv tomorrow. "I'll just go on down to the station, just to kibitz. And say hello to my nephew."

Chaz and Liv were left alone. Chaz hadn't said one word since he'd walked into the kitchen, and he was silent on the way to town.

Finally, Liv said, "Thanks for coming to the rescue."

"Just part of the parade."

"I still appreciate it."

"You're welcome."

They reached Liv's carriage house and Chaz pulled into the driveway.

"You were right about not getting involved in the investigation."

"A little late. But better late than never."

"But you were wrong about there not being anything anyone could do about it."

He shrugged. "Good night, Liv."

"Good night and thanks again."

Chapter Twenty-four

....

Three weeks later, Celebration Bay threw a very special party. Victor Gibson had returned from the dead. The state detectives had been recalled. And a speedy investigation aided by Anton and Andy had ended in a verdict of accidental death.

The party was held on the village green and was attended by hundreds of people. Later that night a smaller group met at Andy's house for a private send-off. Liv was gratified and flattered that she—and Whiskey—had been invited.

The men had gravitated to the parlor, laughing and enjoying a round or two of some of Joss's home-brewed hard cider. The women bustled around the steamy kitchen, preparing a feast under the direction of Amanda Waterbury, who had made the most delicious-looking lasagna Liv had ever seen. Dolly had outdone herself with a going-away cake that was hidden away in the pantry.

Liv was tossing salad, the extent of her culinary skills, when Roseanne walked over and handed her a jelly glass of some dark amber liquid.

"Dad said to give you this. It's hard cider. I think it's pretty nasty, but he wanted you to try it."

Liv took a sip. The inside of her mouth puckered and for a second she couldn't get her breath.

Roseanne watched her closely, then smiled. "See what I mean."

"Definitely an acquired taste. Like brandy," Liv added. "Thank him for me."

"I will." Roseanne moved a little closer. "I'm so glad it's all over; aren't you?"

"Absolutely."

"But I feel bad for Junior—I mean Victor. To have to go through life looking like that because of what my uncle did. I wish he weren't my uncle."

"One rotten apple," Amanda Waterbury said, coming up to them. "It has nothing to do with us. You just look at your father and know what a fine family the rest of the Waterburys are."

She continued into the dining room with a huge bowl of steaming vegetables. Everyone gathered around the long farm table. Joss said a quick but heartfelt blessing and everyone dug in.

As soon as dinner was over, the men returned to the parlor and the women took all the food back to the kitchen. When the dishes were washed and put away, the women joined the men in the parlor. Liv wandered over to where Ted, Andy, and Joss were talking to Anton and Victor.

"Your mother paid on that insurance policy all her life. She wanted you to have it," Ted was saying. "I put it in a savings account. I didn't think you would come back, but I didn't have the heart to spend it myself. It's yours."

Victor looked at Anton.

"It is up to you, Junior. You are a wealthy man. You can have surgery, stay here among your old friends."

"I'd love to have you stay at the farm," Andy said.

"Or with us," Joss said.

"I have a space over my garage that would make a great apartment," Ted said.

Junior smiled, the half of his face that was unscarred looking almost joyous.

"Thanks, Ted. And Andy and Joss. And everybody. I appreciate it. It was good to see everybody as myself and not just someone passing through, but Anton and Serge and Georgi are my family now." Victor turned to Andy. "I never got a chance to thank you for what you did. You saved me from Pete twice."

Andy blushed. "Anybody would have done the same."

"No, they wouldn't. And not just for that, but also for being my friend."

"I'd do it again. But, Victor, why didn't you come back, at least let us know you were alive?"

"I couldn't." He looked around the crowd, then lowered his eyes. "Andy tried to hold them off while I got away. I ran as far as the lake before they caught up with me. They started hitting me and I said I knew what they did and they'd better stop or I'd tell.

"It was a stupid thing to do because then Pete said if I told, he'd kill me and then he'd come after Ma. They just kept beating me until I couldn't fight back and they threw me in a boat that was moored there. I tried to get out, but Pete grabbed one of the oars and swung it at my head.

"That's the last thing I remember, until Anton found me. And I didn't remember that much for a long time. I never knew Pete had left town. Never knew it was safe to come home. And now I have a new home. But I'll always remember you, Andy, Uncle Ted, all of you."

Anton rested his hand on Victor's shoulder, affectionate and proprietary and strong. "Come, Victor. We must get to bed if we are to have an early start tomorrow."

"Good-bye, Uncle Ted. Thank you for taking care of my mother. Good-bye, Andy." He knelt down and scratched Whiskey's ears. "Good-bye, little dog."

"Where will you go next?" Andy asked.

"Florida," Anton said. "Our parents have a house there and they are eagerly awaiting our return." He stopped to shake Ted's hand and Liv saw Ted slip him what looked like a bankbook.

"Our mother will see that he gets the surgery. She has always meant to, but there was no insurance and never enough money until now."

They all followed the Zoldoskys out into the yard and watched them walk back to the trailer parked near the trees.

The next morning Liv and Dolly were standing at the bakery door when the silver Airstream drove past on its way out of town. At Liv's feet, Whiskey dropped his pumpkin-shaped dog biscuit and yipped at the face peering out of the trailer's window. Victor smiled and raised his hand in farewell.

Several people stopped to wave good-bye. The residents were no longer blaming their ills on the outsiders, but they were definitely relieved to see them go.

"Well," said Dolly. "All this hoopla. It should be a lesson to us all. Not to be so quick to judge. Why, I saw that Ruth Benedict talking to the one with the broken arm at the Price Chopper yesterday like they were bosom buddies."

"Is that the Ruth who was giving you the hard time about hiring Victor at the bakery?"

"One and the same." She sighed. "Poor boy. I guess I should say 'man,' but Victor just seems like a boy to me. I'm sorry for him, but I think it was wrong of him not to come home sooner, even if he was scared of Pete. We would have protected him."

Liv had no doubt of Dolly's words. Celebration Bay was a special place. They took care of their own.

"But I'm glad he's found a family. One that loves him and takes care of him."

They watched the silver Airstream make its way past the park. The roof glinted in the sun before it rounded the corner and passed from view.

"I'd better get to work," Liv said.

"Me, too," Dolly said. "Sold every one of those orange-frosted cupcakes yesterday. I'm going to try some with a licorice icing today."

Whiskey retrieved his biscuit and trotted alongside Liv to the Buttercup, where she picked up her morning order from BeBe, then headed to town hall.

"Well," she said, handing the drinks to Ted. "Things are rapidly returning to normal. The whole town is preparing for the weekend."

"And with the Zoldoskys gone, everyone is more than satisfied to bicker among themselves."

"Are you sorry that Victor chose to go with Anton?"

"A little sad. Mainly because Eleanor didn't live to know he was alive."

"Maybe she did know . . . in her heart. I know that sounds corny, but I think mothers sometimes do."

"Not corny at all. But speaking of corn. Somebody stole all the decorative cornstalks from Dexter Kent's nursery last night."

"Oh dear."

"Seems they showed up at the Delarosas' farm stand for a dollar cheaper. Evidently Benny D and Dexter had a fight over the price last week. Dexter is accusing Benny of stealing them. Benny is refusing to give them back." Ted chuckled. "Says it's impossible to tell whose cornstalks are whose. That's just like Benny. He'll end up giving them back but not before he gives Dex the runaround."

"Bill, I suppose, is caught in the middle."

"You betcha. Life as we know it."

Yes, thought Liv. *Life as we know it.*

"Ted?"

"Yeah?"

"There aren't any other missing persons that might show up dead anytime soon?"

Ted grinned. "Not that I know of." He leaned over. "Now, who's my favorite dawg?"

Liv smiled as she walked into her office. Haunted October was running very successfully. Preparations were under way for Thanksgiving.

They had a lot to be thankful for. It had been a near thing, but it had all worked out. And with the hiring of the new security team, they'd never have to worry about murder again.

Liv pulled up her Christmas folder. Time to get cracking. December was just around the corner. Maybe Ted could teach Whiskey to sing "Jingle Bells."

"Bring it on," she said out loud. "Deck the halls with . . ."